SNOW MELTS
IN SPRING

DEBORAH VOGTS

SEASONS *of the* TALLGRASS

SNOW MELTS IN SPRING

BOOK ONE

ZONDERVAN.com/
AUTHORTRACKER
follow your favorite authors

We want to hear from you. Please send your comments about this book to us in care of zreview@zondervan.com. Thank you.

ZONDERVAN

Snow Melts in Spring
Copyright © 2009 by Deborah Vogts

Requests for information should be addressed to:
Zondervan, *Grand Rapids, Michigan* 49530

Library of Congress Cataloging-in-Publication Data

Vogts, Deborah, 1965–
    Snow melts in spring / Deborah Vogts.
       p. cm. — (Seasons of the tallgrass ; bk. 1)
      ISBN 978-0-310-29275-3 (pbk.)
       1. Women veterinarians — Fiction. 2. Rural families — Kansas — Fiction. I. Title.
    PS3622.O363S66 2009
    813'.6 — dc22
                                    2009000993

Published in association with the literary agency of WordServe Literary Group, Ltd., 10152 S. Knoll Circle, Highlands Ranch, CO 80130.

Interior design by Christine Orejuela-Winkelman

Printed in the United States of America

09 10 11 12 13 14 15 • 23 22 21 20 19 18 17 16 15 14 13 12 11 10 9 8 7 6 5 4 3 2 1

To Mom and Dad, for nurturing my love for writing
and always standing behind me on this journey.
And to Christopher, for allowing me to pursue this dream.

I HEARD THE PRAIRIE CALL TO ME,
ITS WORDS A WHISPER ON MY HEART,
AND I KNEW THAT I WAS HOME.

ONE

Red lights flashed like fire in the murky shadows of the night. Mattie Evans slid from the seat of her truck and made her way to the accident scene, tuned to the shrill, intermittent static of the emergency radios.

What a way to start this early Sunday morning, not even a week into the new year. *Lord, give me strength.*

As she neared, the crushed sedan came into view. A ghostly chill crept up her spine. She noted the shattered glass, a trail of blood. Paramedics worked to pull the driver from the car and transferred the motionless boy to a stretcher.

At the sight of the victim's marred face, Mattie pressed her hand to her mouth. Another body lay covered on the ground.

"Thanks for getting here so quickly, Doc." The county sheriff met her on the dirt road, and Mattie forced herself to regain control. "Got ourselves a bad one. Two drunk teens hit a horse with their car. One's dead, the other ... well, it don't look good. As for the horse, I doubt you can save him."

With his flashlight, he cleared a path through the dense fog, and Mattie followed to the edge of the road where her patient lay. Blood stained the gravel.

"They probably didn't even see the animal until it was too late," he said. "Don't know why the horse was on the road—must have a fence down." He shined a beam into the dark pasture. "Likely spooked and jumped toward the vehicle, then smashed into the windshield. Still breathing, though."

Mattie knelt for a closer inspection. Someone had tried to stop the massive bleeding with towels, to no avail. She stroked the horse's neck, and the gelding raised his head. The white of his eye showed pure terror, dilated from shock.

"He's lost a lot of blood." The sheriff drew the light over the animal's body.

Mattie took a deep breath and reached into her bag for a syringe. Once she had the horse sedated, she removed the towels to examine him. Her heart sank at the extent of the damage.

The impact of the windshield had lacerated his right shoulder, withers, and limb. Corneal rupture of the right eye and massive skull fractures. A quick check of his mouth revealed his old age. She noted the paleness of his gums.

At times like this, she hated her job. Such hopelessness. Angered by the senseless destruction, she fought back tears, her teeth clenched as the horse lay wheezing his every breath. Despite her oath to save animals, Mattie knew the horse would require extensive treatments, and even then, his chances for a full recovery were slim.

"He's in a lot of pain." The nagging worry from her recent loss caused her to doubt her abilities. "There's no reason to make him suffer. I recommend putting him down."

"Can't do that, Mattie," a gruff voice answered close by.

Her gaze jolted to see her friend John McCray slumped over his cane. "Didn't you just get out of the hospital? You shouldn't be out on a night like this."

"That's my fault." Another man stepped from the darkness, and Mattie acknowledged John's hired hand, Jake. "When I heard the car horn blaring and realized what had happened, I called the ambulance. Figured the boss would want to be here."

"This is Gil's horse." John gripped her shoulder. "You have to save him."

Mattie had heard stories about Gilbert McCray from her older sisters, though John hardly spoke of his son. Some said he could have been a professional team roper, but he'd left it all to become a football hero in California. A stupid move, as far as she was concerned. Why would anyone give up being a cowboy for a football career?

She shook her head. "I don't know if I can." She studied the horse's wounds again, then glanced up at John McCray. Mattie recognized the look of regret, the kind that left people empty. She also acknowledged the uncomfortable tightening in her stomach. If she tried to save the horse and he died, could her business or her heart handle another fatality?

THE TEAM MANAGER FOR THE SAN FRANCISCO 49ERS OPENED THE door to the trainer's room, and the musty stench of sweat crept in and mingled with the odor of medicine and bandages. "Gil, your dad's calling on your cell. I figured you'd want to take it." His booming voice broke through the racket of the locker room next door as he tossed the phone to Gil.

Gilbert McCray slid off the table and apologized to the attendant taping his ankle. He checked the caller ID and couldn't imagine why his dad would be calling just hours before a playoff game—unless it was an emergency.

He flipped the phone open. "Hey, Dad, what's up?"

A raspy cough sounded on the other end. "I have some bad news for you, Son."

Gil stepped into the hallway for better reception. "Is everything okay?"

"It's Dusty," his dad said. "He was in an accident early this morning. I hated to call you, but they're not sure if he's going to make it. I thought you should know."

Gil frowned at the mention of his chestnut gelding. "What happened?"

"He was hit by a car. Got through the fence and must have been on the edge of the road. Too foggy. The driver didn't see him."

Dusty. Gil swallowed the emotion threatening to clog his throat as the memories whooshed back. He and the horse had been a team. Gil trained Dusty from a colt, learned some great techniques on his back, and won plenty of high school championships with him. The old boy was dying? Though he hadn't ridden the horse for two years, the news caught him off guard.

"Is he in much pain? If we need to, I'll hire the best vet in the country. Fly him in." The familiar catch in his voice reminded him of his boyhood when he'd asked for simple favors, believing his dad could do anything.

"We've already got the best, Son. I just thought you should be prepared."

After he said good-bye, Gil slammed his fist against the wall. A burning sensation shot through his shoulder to his palm. He'd give anything to see Dusty one last time. Unfortunately, two hours from now, he had a date with destiny, an appointment at Lambeau Field. If his team won the Division Championship against the Green Bay Packers, they'd be one game closer to the Super Bowl. If they lost, this would be the last game of Gil's career. Funny, he was about to retire from a game he loved, and his old friend was retiring from the game of life.

GIL WAITED ON THE SIDELINE WHILE THE DEFENSE PLAYED THE FIELD. In all his years as quarterback, he'd never experienced the chaotic feelings tumbling over him this first half. Two decades ago, he'd left everything for the game of football. Rodeo. His dad. With no regrets. Or maybe he'd never allowed himself that luxury until now.

He stared out at the field and watched as one of their linebackers intercepted Green Bay's pass.

Offense's turn.

The lights glared down as Gil blocked the roar of the spectators from his mind. Silence. His offensive line crowded around, waiting for his call.

"Go on two." His breath turned into a puff of vapor in the brisk night air. Gil walked to the line of scrimmage, adrenaline pumping.

"Down, set, hut, hut ..."

The ball snapped into his hand. He dropped from the line of scrimmage and looked for his primary receiver. Covered. The defense had his running backs blocked as well.

No clear path—either throw or run.

No time for debate.

He tucked the pigskin into his arm and faked a sweep, rolling over the first lineman coming his way. His legs careened him up and over the defense as they'd done a hundred times before, and he flew down the field like a horse after a steer let out of the chute. A cornerback charged him from the side. Gil slid to the ground.

"First down," the referee called out.

Gil saw the official's signal and should have been thrilled. Instead, he stole a glance at the hostile Packer crowd and caught sight of a man who looked like his father. His breath stilled.

Impossible. His dad didn't attend his games. He didn't care enough to.

"Do you even see what's happening out here?" Johnson jammed his fists into Gil's padded shoulders. "It's like you're in another world."

Gil stared up at the lights.

Concentrate. Keep your mind in the game.

He went to set up another formation and listened for the radio signal in his helmet. Receiving his coach's instructions, Gil pitched his hands into the huddle, felt the determination of his teammates as the heat rose off their bodies. He refused to let them down. "This time we'll go for a 40/50 sprint draw. On one."

He moved into position behind his center.

"Red, blue, 40 – 50, set hut."

The ball swept up into his hands. Gil sensed a blitz and passed to his wide receiver. Missed. Incomplete.

He tried again. This time when Gil got the ball, he maneuvered it to feel the roughened leather of the seam and pedaled back. He snaked to the left to hand off to Johnson, his halfback. The ball barely left his hand when three defensive linemen dropped him to the ground.

Everything went black.

TWO

In the glow of the barn lights, Mattie examined the horse's sutures, the fatigue from the last eighteen hours crashing over her like a thunderstorm. She checked the IV bag once more before calling it a night. The surgery had lasted five hours, but the horse was a fighter. He was alive. Although thankful he made it through the procedure, Mattie knew Dusty's recuperation would be long and difficult. Had she made the right decision by trying to save his life?

She gave the chestnut gelding one final glance before leaving the pen. His worst injury was the loss of his right eye, which she'd removed. The severe lacerations on his chest and leg would heal in time, and she prayed the trauma to the suprascapular nerve in the shoulder wouldn't be permanent. The horse had suffered acute muscle inflammation from the brunt of the car, and his kidneys would need to be monitored throughout the night.

Little sleep for her.

Mattie came in from the barn and shut the door on the chilly night air. "You might as well go home, Travis. The others are probably already watching the playoffs."

"What about you?" Her college intern from K-State stepped from behind the counter. "Aren't you a football fan?"

Mattie laughed. She couldn't remember the last time she'd sat in front of a television. "I have no desire to watch a bunch of grown men chase a leather ball for three hours. Even if one of them is a local hero."

"You sure you don't want some help?"

Mattie saw her technician's concern and shook her head.

Once he left, her mind reverted to the owner of her newest patient. She could forgive Gil McCray for not being here for his horse, but why hadn't he visited when his father suffered a heart attack less than a month ago? Gritting her teeth, she stepped into the back room to inspect the dogs and cats caged there.

She knelt beside a yellow Labrador and crooned assurance to the young stray. The smell of disinfectant wafted up as she opened the stainless steel door. "How are you, girl?" She stroked the trembling dog's fur, and her fingers moved to the fresh suture line. No sign of infection. The dog inched closer and pressed her head against Mattie's hand. Her heart warmed at the trust in the golden-brown eyes.

Exhausted, Mattie checked the rest of her patients, then turned out the light and ascended the stairs to her small apartment above the clinic. Not bothering to turn on any lights, she unclipped her cell phone from her jeans and punched in the number she knew by heart.

"Hey, John. The surgery went well."

"It's about time you called. Been sitting here flippin' through channels, worried about you and that horse."

Mattie pictured him in his old recliner, yelling at the television. "Dusty's recovered from anesthesia and resting. He's heavily sedated."

"How long will he need to stay there?"

"That depends on how he responds to treatment. I'd guess three to four weeks." Mattie had no idea how John would physically handle nursing the horse to health. "We can discuss his home treatments when you come in."

"Why don't you drive out tomorrow? I have a heifer I need you to look at. Foot problems. I'll tell Mildred to set an extra plate for breakfast." His words came out short and choppy.

Mattie hesitated. Normally, she wouldn't agree to leave a patient at this stage of recovery. It was too soon. Her intuition, however, told her to visit the man who was like a father to her. "My technician arrives around seven. I'll drop by after that, but I can't stay long."

"You work too hard."

She smiled at the affection in his voice. "Have I told you lately how much I appreciate all you've done? You convinced more than a few ranchers to hire me. I wanted to thank you—again."

"Get some sleep and I'll see you tomorrow."

When he said good-bye, Mattie tossed the phone on the couch and followed right behind. She unwound her long, thick braid and dug her fingers into the soft, red curls to massage her scalp. Though her mind reeled with thoughts from her day, she reclined onto a throw pillow, longing for rest before her next shift in two hours.

WITH TEN SECONDS LEFT IN THE GAME, REFEREES CALLED THIRD down on San Francisco's forty-yard line. The fans went wild in the stands.

Gil knew their only chance was a Hail Mary.

A high-risk pass, but if it succeeded, it would mean victory.

In swift succession, he called the play and lined up behind the center. As soon as Gil felt the snap, he gripped the ball and lunged back. Seconds later, he released it into the air with as much force as he could muster, praying Charlie or one of the other receivers would sneak behind the defense. His opponents knocked him down, the air stolen from his lungs one last time. Despite the pain, he struggled to watch the play unfold.

The leather ball flew sixty yards as though in slow motion and descended near the end zone where his wide receiver was headed.

15

With cat-like agility, Charlie leapt into the air and caught the pass as though he had glue on his fingers. *The game was theirs.*

In the next instant, Gil heard the roar of the Green Bay crowd and knew something had gone wrong. Charlie must not have been able to keep his hold on the football. Gil closed his eyes and toppled back onto the field in misery.

It was over.

THREE

John McCray's housekeeper greeted Mattie at the ranch house the next morning and led her down the hallway to John's room. Mattie knocked lightly on the wooden door, which opened at her touch. A beam of sunshine streamed in from a slit in the dark drapes, illuminating the frail gentleman propped on an oversized pillow and lying on what he affectionately called his "deathbed." She stifled a giggle. John McCray was far from dead.

"My boy's team lost. Twenty-one to fifteen." He threw his copy of the *Wichita Beacon* onto the covers. "Too bad about that final pass."

Mattie already heard from her employees how the winning team had pummeled Gil's receiver, knocking the ball loose and costing the 49ers the win. "Is this how it is now that you're home from the hospital? You stay in bed all day?" She strode to the window and pulled back the heavy curtains.

"I don't need another sassy woman telling me what to do. Mildred's always trying to make me eat those counterfeit eggs. Says I need to lower my cholesterol."

"You'd better watch how you talk about your hired help. If you lost Mildred, you wouldn't know what to do with yourself." Mattie moved to his bedside and handed him his flannel robe. "Let's go out on the veranda. It's a beautiful morning, even if it is the thick of winter. I heard on the radio that it's already fifty-six degrees." She held onto his arm and helped him from the bed. "If that doesn't entice you, I brought you some of Clara's apple muffins."

His mouth opened in surprise. "You didn't bake them yourself?"

"Nope, I've been too busy with that horse of yours. You'll have to settle for these." She held a white paper sack in the air. "I have Clara's word they're made with real eggs."

Mattie ignored the man's grumble and escorted him to the veranda. When he'd settled into a chair, she placed an afghan across his lap and took a seat beside him at the wrought iron table. She loved the atmosphere of the Lightning M Ranch with its large native limestone house and seven thousand acres of prime grassland. The daughter of a cattleman, she'd grown up on a ranch not far from here and couldn't imagine living anywhere but in the Flint Hills. Of course, she lived in town now, but someday . . .

"I wanted to talk to you about Dusty." She waited as Mildred brought out a tray for breakfast, her yellow apron fluttering in the morning air. The older woman set two plates before them filled with waffles, bacon, and scrambled eggs, along with orange juice and a thermos of coffee.

"Thank you, Mildred." Mattie smiled at the devoted employee.

John didn't offer his thanks, his face as sour as ever. "I suppose this is some of that fake turkey bacon you like to give me. What's wrong with feeding a man real eggs and meat from a hog? I'd give anything to sink my teeth into a piece of real fried bacon, cooked in its own grease."

Mildred squeezed Mattie's shoulder. "It's a pleasure to cook for someone who appreciates my efforts." The woman wrinkled her nose at her employer, who shuffled his eggs to the edge of his plate, making it clear he had no intention of eating them.

"Have you heard how the Marshall boy is?" John changed the topic in his usual abrupt manner.

Mattie's smile faded as Mildred went inside the house, the screen door slamming behind her with an unnecessary *whack*. "I heard they took him to Emporia, but his prognosis didn't sound good."

"He was lucky he didn't get killed. When I was a boy, if you got half-cocked on Jack Daniels, your folks would have skinned you alive. 'Course, back then I rode my horse to school. Things were different in my day."

"Sometimes I think we'd be better off without some of the conveniences we have now," Mattie said. "But if that were the case, your horse would be dead, which is what I wanted to talk to you about."

"Got my bill figured up already?" The elderly host sloshed juice onto his plate, and she quickly mopped up the orange liquid with her napkin.

"Let's discuss the care Dusty will need when he comes home."

"I haven't thought that far ahead," John said gruffly.

Mattie suspected as much. She took a bite of the sweet, tender waffle and gazed out at the hills, a perfect view from where they sat. Even in the dead of winter when the grass was crisp and brown, she never tired of the rolling plains. In the distance, a mangy coyote traipsed across the hilly terrain. She turned to her friend, who was soaking up a large bite of waffle with the last of his maple syrup.

"You need to think about how you're going to manage Dusty if he makes it through the next few days. He'll be on a special diet and will need medication as well as daily exercise. You might want to hire extra help."

John snorted. "I'll hire you and you can treat him. That makes more sense than paying some greenhorn." The man sniffed the bacon on his plate and frowned. He tossed it onto the ground, and his blue heeler Hank chomped the strip of meat at once.

Mattie's gaze shifted from the small cow dog to the open prairie. As a girl she'd ridden with abandon on every acre of her father's land, embracing the wind as her horse flew over the lush bluestem. "I'll consider that offer if you allow me to ride your pastures."

"Shoot, girl, you can do that now." His steel gray eyes narrowed in on her. "You look tired. Didn't you get any sleep last night?"

She chuckled and swallowed the last of the pulpy juice. "Rest will come. Right now, I should get to the clinic to check on your horse."

"Not my horse. Gil's. If you're needed, they'll call on that fancy gadget you carry on your hip. Besides, I have a heifer I want you to look at."

"I thought that was an excuse to get me to come over." Mattie smiled, but the usual wave of guilt set in as it always did when she was tempted to do something for her own enjoyment, even if it was under the guise of work.

"I'll have Jake saddle up my mount. She hasn't been ridden for a coon's age." The man scooted from the table, his face lit with excitement. "A little exercise will do her good. She might be a tad fresh, but from what I remember, you can hold your own on a horse. I warn you, though, she likes to jump fences." A low chuckle issued from his chest, and Mattie smiled at how good the hearty laughter sounded.

"You mean Tulip?"

"Don't make fun of my mare. She might not be much to look at, but pretty is as pretty does. The way she handles, she's worth her weight in gold."

Laughter bubbled in Mattie's throat. "Okay, I'll check on this heifer of yours, but then I need to get to the office." She reached into her sack and pulled out a muffin. "I'll take one of these to your foreman Jake, but you can have the rest . . . on one condition."

"What's that?"

"Apologize to Mildred for your mean behavior."

John's mouth gaped. "She knows I don't intend any harm."

"No." Mattie tossed him a muffin, and he surprised her by catching it in midair. "I don't think she does."

J<small>AKE MET</small> M<small>ATTIE AND</small> J<small>OHN AS THEY WALKED TO THE BARN,</small> <small>HIS</small> beat-up Stetson perched low over his eyes to block the sun. "Aren't you a sight for sore eyes?" The grizzled cowboy grinned as he walked toward them.

Mattie handed him a muffin and a cup of coffee. "Compliments of Clara's Café."

"Mighty thoughtful of you."

Jake reminded Mattie of a greeting card cowboy. His legs were bowed, his hair a coarse gray, and his skin had been wrinkled by age and wind. He had a wide, crooked nose that looked like it had been broken a few times, and his bright blue eyes had seen plenty of living.

"How's Dusty?" Jake asked.

"We'll know more in a few days."

The ranch hand turned to his boss, who leaned heavily on his wooden cane. "I've checked the fence where the accident happened, and sure 'nough, it was down. I thought I'd go around the section today to see if there are any other gaps."

"That'd be good. Sorry I can't help." John tucked his chin to his chest. "This young lady wants to look at that heifer with the bad foot you've been worried about. Saddle Tulip for her, then help her get the heifer tied down in the pasture." He turned to Mattie and frowned. "Can't even saddle my own horse no more. What's a man good for if he can't do the things he loves?"

Mattie squeezed John's arm. "You're already doing more than your doctor expected. Have a little faith." She rose on her tiptoes to kiss his leathery cheek.

Jake nodded and stuffed a wad of chewing tobacco against his lower gum. "Yep, ya gotta have a little faith, is all. Things will right themselves sooner or later."

Descending from two thousand feet in a private Cessna, Gilbert McCray stared at the terrain below. From this vantage point, the white flinty rocks embedded in the hills of his father's ranch stood out even more than he remembered.

"Thanks again for doing this, Roger. If it hadn't been for you, I'd still be sitting in an airport terminal waiting for my flight."

"No thanks necessary. I like getting the old girl out every now and then to stretch her wings. Besides, I owed you a favor."

Gil chuckled. He and Roger were friends from way back when they played for the Denver Broncos, his first pro team after college. "I don't believe in owing favors unless they're my own. Thanks the same, but I'll pay for this ride."

Roger nodded. "Tough break last night. If your guy could have held onto that pass, the scoreboard would have been yours."

Gil shrugged. "You win some, you lose some."

He hated losing. Success had blown in like the wind with the NFL draft in Denver, microphones in his face, an overnight celebrity. He knew it would blow out as fast. "Hudson's grass landing strip is over there on your left. My father's neighbor is a crop duster. I rode with him when I was kid."

"You like living on the edge, don't you?" Roger reduced the throttle to increase the rate of descent. "Football, low-flying airplanes, wild rodeos."

Gil's mouth tilted into a smirk. "What can I say, life's an adventure."

The plane angled and as it turned, Gil whispered under his breath. Below him, racing across the prairie, was a red-haired vision on a gray horse, her long hair dancing in the wind like the mane and tail of the creature she rode.

"Who is that, and what is she doing on my father's property?"

FOUR

BRISK AIR WHIPPED THROUGH MATTIE'S JACKET, REMINDING HER IT was still winter despite the fair weather. Now that Jake had gone on to fix fence after tending the heifer, Mattie gave the dappled mare free rein and rode across the dry prairie, careful of the large clusters of flint rock. She stopped on one of the taller mounds and gazed out at the land, which stretched for miles in every direction. A flock of Canada geese flew overhead, and Tulip's ears perked at their haunting call.

Acknowledge and take to heart this day that the Lord is God in heaven above and on the earth below. There is no other.

She breathed in the fresh air, and her lungs tightened from the cold. Then the hum of an engine broke through the stillness as a small aircraft descended overhead. Curious, she raced Tulip down the hill for a closer look.

Minutes later, Mattie slid the horse to a halt as a man in jeans and a red jacket tossed a large duffel bag over the fence of the Mc-Cray property. He climbed through the barbed wires as though he owned the place.

She'd heard about money-hungry businessmen scoping out ranches and getting their grubby hands on every stitch of tallgrass left in the county. It reminded her too much of her own family's ordeal.

"What do you think you're doing?" She pitched the mare forward with every intention of running over the intruder. "This is private property. No trespassing."

The tall, haughty man didn't seem the least bit disturbed by the close proximity of the horse. Instead, he smiled and hitched the bulky bag onto his back. "I could tell you the same."

Mattie glared at the stranger. "I don't know who you are, but you don't want to mess with John McCray." She motioned toward the aircraft now setting up for lift-off. "I suggest you hurry, or you're going to miss your ride."

The broad-shouldered man instead began walking in the direction of the house. After a few moments, Mattie dug her heels into Tulip's side and caught up with him. She guessed the fellow to be in his late thirties and couldn't help but notice how the brown curls against his forehead accented his blue eyes. "What did you say your name was?"

He stopped and turned. "I didn't, but since you brought it up, who are you, and why are you riding my father's horse?"

Mattie's eyebrows scrunched in doubt. Could this be the star quarterback the whole county admired? The man who abandoned his father's ranch, who couldn't call his own dad in the hospital? Upon closer examination, he did bear a grand resemblance to John. They both possessed thin upper lips, bushy eyebrows, and the very same cleft in their chins.

"Gil?"

"One and the same."

Mattie wished she had a cowboy hat to cover her embarrassment. "I'm sorry. I had no idea."

"That's quite all right. It's refreshing not to be recognized for a change, Miss..."

"Mattie Evans. I'm a friend of your father's."

Gil's brow wrinkled as though trying to put a face with the name, then his lips flattened into a straight line. "That's funny—I didn't think the old man had any friends." He continued his trek across the pasture.

Unable to let the comment pass without rebuttal, she clicked her tongue to move Tulip forward. "Not that you'd know or care, but your father has lots of friends. It's a shame he can't say the same about family."

Gil stopped abruptly. "What are you implying, Miss Evans?"

"Only that you couldn't be bothered to visit your father when he needed you most." Mattie raised her chin, daring him to deny the statement.

"What makes you an expert on my family?" His sudden irritation could have torn the hide off one of John's steers.

"I told you—I'm a friend. I care about your father."

"And I don't? You don't know the first thing about me and my father—how things are with us."

Mattie fidgeted in her seat. Perhaps she'd gone too far. "I know this. If you walk up to your father's doorstep unannounced, you'll likely send him into cardiac arrest."

Gil's sudden arrival had certainly jump-started her heart. In fact, it took her breath away. She hated to think what John's reaction might be. Patting the mare's sleek neck, she stole a peek at the quarterback's chiseled face.

"If you don't mind, I'll ride ahead and let John know you're here."

"I'd be obliged if you would," Gil said, a forced politeness in his tone. "I could use a little time to get my thoughts in order."

"I imagine your dad would appreciate the same." With a flick of the reins, Mattie moved ahead of him, past a squeaky windmill.

"The prodigal son returns." His sarcastic tone echoed against the clear blue sky.

Mattie glanced back and saw his cynical grin. Galloping onward, she whispered a prayer that the two McCray men wouldn't butt heads like two bulls in a pasture.

MATTIE LED HER MOUNT INTO THE McCRAY BARN, SURPRISED TO see John sitting on a hay bale.

"How did Tulip do? The mare didn't fool you into thinking she was tired, did she?" John teased, a muffin crumb stuck to the stubble on his chin.

"No, she didn't pull any tricks." Mattie took her time unbuckling the leather saddle strap, unsure how to inform the man of his son's arrival.

"Tell that to Gil. Last time he was here, he wanted to sell her. Insisted Tulip was too lazy to catch up to those steers. A lot he knows — got sidetracked with football and lost interest in cowboy ways."

Mattie remembered going to the local rodeos as a girl but was too young to recall Gil. "My sisters said he could have gone pro."

The aged rancher stood and leaned on his wooden cane. "I guess he had other ideas." John's heavy fist slammed against Tulip's saddle with a loud smack, causing the horse to prance to the side. Mattie shoved the mare back into position.

"If you ask me, football ruined him." John's displeasure carried through his gruff tone. "Those college coaches with their fancy scholarships got their hands on him, and he got too big for his britches. Didn't give ranch life a second glance after that. Just off and left for bigger things."

Mattie had seen in her own family how pride and fortune could bring a person down and guessed that's what had happened to Gil. "Speaking of Gil—"

"One of these days, some cowboy's gonna sweep you away from here too, Mattie. I feel it in my bones. My luck, I'll already be in my grave and will miss hearing your sweet voice say *I do.*"

Mattie laughed. "I swear you're worse than my daddy."

"Don't think marriage won't happen. You're a dandy girl. Don't settle for second best."

"I'm content to live the life God's given me right here in Charris County. Especially if I can wake up to these hills every morning."

John chuckled, then his expression turned sober. "These hills won't keep you warm at night. I know that for a fact."

Mattie's cheeks flushed at his remark. She heaved the sturdy saddle off the mare's back and eased it onto a stand, glad for the excuse to exert a bit of energy. Fearing the subject might change again, she forged ahead with her news. "You'll never guess who I saw coming down out of the sky, right there in your pasture."

John's eyes gleamed. "Superman?"

She took Tulip's lead rope and headed to the stall to feed the horse a little grain. "No, it was Gil. He's walking up to the house right now. Should be here any minute."

John's face paled. He looked at her as though she'd hit her head on a rock in the pasture and given herself a concussion. "What are you talking about? Gil's in Wisconsin."

A hulking shadow appeared in the passageway of the barn. "No, Dad, actually, I'm not."

FIVE

Gil set his duffel on the ground. "A friend of mine gave me a lift in his plane." Gil jammed his hands in his jean pockets, feeling strangely awkward being back home. He studied the man he hadn't seen for so long, surprised by how much he'd aged. What was his father now, seventy-two?

Not wanting to stare, Gil turned to the red-haired woman lingering in the horse stall. Pretty and strong-willed, as already evidenced by her dramatic welcome in the pasture, why would she befriend an old man like John McCray? At least, he hoped they were merely friends. His mother had been gone for a couple of years and no doubt his father suffered bouts of loneliness. It wouldn't be the first time an old-timer hooked up with a girl less than half his age. The idea sickened him.

"I probably should have called, but with the game and all ..."

"No need to explain." With the help of a cane, his father moved closer, then stopped.

At this range, Gil saw the deep lines etched in the weathered face. Again, he looked away, this time at his brown leather loafers — not the worn cowboy boots he used to wear as a teen. Another reminder of how much things had changed.

"I'm surprised you came, considering how busy you are."

Gil lifted his gaze to stare into eyes that mirrored his own. "I would've come sooner if I could have."

His father scowled. "I've heard that before."

The comment hit Gil harder than any linebacker ever had. "You know I had no choice then. I did everything I could to get home before she died."

"Whatever you say." His father waved his hand in a disgusted manner as Miss Evans eased her way from the shadows. "I guess you've met Mattie."

"She's a better watchdog than Hank." Gil kicked his heel against the dirt floor and watched as the woman neared. "So, Miss Evans says she's your *friend*?" He tried to keep the revulsion in the pit of his stomach from coloring his tone.

"Miss Evans is the vet I told you about. The one caring for your horse." The answer came out clipped, a biting punishment for thinking the worst of his old man.

Gil's jaw dropped from embarrassment and surprise, and he fumbled for his next words more than he'd ever fumbled a football. "I'm sorry ... Dr. Evans ... I didn't realize."

Mattie's face lit with amusement. "That's quite all right. It's kind of nice to be recognized as a woman instead of the town veterinarian."

Eager to recover from his blunder, Gil reached out his hand to greet her. "How's Dusty doing? You operated on him, right? Are you sure you did everything you could?"

The doctor's expression grew taut as she removed her hand from his. "Last I checked, your horse was still breathing." She brushed past him without further explanation.

Gil noticed the steadiness in her gait as well as her petite frame and build. She rode a horse well too. "Tell me, was the operation a success? How bad were Dusty's injuries? You're a small woman. How many large animals have you handled, anyway?" He trailed the doc to a white Ford pickup that had a metal box in the back for supplies.

"I'm on my way to the clinic if you'd like to see for yourself." She stopped at the driver's door and turned suddenly to face him, closing the distance between them in seconds.

"Let's get one thing straight, though." She poked the center of his chest with a steady finger. "I graduated top in my class and own a respectable practice, despite men like you who shy away from female vets. Regardless of what you think, I know how to treat Dusty's wounds, but until I have your cooperation, I'm not laying another finger on your horse. Do you understand what I'm saying?" She glared at him, her squared-off shoulders only reaching to his chest.

Not wanting to feed her anger, Gil tried to force down the grin that threatened to appear. She was cute when she got her dander up.

"You're free to take Dusty to K-State. The veterinary college has better facilities than mine." She spun on her heels to return to her truck.

Gil reached for her shoulder and felt the fragile bones beneath. "That won't be necessary, Dr. Evans. I'm sure your care will be satisfactory. After all, my father says you're the best."

This seemed to mollify the doc's irritation, but rather than concur, she climbed into the truck and slammed the door. "In that case, hop in." She turned the key in the ignition and revved the engine.

Gil rushed to the other side and struggled to climb aboard as she spewed dust in the air with her tires.

He looked back to see his father raise his cane in farewell.

Gil gripped the door. "We'll talk later," he called out, all the while wondering about the mean-spirited woman who'd just tried to run over his toes. "That is, if I make it back in one piece," he muttered to himself.

When they reached the end of the lane marked by a limestone

fence, Gil decided to ask the question foremost on his mind. "You're not related to Owen Evans, are you?" He knew the answer before the words were out of his mouth. How many Evans could there be in Diamond Falls?

"He's my father."

"You're Bridgett and Jenna's sister?"

"That's right." Mattie glanced at him, and he noticed her eyes. Wide set and a deep shade of green, like turf on a football field. "Didn't your brother date Jenna? I remember him coming over when I was a kid."

Gil nodded. "Yeah, they dated." He faced the passenger window and shut his eyelids in an effort to block the painful memories.

"I'm sorry about your brother. Your dad speaks often of Frank."

Animosity roused within. "I'm sure he does." Frank and his father had shared a special bond ever since Gil could remember.

"I think he misses him and your mother more each year. Especially since his attack."

Gil jerked to attention. "What do you mean, *his attack?*"

Mattie's eyes narrowed. "Your father had a heart attack right before Christmas. Surely you knew that?"

A wave of nausea tore through Gil as he tried to mask his shock. He recalled his father's cane, his frail condition. "I guess it wasn't something he cared to share with me," he said, trying to keep the bitterness out of his voice. "So, tell me about your sisters. Do they still live around here?"

"I'm the only one who had the sense to stay. My folks live in Kansas City near Bridgett, and Jenna moved to Texas after she married."

Gil's heart thudded. He wanted to know more about the oldest sister, but hated to ask. "What about the home place? Is that where you have your practice?"

"It sold at auction." Mattie's lips tightened, and he could have sworn she aimed for the next pothole with perfect precision, crowning his head on the roof of the cab.

"Go easy on those ruts. You'll give this truck a flat tire, and I'll have to change it." Gil braced himself against the door in anticipation of the next jolt, but she surprised him by slowing down.

"I don't need a man to do the work for me." She frowned. "When I think about my parents' ranch, my blood boils. Three generations of hard work, all for nothing."

Gil studied the woman across the seat and wondered if she was anything like her sister. He never remembered Jenna being concerned about the land. "Where do you live?"

"I bought Doc Bryant's place when he retired."

The old vet's practice had never been a thriving business. More like one about to crumble, and that was twenty years ago. "Tell me about Dusty. Is he in a lot of pain?"

The truck jostled onto a paved road, and Mattie headed toward town. "Like I said, the damage was extensive. He lost a lot of blood and has substantial swelling. You'll see for yourself soon enough." Her cell phone chimed then, and she answered the incoming call.

As the doc's voice faded into the background, Gil stared out the passenger window at the familiar landscape. He thought of the many times he'd driven this road, pulling Dusty in his trailer. Ever since he'd heard about the accident, Gil had been unable to stop the deluge of memories — of riding rodeo with Frank, of his mother — and of Jenna.

He rubbed his forehead and allowed the memories of his youth to rush back.

The people in the stands became a blur as Gil and Dusty broke from the box, Frank right behind in the arena. Swinging his lariat, Gil chased the steer less than fifty yards and nailed him on his first try. Frank heeled the steer immediately after.

Still on their horses, they both listened for the official time. Once announced, Gil glanced over at Frank. "*Think we stand a chance at Nationals?*"

Frank smiled, his pupils dark with their usual intensity. "*Are you kidding? We're undefeated.*"

Mama waited with the others at the chutes, her hair pulled low in a ponytail. "*I guess all the rodeos we took you to are finally paying off.*"

"*Those late night ropings didn't hurt either, did they, Son?*" His dad looked up at Gil and slapped his horse on the flank. "*Even if it did interfere with your homework, or datin', or even those darned football practices. I'd say making it to the National High School Finals Rodeo is more important than some football game, wouldn't you?*"

Frank jumped off his horse and into Jenna's open arms. "*No comparison in my book. Never have understood what you see in that sport.*" Frank liked to tease, but Gil knew what attracted him to football. It was the one thing Frank didn't excel at, the one thing Gil could hold over his brother . . .

The doc's truck swerved onto the main street in Diamond Falls, and Gil's forehead thumped against the passenger window, bringing him back to the present. Though tempted to run from the mounting complications, Gil vowed to see this visit through, even if it meant putting up with his father, the memories, and Dr. Mattie Evans, the sister of the girl he'd used to betray his brother.

SIX

MATTIE FOLLOWED GIL INTO THE CLINIC BARN, AND THE VOICES OF her employees hushed upon their entrance. Disregarding their adoration for the local superhero, she noted the emotion that flashed across Gil's face when he viewed the chestnut gelding. Her throat tightened. Dusty lay motionless on the straw bedding, his chest swollen and his head wrapped in bandages. She'd witnessed scenes like this before, and in an effort to keep her sympathy from impeding her judgment, she'd learned to detach herself from the situation. With steady fingers, Mattie checked the horse's IV and fluids, then turned to her technician to get a report on the last two hours.

Gil rested his cheek against the horse's neck and whispered words she couldn't make out. She grasped her clipboard and faced him.

"We've enucleated his right eye. I inserted an intraorbital prosthesis before sewing the skin shut. The fractures to his skull were significant. I repaired as much of it as possible, especially around the eye and sinus area." Mattie gazed up at the hayloft where sunlight filtered in through the fractures in the wood. She wanted to be professional, collected, but the torment on Gil McCray's face could not be ignored.

Mattie put the clipboard down and knelt beside him on the straw.

"Look, right now my main concerns are Dusty's kidneys and the injuries to his shoulder. He's on heavy fluids and anti-inflammatories, but it's too soon to know how extensive the internal damage is."

"Will he live through this?" Hope cracked his voice.

Mattie shielded her expression to offer encouragement. "I've seen horses older than Dusty come out of worse conditions. It depends on his strength—his determination to live." Some horses had all heart, went full blast until they breathed their last lungful. She prayed this patient might be among that rare breed.

"I raised him, you know."

"John mentioned that." Though the sun warmed the air outside, Mattie felt chilled in the barn and zipped her jacket. "You should know I recommended putting him down the night of the accident. Your father wouldn't allow it."

Gil returned his gaze to the horse resting with his nose to the ground. "How long before he'll be up and walking?"

"I'd like to see Dusty stand within the next ten hours. If that doesn't happen, we'll try other measures." She met the resolve on Gil's face with her own. "I'm a firm believer in prayer. That and positive thinking. Maybe your presence will help Dusty heal."

"You think he knows I'm here?"

"I know he does." She stood to check the horse's monitor and recorded the increase in heartbeat. "How long since you've seen him?"

"Two years ago August. I counted it up last night at halftime. The way my mind rambled, it's no wonder we lost." He got up and walked to the barn door, staring out at the graveled parking lot. "It was my mother's birthday, and she insisted I go for a ride. She died two months later."

Mattie wondered what drove Gil from the ranch. The shock when she'd mentioned John's heart attack and his obvious torment suggested a soft spot in Gil's heart for home. She knew better than to get involved but was intrigued.

"I'm sorry I never met your mother. From the stories your dad tells, she sounded like a wonderful woman."

Gil turned back to her and jammed his hands into his jean pockets. "Mind if I stay with Dusty for a while?"

Mattie removed the near-empty bag of fluid and replaced it with a full one. "I'll check back later." She gathered her instruments and set them in a bucket. "For what it's worth, I'm glad you're home."

A momentary look of surprise creased Gil's brow. Reminding herself to stay out of other people's business, Mattie left her client to deal with whatever haunted him.

GIL RETURNED TO THE LIGHTNING M RANCH LATE THAT AFTERNOON. He knocked on the heavy, wooden door to his father's room, and it screeched open. Gil stared at the man on the bed, his dad's face more pallid and drawn than it had been earlier that day. Moving closer, he touched the wrinkled hand, surprised at how fragile it felt under his own.

"Why didn't you tell me about the heart attack?"

John McCray's thick lids opened, his eyes glazed from sleep. "What's the matter? Afraid I might die, and you'd miss out on your inheritance?" He jerked his hand away. "Don't bother." His dad hacked out a deliberate cough and glanced at the door. "Did Mattie bring you?"

"One of her staff gave me a lift. Dr. Evans stayed at the clinic."

"She's a hard worker. Real serious about her job, especially with her run of bad luck."

Gil's interest perked like a horse's ears at an unfamiliar sound. "What sort of bad luck?"

"Nothing that amounts to a hill of beans. 'Course, she don't see it that way, but she's young. She'll learn."

"You know she's Jenna's sister?"

"Do I look stupid? What does that matter?" His father sat up and reached for the glass of water on the nightstand. Gil noticed a prescription bottle of pills.

Some things were better left in the past. "I'm not here to fight." He glanced up at the high ceiling and watched the cobwebs sway in the drafty currents.

"Why did you come? I'm sure you have more important stuff to do than visit a sick man on his deathbed. Don't you have parties or press conferences to attend?"

"Not much to celebrate, remember?" Gil shifted his weight on the wingback chair. Thoughts of last night's game resurfaced. If he'd kept a clear head, made better calls, his team might have gone on to the championship game. "My legs and arms aren't as quick as they once were. I'm thinking it's time to retire and settle down."

The old man sipped his water. "You ever gonna marry and give me grandsons?"

"Don't start that again." Gil knew plenty of women, but his first mistake with love soured him on commitment. Besides, he'd never met a girl who could come within yards of his mother's character and gentleness.

"What's the matter? Don't women hang all over you?"

"Some guys like that sort of thing."

"Well, you'd better get a wife if you're gonna retire."

"I'm more concerned about getting you back on your feet so you can run this ranch. This place is falling apart." It had pained Gil earlier to see the deterioration of the fence and barns. "Did you let go of all your hired hands?"

His father scowled. "Jake and Mildred are the only help I can afford. I ain't got no sons to help me."

Gil sucked in air from his dad's verbal punch. "Been here five hours, and you're already complaining. I should've known you wouldn't change." He took a deep breath and worked to hold his temper. "I know it's not easy. Jake's old, and your health's poor. I'm not surprised the place looks like it does."

The man shifted restlessly on the bed, his thick brow even more furrowed than before. "Thanks for your expert opinion. Remind me to compensate you at the end of the month when I write out the paychecks."

"Oh, come off it, Dad. The fence needs repaired, the machine shed's about to collapse. I'm scared to think about the pasture. Have you grubbed off all the bluestem yet?"

His father shook his fist in the air. "Boy, this land's been in the McCray family for four generations. My great-granddad settled here in 1885, and we've taken care of the pastures ever since, grazing it the way it's meant to be." He wiped the spit from his mouth, his face growing redder with every word. "You go off and move to California without one care for us folks here, and then show back up out of the blue to tell me I don't know how to take care of this land. Boy, you got no right."

Gil stood up, his own temper heated. "That's great. Try to offer some helpful advice only to have it thrown in my face. I don't need this. I'm out of here." He strode across the room, regret chasing him with every step.

"That's right. Run like you always do." The angry voice followed him.

"I'm going into town before I say something we'll both be sorry for." He slammed the door on his way out. The echo reverberated in the aged walls, and the black-and-white photos of his ancestors rattled in his ears as though chanting good-bye.

SEVEN

GIL OPENED THE DOOR AND THE JINGLE OF THE BELL ANNOUNCED HIS arrival in the café. Memorabilia covered the walls, and it didn't take long to notice his retired high school football jersey, No. 12. The green and yellow shirt hung center stage in the restaurant, complete with an autographed picture of him in his 49er uniform.

A handful of patrons dotted the small establishment in booths, tables, and at the counter, where employees served old-fashioned fountain drinks. The smell of grease hung in the air, mingled with small talk. Gil prayed no one would recognize him, and that he might be able to eat in peace for once.

He sat in an abandoned booth, and before he opened a menu, one brave soul from across the room sauntered over, an icy cola in hand.

"Aren't you Gil McCray?" The giant stranger could have been a football player himself. "That was a tough break last night. What are you doing in Diamond Falls? Visiting family?"

Gil nodded and glanced through the menu items, craving a double cheeseburger with bacon and all the extras.

"You ought to try the cottage fries. They're made for real men."

The guy pushed a piece of paper toward Gil. "Would you mind signing this for my son? He plays football at the high school."

Gil smiled, like always. "Sure, what's his name?"

"Girard." The man grinned and stood a bit taller when Gil returned the paper. Two more patrons lined up behind him, napkins in hand.

A young waitress came to take his order, unaffected by the commotion at his table. He saw the moment recognition dawned, when her face lit with excitement.

"What can I get you, Mr. McCray?"

As Gil gave his order, another customer walked in, and he noticed the familiar face. She gazed at his little following, and he waved. Dr. Evans didn't return the gesture, but walked to the counter and took a seat on one of the swiveling stools. He got the impression she didn't share the community's awe at having a celebrity among them. If anything, his presence seemed to trigger the opposite response.

Annoyance. He remembered how her red hair flew wild in the breeze as she rode his father's horse. Now it was bound in braids. Not as pretty as before, and it seemed almost to protest, as several curly strands fought their way to freedom.

Gil excused himself from his admirers and made his way to the counter. "Any change in Dusty?"

The lady vet stared ahead at the mirrored wall. "If we don't get him up on his feet soon, all our efforts may have been for nothing."

He straddled the stool beside her. "It's that bad?"

She turned to him, dark shadows under her eyes, her shoulders slumped. "You don't believe me?"

"It's not that ... it's just I thought he was doing okay this morning."

"Your horse is far from okay." She rose from her seat and drummed her fingers on the counter. Within minutes, the waitress returned with her carry-out dinner. "Put it on my account, will you, Clara?"

"Sure thing," the woman said. "You take care of yourself, Mattie, and next time maybe we can visit longer—"

The doc had already headed for the door.

"Mind if I join you?" Gil called out before she slipped away. "To help with Dusty, I mean?"

Mattie stopped and nodded toward those who waited at his table. "I wouldn't want to take you from your fan club."

Gil groaned and hurried to the booth to grab his coat. The door chimed and he knew Mattie had left the restaurant. Apologizing to those around him, he threw a twenty-dollar bill on the table, then followed the doc outside. Puffs of vapor floated in the cold darkness as he ran to catch up to her.

"I wasn't that hungry," he said, realizing he much preferred this woman's company to the fans inside the café.

"Suit yourself, just don't get in the way." She hopped into her truck and backed onto the brick street.

Gil followed in the pickup he'd borrowed from Jake and drove the three blocks to the clinic. He parked outside the barn where light streamed from the windows. Upon entering, he felt the warmth from a portable gas heater that kept the chill from the shed.

Mattie and her technician were trying to nudge Dusty to his feet. "Come on, boy," Dr. Evans coaxed.

Gil joined her. He hated seeing the look of defeat in his horse's one remaining eye. "Let's go, Dusty. Get up, boy."

The aged gelding lifted his head, and his ears angled toward Gil's voice. He rocked forward, but immediately fell back from exertion. After two more tries, Dusty struggled halfway up on wobbly legs. Unable to hold himself, he lunged and his knees buckled onto the soft bedding. With a heavy groan, he laid his neck on the straw, his breath labored.

"Can't we lift him with straps or some sort of leverage?" Gil's heart ached for the injured animal.

"Let him know you love him, that you still care." Mattie pressed her hands on the gelding's rump and goaded him to sit up.

Gil faced Dusty and their vision locked. In that instant, Gil thought of the many times he'd pushed Dusty to go one more circle, trained him with his very heart to dig deeper, turn shorter, and run with greater speed and precision. He knew the horse was in pain, but he urged him on now, the consequences of failure too great.

"Come on, boy. Do this for us, for all we've been through. Show these folks what champions are made of." This time when he called Dusty's name, the horse made a grand effort and slowly rose to his feet.

Overcome with gratitude, Gil punched his fist in the air.

The doc tended to Dusty at once, and when she got him stabilized, he hung his head to the ground, his back arched in pain.

Gil stroked the gelding's neck the way he'd always done when the horse achieved a goal.

Dusty turned his head and nickered. To Gil, that one response told him his horse hadn't forgotten. That he needed his master's help once more. Gil silently begged God's forgiveness for abandoning Dusty all those years ago. At the very least, he should have visited more often or rented a stable in California.

"He needs exercise." Mattie moved from behind the horse and grabbed a nearby pitchfork to clean the stall. "Get him to take a few steps if you can. He's a bit skittish on his blind side, so always let him know you're coming. Even if he stands only a few minutes, he'll be that much stronger."

THIRTY MINUTES LATER, MATTIE SAT WITH HER BACK AGAINST THE wooden stall and faced the chestnut gelding, which rested on a fresh bed of straw. She opened the sack from the café and pulled out a handful of fries and the half-eaten hamburger.

"I heard you've had a run of bad luck." Gil settled down beside her, uninvited. "Mind if I ask about that?"

"Yeah, I mind." Mattie took a bite of the fries, now cold, but still tasty to her famished stomach. She licked the salt from her fingers, debating whether to share her troubles with a total stranger. "I guess you have a right to know." Realizing he hadn't eaten either, she split what was left of her sandwich and offered him a portion.

"No, thanks."

Mattie shrugged and took a bite of the hamburger. When she'd finished chewing, she said, "In the last three months, several of my patients have died. Of course, that happens in this business ... but rumors are starting to spread."

Gil's eyebrows rose, and Mattie figured he was weighing whether his first instinct about her might be accurate — that she was an incompetent female, not capable of practicing good veterinary medicine. "You don't come off as one who'd worry about rumors. How many patients have you lost?"

Mattie blew out a deep breath and brought her knees to her chin. She nibbled on her hamburger. "In September, I lost a horse that had broken his neck by getting caught between the bars of a pipe fence. Then two fillies died from the West Nile virus ... Need I go on?"

She wiped her mouth and attempted to stand, not willing to sit a moment longer and allow her pity party to flame the fire within. Gil caught her arm and pulled her down. His greater strength was obvious, but even stronger was the tingling sensation that rushed up through her shoulder and down her backbone.

"That doesn't sound so bad. I've seen football teams with worse streaks than yours."

"Yes, but then in December, I treated six head of cattle over at the Carter place that had pneumonia — and lost three. To top it off, last week a seven-year-old Rottweiler died. His hind leg had been shot off during hunting season."

Mattie's body tensed, reminded of the painful moment. "I thought the dog was on the mend, that he would make it." This one time, she'd allowed herself to become attached to a patient. She'd let that big dog into her heart and paid the price. "I went to feed him the next morning, and he was gone. Just like that." She snapped her fingers in the air.

She stared at the gelding, which had slipped off to sleep. "Treating your horse isn't easy for me. It seems like such a long shot."

Gil picked up a piece of straw and stripped it down the middle. "Few things in this life are easy. I think God teaches us with the hard lessons."

His statement caught Mattie off guard. "Are you a Christian?" In all her visits with John, he never mentioned one word of religion. It surprised her that his son would do so now.

"My mother took Frank and me to church every Sunday, sometimes against our will." He grinned, and she noticed his even white teeth. "I don't think I understood what it meant to be a Christian, though, until a few years ago when a teammate asked me to go to Bible study with him. It's a lot more than going to church." Gil laughed, and his eyes lit with pleasure. "Most people don't associate football with religion, but you'd be surprised how many Christian athletes there are."

This piece of information added a new dimension to Mattie's estimation of Gil McCray. She tried not to let it impress her. "Why did you return?"

"That's the second time I've been asked that today." Gil stretched his long legs out on the straw and shook his head. "I honestly don't know. To see Dusty, my dad — to have closure. Like I said — hard lessons."

Mattie found herself wanting to know this man better, even though he'd abandoned his family and played a sport that seemed senseless to her. "How long will you be in Diamond Falls?"

"Actually, I need to leave in a few days to take care of some team business."

Of course. Why would he stay? She tried not to let this bother her. "Will you come back?"

Gil kneaded his forehead. "How long will it take Dusty to heal?"

Hadn't the man heard a word she'd said? Right now, her record with high-risk patients equaled that of a losing football team. She took one last bite of her hamburger and shoved the remains in the sack. "Your horse has heart, but he has a long haul ahead of him. With no further complications, Dusty could be out of here in four weeks, sooner if he receives the love and care of someone he trusts."

"Will you take care of him while I'm gone?"

"That's my job."

"No, I mean, will you encourage him to get better? Treat him like he was your own?"

Mattie's throat tightened. "Dusty's your horse. He'd be more receptive to your attention than to mine. If you want what's best for him, you should consider staying longer."

"That's not an option, at least not now. Will you fill in for me? Until I can get back ..." His brow furrowed with expectation. "I'll pay for the extra effort."

Gil knew, as she did, that Dusty's chance of healing would increase if they added love to the equation. Someone who cared. But after so much recent loss, her only defense had been to distance herself from her patients. How could he make such an unfair request? She closed her eyes and felt assurance that she was not alone.

"Well, Miss—Doc Evans?"

Mattie stood and tossed the paper sack into an aluminum trash bin. Her intuition told her not to become involved in such a precarious situation, but how could she not? She wanted Dusty to live too.

"I'll do my best. But I warn you, Dusty might not be alive when you get back."

EIGHT

GIL CLIMBED INTO JAKE'S TRUCK AS THE TOWER CLOCK ON THE courthouse chimed eleven. He sat in the chilled cab and stared out the front window until the glass fogged with steam. Though late, he had one more thing to do before going back to his father's ranch.

The yellow headlights shone on the brick paved streets, and a few blocks later, they lit the way down the gravel road. A lone cedar marked the small cemetery he last visited for his mother's funeral.

With trembling fingers, he shut off the motor and made his way in the faint moonlight to the family headstones. Synthetic poinsettias decorated each, and Gil wondered if his dad had brought them, or someone else. He knelt down and pulled the faded flowers from the moist ground.

"I'll bring you fresh ones next time, Mama."

Gil fingered the inscription on the cold marble stone. *Emily Jean McCray, loving wife and mother.*

"I'm sorry for worrying you all those years ago and causing you grief, Mama. I wish I'd been a better son." His voice sounded foreign in the crisp night air as he stared up and watched a shooting star trail its way across the atmosphere. He edged closer to his brother's grave.

"Why did you have to go and die, Frank?" He picked up a clump of dirt and threw it into the dark, heard it hit against the dead grass. "We could have gone on in rodeo; you might have married Jenna. I could have stayed home to take care of Mama."

Gil gripped the edge of the headstone until his fingers tingled from the pressure. A sob escaped his mouth. Frank had always been good at everything he did—his father's pride and joy. Gil figured that was the reason for his own secret fascination with Jenna. But he never wished his brother dead.

Jenna. He compared Doc Evans to her sister, but the resemblances seemed few. Jenna was tall, with dark hair and an unpredictable hunger for mischief that matched Frank's. Gil thought back to that reckless summer night when his life had turned into one big ball of barbed wire.

A huge, tangled mess.

An owl screeched high overhead, and at the shrill sound Gil lived the nightmare once again ...

He and Jenna had been skinny-dipping out by Coover's Bridge less than a mile from the highway when they'd heard the first siren. Gil ignored the intrusion and reached out for Jenna, more interested in holding her glistening curves close to his body. The moon shone down on them, and her creamy skin glowed next to his.

"How come you stayed with me tonight, 'stead of going with Frank?" Gil rested his hand on her cheek and kissed her neck, tasting the muddy creek water on his lips.

Jenna's laughter rose to the top of the cottonwoods. "Frank's such a bore. A midnight swim sounded more fun than sitting around with a bunch of guys drinking beer and talking about rodeo. Besides, I've seen the way you look at me."

The girl played with fire, but she had no idea how hot the coals burned. He picked Jenna up and twirled her in the waist-high water, the celebration in his heart bittersweet. He'd betrayed Frank by making love to this girl, and nothing would ever be the same again.

Not ready to give in to his conscience, he kissed Jenna hard on the mouth, and they both fell into the water. In a fit of laughter, they splashed each other until two more sirens interrupted their fun. Curiosity aroused, they grabbed their clothes on the bank and hopped into Gil's half-ton to follow the flashing red lights to the site of the accident.

A beat-up Chevy truck lay overturned in the ditch. Gil recognized the vehicle at once, and he and Jenna raced down the steep hill, their clothes clinging to their wet skin. The passenger had received a fatal blow against the windshield, and paramedics worked to pull the teenage boy from the crushed cab. The driver, thrown from his window, lay covered on the ground.

Drawn by pure terror, Gil tore the white sheet from the body and nearly retched. The lifeless form of his brother lay bloodied and mangled on the ground. Tears streamed down his face as he fell to his knees. Gil held Frank's limp frame close to his chest and willed himself to feel the warmth of life in his veins, the beat of his heart, which failed to oblige. Unable to believe his brother dead, Gil rocked him in his arms and called out Frank's name in the dark night . . .

Haunted by the memories, Gil swayed back and forth on the cold cemetery ground.

Again, he heard the owl's shriek. He'd been wrong to come here. The pain was still too great. Grief left him numb, yet the torment of what he'd done to his brother gnawed at his stomach until he wanted to cry out from guilt.

Christian or not, could there really be forgiveness for such a crime?

With doubt hounding him, he lumbered to the truck and followed the winding road to his father's home.

As the miles crept by, Gil thought about the kids who'd hit his horse two nights ago. He'd heard the driver had been intoxicated and that the other boy had died. The notion to visit the teenager who'd lived through the accident weighed on his shoulders, and he resolved to go to the hospital the next day. Barely able to keep his eyes open, he arrived at the ranch too tired to find his way into the dark house. Instead, he stretched out on the seat of the truck and slept.

The next morning as the sun shone down on Gil's face, the passenger door screeched open, followed by a low whistle.

"Whoo-wee, I ain't seen nobody do this for a long time. You okay there, Son?" Jake asked.

Gil lifted his head, his shoulders pinched from lying in such an awkward position, his toes and fingers nearly frozen. "I didn't want to wake the old man last night."

Jake nodded thoughtfully. "He's gettin' older. Probably wise to let go of hard feelings. Start afresh."

Not up to a lecture, Gil cocked an eyebrow and rubbed his neck. "Does Mildred still make breakfast for you? I'm so hungry, I could eat a horse."

The ranch hand chuckled. "I'm headed that way now. Tuesday mornings she makes biscuits and sausage gravy. 'Course it's turkey sausage, but it beats cold cereal."

Gil rolled out of the side of the truck and walked with Jake to the house. "Thanks again for letting me borrow your wheels last night."

"Use it any time you want. I'm glad to have you home." Jake patted him on the shoulders. They entered the kitchen through the back, and the screen door slammed behind them.

Mildred turned from the stove, her hands on her hips. "I wondered where you were. I made your bed up last night. Noticed you didn't sleep in it."

"He dozed in the truck," Jake intercepted, "but I reckon he's paying the price for it now." The old cowhand sat at a wooden table and picked up his silverware.

Mildred set a plate of steaming biscuits beside a bowl of creamy white gravy that smelled like heaven. Gil said a quick prayer, then reached for one of the tender, golden tops.

"It's good to see you pray before a meal." Mildred handed him a dish of fried sausage links. "Your mama always said grace, but that seems a long time ago."

Gil studied the blue patterned bowl and recognized the piece from his mother's collection. She always insisted using the china dishes she'd called Blue Willow, even though they might get chipped or broken with daily use. Odd how certain things stood out in his memory.

"It's been a while since I served you breakfast." Mildred grabbed a jar of jelly from the refrigerator and joined them at the table.

"Too long." Gil looked toward the hallway and wondered when his father would appear. "Shouldn't Dad be up by now? I never knew him to lie in bed past sunup."

"Things are different since his attack."

That was an understatement. Gil had never known his father to take an afternoon nap, nor could he imagine him relying on a cane to walk. A moment of sadness swept over him at the toll the years had taken on his father and how much Gil had missed. He set his jaw and forced himself not to dwell on events he couldn't change. "How's the ranch, Jake? If you don't mind my saying, things look a bit rough around here."

Jake sliced into a biscuit, and Gil watched the steam rise above the knife. "The place is a little worn down, but not so much that it can't be repaired."

"Who's going to do the work? Dad's not up to it, and you're too old to manage by yourself."

The grizzled cowboy shook his head. "Your dad's seen harder times than this. He'll have things in order soon enough. Nobody wants that more than him." Jake took a bite that left a smudge of gravy at the side of his mouth. "What about you? If you have a mind to stay awhile, maybe you could help get the ranch on its feet?"

Gil ducked his head, plagued by all the reasons to stay, yet spurred by his inner desire to flee. "I need to head back to the city later this week to take care of some business."

"Business, huh?" Jake's disappointment was evident. "Well, until then, it's gonna be nice having you around. Ain't it, Mildred?" He went back to his breakfast, smiling like a little kid. "Whoo-wee, just like old times."

"What's all the commotion about?" John McCray lumbered into the room with his cane, his eyes fastened on Gil. "I figured you'd be gone by now."

"I'll be out of your hair in a few days." Gil noticed the deepening crease in his father's brow and wondered how he would manage his dad's company for that amount of time.

"I'm surprised you're staying so long—surprised those football folks of yours ain't called you back already."

Gil tried not to let the spiteful words anger him, and he tried not to think about football. How would he handle retirement? No morning meetings with the guys, no afternoon practice, no game plans to study. From now on, everything would be different.

He smeared cherry jam on one of the biscuits and smiled at Mildred's cooking, sure it could take his mind off his problems. She was the one woman who might come close to his mama in the kitchen. "Did you make this jam yourself, Mildred?" He bit into the warm bread and savored the tart flavor.

"That's some of the preserves Mattie gave us this fall. She's a good cook, that girl."

Gil's brow puckered as he took another bite from the biscuit. He thought of the red-haired doctor and then of his horse. Baffled by how good the jam tasted, he shoved the last morsel into his mouth. "I planned to drop in and see how Dusty's doing this morning. Mind if I take Dr. Evans a few of your tasty biscuits?"

Mildred smiled at the compliment and nodded. "She probably

didn't bother to eat before work this morning. All skin-and-bones, she is."

From what Gil had seen of the Diamond Fall's veterinarian, he was inclined to agree. He wrapped two biscuits in a paper napkin, then rubbed the stubble on his chin. Maybe he should freshen up a bit first.

"I don't know what to think about your busy schedule," his father said. "Never any time to sit and talk."

"We'll have plenty of time for that later." Gil hoped he and his dad could be civil long enough to have that visit, but not now. "Jake, can I borrow your truck again?"

The old cowboy got up from the table and placed his hat on his head. "I've got heifers to check, so I won't need it."

"I appreciate the favor."

"You could borrow my truck," his dad said. "Or your mama's car is parked in the garage."

"My luck, I'd put a dent in one of them, and you'd cuss me up one side and down the other." Gil chuckled, only half-teasing. "Jake doesn't have to worry, 'cause he'd never know a new dent from an old one."

Jake grinned broadly. "Whoo-wee, I do believe our boy's home."

NINE

MATTIE STEPPED OUT INTO THE MORNING SUNSHINE AND HER COFFEE
steamed in the cool air. In another month, it would be calving and
foaling season. Business was bound to pick up. When she entered
the barn, she found the chestnut gelding sitting up. A good sign.
Nearly forty-eight hours had passed since Dusty's surgery, and his
body was responding well to treatment. She knelt beside him and
slid her palm against his neck.

"Hey, Dusty. How are you doing this morning?" She eased her
hand down his chest and right leg, pleased the swelling had lessened. "Let's see if you're ready to stand." With a slight tap to his
backside, she gave him a gentle push, urging him to his feet. The
horse didn't budge.

"Haven't I seen this before?"

Mattie recognized the man's voice instantly and rose from her
knees. "Are you going to stand there and gawk or are you going to
help?" she asked, unable to keep the smile from her face.

"I'm here to serve." Gil laid a sack beside her coffee on the
wooden bench, then stood beside Dusty and nudged the horse's side
as he'd done the night before. "I don't know what you're going to do
when I'm not here, Doc."

"I can always steal one of the posters they display of you in town. That ought to do the trick." She wanted to cheer when the horse wobbled up on all fours.

Gil chuckled. "What do you have against football players, anyway?"

"I don't have anything against big, bulky men who strut around in skintight pants." She grinned teasingly. "Rodeo's a whole lot easier to understand."

"Did you rodeo?"

"Barrels and poles. Tied some goats," Mattie said. "I understand you had a future in rodeo. Why'd you quit?"

Gil looked away. "Football offered me a better deal."

"Do you miss it?"

"I've participated in a few charity ropings. It's a good way to raise money for kids who need it."

Mattie knelt to examine Dusty's front hooves, surprised Gil would be involved in charity work. "What else do you do when you're not playing football? Television commercials? Let's see, maybe prance around in men's underwear or sell deodorant?" She glanced up to see if this embarrassed him.

"I never prance. I own investments and sponsor a foundation." He slid his hands into his jean pockets, then smiled. "I once did a milk commercial, but I take it you've never seen it?"

Feeling the warmth of her own embarrassment, she turned her attention to the horse. "I don't watch much television."

"And when you do, Sunday Night Football isn't on your list of priorities, right?"

"Smart guy." She rose and went to the other side of the horse to distance herself from this imposing man who made her feel like a Shetland pony next to a Percheron stallion. "What brings you here this morning, anyway?"

"I brought you some of Mildred's biscuits. I figured after the cold hamburger last night, you might enjoy a warm snack."

Mattie smiled at the gesture. "All I've had is strong coffee." She put a rope around Dusty's neck, and the thought of the freshly baked biscuits made her stomach growl.

"If you want, I'll heat them in your microwave."

"That won't be necessary." She'd eat the food cold before she'd allow this man to see the dirty dishes on her kitchen counter and clothes lying in a heap on the floor. "Dusty's swelling has gone down some. The more he moves, the less stiffness he'll have."

"Should I try to walk him while you eat?"

"Some sunshine on his back would be good."

While Gil managed to lead Dusty out of the barn, Mattie washed up, then settled on a bench to watch. She took her first bite, savoring the buttery flavor as well as the morning sunshine.

"Tell me, Doc. What makes a young woman like you want to stay in a rinky-dink place like this? You'd have more business if you lived in a city."

Her eyes trailed Gil and his horse. He sounded like her parents. They were always notifying her about vet positions in Kansas City. Thought she'd make more friends and marry if she lived in the city. "I've never had any desire to leave these hills."

"You don't crave big malls or supermarkets? Theatres or nice restaurants? Don't you get lonely for people your own age?" Gil stopped to rest Dusty, who nosed a clump of fescue but didn't eat.

"I have lots of friends. And if I want to shop, all I have to do is hop in my truck and drive forty miles to Emporia."

"I grew up here, remember ... I know the population per square mile, and most of the people are over fifty."

Mattie stopped chewing. "By people, I assume you mean single men. What makes you think I wouldn't be interested in someone older? Like your father, for example." Her eyebrows rose as she waited for his response.

The register of shock made her want to laugh. "Did you think your dad and I were an item?" His sheepish expression told her the answer before he opened his mouth.

"I had my suspicions."

"I thought so." Mattie lowered her head, and a wispy curl fell in her face. She couldn't deny that she longed for romance. But pursue a man more than twice her age? She didn't think so. John McCray was like a father to her, not a beau.

Although he did own a respectable portion of the Flint Hills . . .

She bit into the flaky biscuit as though biting into a dream. The McCray property was a worthy investment. Established acreage with a house and outbuildings. Though the thought had its advantages, marrying a gentleman for his land was out of the question. "If God wants me to remain single, that's what I'll do."

Gil squatted and pulled a few slivers of grass from the ground. He placed them against Dusty's muzzle. "You'd be content with that?"

Mattie tore at the biscuit. "I have my work. Freedom to come and go as I please." *And my honor.*

Gil looked at Dusty, and the horse nickered, his ears twitching back and forth. "You make a good point. Who needs relationships when you have all this?" He extended his arms to the open prairie at the edge of town.

Mattie agreed. She might not own a ranch, but she had one of the better views of the Flint Hills right here from her clinic property. "What about you? Have you ever married?"

The man sobered. "I never let a woman interfere with the game. I didn't care to have the distraction."

"Even off-season? I find it hard to believe a man like you wouldn't want someone to come home to, little feet to pad the halls of your three-story mansion." Mattie looked away, hating her jealous heart. She thought of her sisters with their suburban homes. Even her best friend, Clara, still had her children to hug at night, despite a painful divorce.

This is the life you've given me, Lord. Help me be content.

Gil stood and tossed the grass to the ground. "I live in a two-bedroom townhouse near the Bay, but I've considered buying a ranch in Sonoma County to raise horses on—not children." His mouth curved into a twisted grin. "California isn't so bad once you get out of the city."

"Why not move back here and take over your dad's ranch?"

"I don't think so."

Her stomach tightened. How could Gil not take advantage of the opportunity? She'd have done somersaults to go into ranching with her dad—if she'd had the chance. Only a fool would give that up without a fight.

"Like I said before, you don't know how it is between me and the old man." He led Dusty to a bucket of water and waited. The horse sniffed at the plastic container.

You can lead a horse to water, but you can't make him drink. She figured it must be the same with men. But for the life of her, she couldn't understand it.

TEN

GIL WRESTLED WITH UNEASE AS HE EXITED THE BARN THIRTY MINUTES later. The doc said there was no cause for alarm over the fact that Dusty wasn't eating, but he noted her concern. She'd inserted another IV to treat the gelding with electrolytes. He wondered if colic might be an issue.

Dusty looked thin, but he'd been in a near-fatal accident and had undergone five hours of surgery. The horse would eat when he got hungry, right? Gil shook his head. Did he trust the doc or not?

In football, nearly everything hinged on numbers and odds. He considered Dusty's odds of getting better.

Sixty percent?

Better than half, but not good, given those were the same chances San Francisco had of beating Green Bay in the play-offs. Gil figured blind trust would have to prevail over common sense this time.

Driving to Emporia, Gil went over possible scenarios of what he might say when he met the hospitalized boy and his parents. He knew little about Dillon Marshall's injuries but heard the boy was in intensive care. Upon his arrival, he went straight to the receptionist and asked for directions.

When Gil saw the boy through the window, he shrank back, his heart in his throat. He would never understand the senselessness of drunk driving. The boy lay immobile in the hospital bed, his head bandaged. A man in a rumpled shirt came to the door where Gil stood and reached out his hand.

"I'm Dillon's father." His fatigue lifted slightly into a forced grin. "Nice to meet you, Mr. McCray. I heard you were home, though I never expected you to visit."

Gil tucked the gift he'd brought under his arm and gripped the man's hand in a firm shake, hoping to convey his earnest regret. "I'm sorry about your boy."

"We're sorry about your horse. I understand he's still alive."

Gil nodded. "He's a fighter. Apparently, your son is too."

The father's bloodshot eyes glistened, and Gil looked away.

"Dillon suffered from cerebral bleeding that resulted in a stroke," the man said. "His speech is impaired, and he's paralyzed from the waist down. We figure when your horse hit the car windshield, Dillon lost control and smashed into a rock culvert."

A woman came to the man's side and placed her hand on his arm. "The doctors say our son may never walk again." She wiped her tears with a tissue, then blew her nose.

Gil stared through the window at the boy. "Does he know about his friend?"

The father nodded. "The funeral's tomorrow. He wants to go, but there's no way . . ."

"May I see him?" At his question, the man opened the door for Gil.

The room smelled like disinfectant, a stench he'd grown to despise. He'd been in enough hospitals to last a lifetime, both to visit those who were ill and for his own football injuries. This time was no different. The medicinal odor and confined space made him claustrophobic, made him wish for fresh air.

White bandages hid Dillon's face.

"Hi, there." Gil offered the signed football he'd brought and laid it on the covers. "I understand you're the one who ran into my horse the other night."

The boy's lashes blinked and his head moved ever so slightly.

"I'm Gil McCray, quarterback for the 49ers. I've been banged up pretty bad from my time on the field, but I think you've beaten me, hands down. Are you in much pain?"

Again, the head nodded.

An IV and various clear tubes trickled medicine into the teen. "They probably have you doped up pretty well, and that's a good thing, believe me." Gil smiled, growing uncomfortable despite the many times he'd visited kids in hospitals. Even his work with the foundation, which sponsored anti-drinking-and-driving campaigns in schools throughout the nation couldn't prepare him for the one-on-one talks with kids. Never easy, but especially difficult this time.

He sat in the chair next to the bed and grabbed the football, wanting a familiar object to give him courage to say what needed to be said.

"I'm sorry about your friend." Gil stared at the bandaged boy, concentrated on the sterile dressings rather than the inner wounds. "I know what it's like to lose someone you care about. When I was your age, I lost my brother. He died in a vehicle accident the same way your friend did. He'd been drinking, and it cost him his life."

Gil clutched the football with both hands and squeezed it until his fingers turned white. "His accident's haunted me for a lot of years. I don't want to preach, but I hope you understand the magnitude of what's happened. Your friend died, but God's given you another chance . . ."

THAT EVENING AFTER SUPPER, GIL LOUNGED ON THE SOFA, HIS FEET propped on the coffee table. His dad sat across the room in his recliner, the television remote in hand.

"How is the Marshall boy doing? Jake said you went to see him in the hospital."

Gil's lips scrunched together as he stared at his leather loafers. "Not good. He's alive, but he doesn't have much to look forward to. Won't be scoring any touchdowns, that's for sure."

"Or roping any calves?"

Gil glanced at his dad and wondered if the jibe was intentional. "The doctors aren't giving him much hope to walk again." He shook his head, sickened by what the boy and his family had to deal with, besides the legal repercussions of drunk driving.

"Do you ever think about Frank?" Gil knew the answer already. How could his father not, when surrounded by the memories? Everywhere Gil looked, Frank or his mama appeared ... in photographs, china plates, or even a smell. In the last few hours, he'd detected his mother's scent three or four times, as though it hid in the wallpaper or upholstery and refused to leave.

His dad nodded, his wrinkles more apparent than before. "Mostly when I sit around with nothing to do. That's when the mind works the hardest."

Gil understood his father's dilemma. He'd felt the same when he'd been unable to play ball after he had knee surgery three years ago. There were few things worse than being laid up in bed.

He studied the room and noticed the heavy drapes with their sheer panels, the stained glass lamps, and the dainty doilies his mother made for the furniture. Nothing seemed to have changed since he was a boy, except for his dad's big screen television complete with an outside satellite dish. Then he noticed the chess set next to his mother's curio cabinet. "Do you still play?"

Not waiting for a reply, Gil strode across the wool area rug to grab the marble board and pieces. He placed them on the coffee table and began lining up the pawns. "Feel like getting beat in a game of chess—for old time's sake?"

His father lowered the television volume and tucked the remote inside his flannel shirt pocket. "Don't suppose there's much chance of that, but I'm willing if you are."

Gil grinned, ready to show his dad he'd learned a thing or two in the years he'd been away. He was no longer the dumb teenager who didn't have a clue about the rules of the king and his lady.

His dad made the first move, the queen's knight to her right.

As Gil inched one of his black pawns forward, a knock sounded on the front door.

"May I come in?" Dr. Evans peeked inside, and Gil noted her hair hung loose, not braided, this time. Pretty.

"Make yourself at home." His father waved her in from his recliner. "Gil's challenged me to a game of chess. Thinks he's going to whip my butt."

A huge smile formed on Mattie's face, and her eyes danced with laughter. "Maybe you'd like a snack while you play. I brought your favorite cookies." She laid a foil-covered plate on the coffee table and sat beside Gil on the couch.

Gil watched as she removed the silver wrapper to reveal little white cookies sprinkled with cinnamon and sugar. Picture-perfect in size and form, like their maker. He caught the trail of fresh air as Mattie slipped out of her coat and laid it on her lap.

His dad moved his pawn, then reached over and snatched two cookies from the plate. He offered one to Gil. "She makes them the way your mama used to. Chewy and good by themselves, but best with a cup of cold milk."

Mattie laughed. "Is that a hint?"

"Naw." His father's smile revealed even more wrinkles in his tough skin. "What brings you out this way?"

The woman fidgeted with her hands, small hands that looked cold. Gil advanced another pawn.

"I went to visit the Thornton family and took them some cookies. Pretty sad over there." Her face sobered as she stared at the chessboard.

"I imagine so." His dad broke his queen out of the line and captured Gil's bishop.

Gil swore under his breath. Dumb move on his part, he'd left his bishop wide open. How could he concentrate with the two of them gabbing? "I think I'll get us some milk."

"Ha, didn't think I was paying attention, did ya?" His father chuckled and slapped his hand on his knee. The laughter soon turned into a fit of coughing.

Mattie went to his side and patted his back. "You should take it easy. All this excitement will wear you out." She exchanged a look of caution with Gil before he headed to the kitchen.

What did the doc think — that he was trying to make his old man sick? Gil poured himself a cup of milk and downed it in four gulps. All he'd wanted was to have a nice evening with his father. Maybe start to make amends, but then Mattie Evans shows up with a plate of homemade cookies, her hair down, and smelling like sunshine in June. What was she doing here this time of night, anyway?

Prepared to find out, Gil poured two more drinks for his dad and their guest, then returned to the living room. He stopped mid-stride in the doorway.

The young woman sat on the arm of his dad's recliner, their hands clasped and voices hushed as though sharing an intimate moment.

Gil cleared his throat and marched in with the milk. "Tell me if I'm wrong, but Dr. Evans, shouldn't you be at the clinic taking care of my horse?"

ELEVEN

Mattie looked up, surprised by the question. She released John's warm hands and stood. "Actually, I just bid your father good night. I wanted to tell you that Dusty is doing better. The electrolytes seemed to give him a little more energy." Her voice remained steady. She refused to show Gil how much he'd upset her by his insinuating remark.

The man towered above her, but didn't budge. Neither did she.

"I'm glad he's showing progress. All the more reason for you to be there, to monitor his improvement."

Mattie wanted to stomp on the man's foot or punch him in the chin. She crossed her arms in front of her chest and stared him down instead. What was his problem, anyway? This morning, he'd been kind and helpful, bringing her biscuits. Now this?

"I'm a licensed veterinarian, but I'm not chained to my clinic twenty-four hours a day. Every once in a while, I do come up for air, shop for groceries, even visit friends if I choose."

"Whoa, now." John set his glass of milk on the coffee table, and she noticed how his hand shook. "I'm sure Gil's not questioning your ethics."

"No, but it does make me wonder about your recent losses," Gil said. "Perhaps if you spent more time at your business instead of offering everyone snickerdoodles, you'd have a few more patients to care for."

The jab went straight to her heart and pierced it. Gil's words made her want to fall on her knees and weep ... or growl and strangle someone ... someone with a big head to match his large, athletic body.

"My presence obviously bothers you, so I'll head out." Mattie strained to keep her lips from trembling as she offered John a polite smile. She turned to scowl at the younger McCray. "Enjoy your cookies — and your game of chess." She reached for the shiny black bishop that marked John's progress and Gil's imminent defeat and shoved it into the pompous man's hand. With any luck, the old fellow would skunk his son in three moves.

"You know you're always welcome in my home," John called out when Mattie reached the front door. "This snot-nosed son of mine will be gone tomorrow, so you won't have to tolerate his nonsense next time."

His words sang in the foyer and brought a smile to her face. She waved good-bye, but Gil stood stiff as a soldier, like a defender of the king's castle or something. It made her want to laugh.

The man didn't have a clue what he was protecting, let alone whom.

GIL LEANED AGAINST THE SEAT OF THE PASSENGER PLANE AND STARED out the window at the clouds below. Jake had driven him to the airport in Wichita, and as they left Diamond Falls, they'd waited on Jimmy Thornton's funeral procession. Among the many vehicles in the caravan, he'd noticed Dr. Evan's white pickup. She'd apparently taken time off to attend the memorial service.

What had possessed him to harangue the doc the night before — to the point of embarrassing his father, and his father's guest?

He couldn't say, except that it had practically knocked him off his feet to see Mattie and his dad holding hands. Earlier, she'd laughed when he'd admitted his suspicions about their relationship. Now he questioned her sincerity. Could the doc be after his father's land? Or was she an honest-to-goodness friend? He hadn't met many women like her, who seemed to care about the people around her — in this case, the entire community of Diamond Falls. But he'd known plenty who were hot one minute and cold the next, and it usually meant trouble.

Gil looked down at the sports magazine he'd picked up in the airport terminal and saw Green Bay's quarterback plastered on the front page. He set his jaw and felt the ache in his gut. It was time to get on with life. Trouble was, after fifteen years in the NFL that might prove hard to do.

Ten days later, Gil entered the coach's San Francisco office and handed him a folded piece of paper. "How many more of these documents do I have to sign?"

The man's smile revealed crooked teeth. "That's the last of them, if you're sure you want to go through with this."

A moment's hesitation struck Gil before he nodded. "It's time to give someone else a shot at the game. I had my chance."

"The fans will remember you, don't worry. Your numbers are right up there with Young and Montana." The cheerfulness faded in his eyes. "I've scheduled one more news conference with reporters later this afternoon and then you're free to go."

His coach leaned over his desk and picked up a wood-framed photograph of the 49ers in their early years. "Nowadays, it's hard to find players with staying power. You're the last from the old team, who cared more about the game and the team you played for than the money you made. The boys and I are going to miss you."

"You'll probably see me in the announcer's box one of these days and then you'll sing a different tune."

The man laughed and stood from behind his desk. "With you at the microphone, I know we'll be in trouble." He squeezed Gil's shoulder with affection. "What will you do now?"

Gil stared at the oak bookcase in his coach's office, at the many pictures of his team through the years. "I'm not sure. Spend more time with the foundation—maybe buy a ranch up north."

"Why not take some time off and visit your dad? Repair the damage done after all these years."

"I just came from there. I'm not sure I want to go back so soon."

His coach reached into his pocket and pulled out a silver watch. He played with the chain between his thick fingers. "Here, I want you to have this." The gray-haired man pressed the timepiece into Gil's palm. "My first coach gave it to me when I was a boy. You've been like a son to me. I guess it's time to hand it down."

Uncomfortable with the emotional display, Gil shook his head. "I can't take your watch, Coach. You'll never arrive to practice on time if I do." He slapped his coach on the forearm in an effort to lighten the mood.

The man glared at him. Gil had witnessed that determined look often enough to know not to argue. "My dad gave it to me, now I'm turning it over to you. Don't lose it. It keeps good time ... but remember, even the steadiest of us old-timers will stop running one day."

Coach always did have a way with words. Gil gripped the watch with his fingers and felt the smooth metal beneath his touch. "Thanks, Coach. I won't forget."

After lunch, Gil's secretary greeted him as he entered the fifth-floor office space where he ran his private foundation.

"Welcome home, Mr. McCray." The young blonde straightened in her chair, her posture perfect, and her nails a shade of dark pink that matched her lipstick.

"Is everyone here for the meeting?" he asked as he passed her desk.

She smiled and handed him a folder. "The last one slipped in about two minutes before you arrived."

"Good." Gil took the document from her. He appreciated punctuality in his board members. "Hold any calls for the next few hours and don't schedule me for anything this afternoon. Seems I have an appointment with some reporters."

He moved down the hall to the conference room. The second he opened the door, the flurry of conversation halted.

"Good afternoon, everyone. Nothing like a few traffic jams and the smell of exhaust to welcome a person back to the city." He raised his eyebrows, and they chuckled in return. Prepared to go to work, he removed his gray tweed jacket. "Show me what you've done while I've been gone."

For the next sixty minutes, Gil and his five board members discussed possible contributions, as they did every month. At the end of the session, a stack of paperwork sat in front of Gil on the table to review. His role as financier and overseer of the Gil McCray Foundation had been made possible through his football career. Thankfully, he'd built sizeable investments during that time, and he hoped to continue the foundation in the years to come.

He took the folders to his office and reviewed the possible donations—all victims of drunk drivers. About halfway through the pile, the afternoon sun beamed through the spacious windows and bounced rays of light against his desk. Distracted, his gaze settled on the football propped there, and his heart sank at the realization.

He wasn't going to play anymore.

His football career was over.

Too restless to work, Gil walked to the front desk and laid an envelope in front of the secretary.

"Here's a case I'm interested in. Have Jonathan investigate the report and see if it meets our specifications."

"And if it does?"

"You know what to do." Gil pulled his jacket on and straightened his knit collar. "What do you think? Do I look okay for my last appointment with the press?"

The young woman offered a smile and pulled a red necktie from her bottom drawer. She held it out for him, but he declined.

"You know better than that. Ties are reserved for game day."

Gil sauntered out of the office to the elevator, and only then did he allow his smile to fade. No more ties for him. No more game days. What would he do with his life now?

TWELVE

"Hey, he's on." Mattie's new assistant covered the mouth of her cell phone.

"Who's on what?" Mattie glanced up from her prep work, unable to hide the disapproval from her face.

"Dusty's owner, that football guy. He's on FOX-TV. Mom says they're interviewing him about his retirement."

Retirement?

Mattie waved an electric razor in the air, ready to shave a retriever's belly for surgery. She had no time for nonsense. "Katy, we have another hour before we close." Her tolerance for football celebrities had worn thin, as had her patience for the high school help she'd hired. Why would she be interested in anything to do with Gil McCray? Although it did surprise her that he hadn't mentioned his retirement.

"You're going to have to tape it for us, Mom. I've gotta go." Katy tucked her cell phone into her jeans pocket. "Sorry about that. She's a sports fanatic."

"You're excused this time, but from now on, no personal calls at work." Mattie checked the dog's heartbeat on the electrocardiogram and adjusted the level of anesthesia. She took a long swipe at the dog's stomach with the razor and peeled away a strip of reddish-brown fur.

Gil had been gone for over a week, but it seemed like he hadn't even left. Mattie thought of him every time she looked at Dusty, which was a cruel joke, considering the last time she'd seen Gil, he'd blasted her for inappropriate care of her patients. To think the man practically begged her to give his horse an extra dose of love.

Three more swipes with the razor, and she was ready. "If blood bothers you, step away. The last thing I need is for you to faint, because I won't be able to help you once I open her up."

Katy straightened. "I'll be okay."

Mattie sterilized the shaved area and checked the patient's heartbeat once more. With her scalpel, she made a quick incision in the dog's midsection. She glanced at the teenager, whose face had turned a shade of green.

"Better get some fresh air before you wind up on the floor."

Not everyone had a stomach for surgery, which appeared to be the case with her new employee. An hour later the teenager left for a high school basketball game, and Mattie locked the clinic door behind the girl. She wished she had the girl's energy, then maybe she wouldn't feel so old and unappreciated.

While waiting for her patient to come out of anesthesia, Mattie finished cleaning the surgical room and checked the animals in the back. A Siamese cat stretched his long body and brushed his soft fur against the metal bars, while her pet parrot nuzzled a piece of cuttlebone. Mattie filled their water trays and saw the retriever yawn. Once the dog revived, she grabbed her coat and went to the barn to settle Dusty in for the night.

"How are you doing, boy?" She spoke in a soft voice and patted him on his rump, the cold night air causing her teeth to chatter. He wobbled to his feet, and Mattie walked him a few steps. She removed his bandages and applied ointment to his wounds. Though the electrolytes and fluids were keeping the horse from dehydration, they did nothing for his weight loss, which seemed more noticeable today.

"Come on, Dusty. Doesn't this look good?" She held a clump of alfalfa under his nose to tempt him and watched the gelding nip at it. He took a little, then turned away. She patted him for his efforts and led the horse to his pen, noting the overall gaunt look and the more pronounced ribcage.

Dusty stood a good sixteen hands tall and even in his suffering, Mattie could tell he'd been a great athlete. She imagined him in his prime — chasing a steer at breakneck speed, then sliding to a halt with his rump nearly touching the ground. She envisioned Gil on Dusty's back, leaving his saddle in one fluid motion with his hand on the jerk line as he ran down the rope to flank the calf. Her heartbeat quickened as she pictured the two as a team.

Then reality surfaced.

Her pleasure turned to sorrow as the injured animal hung his head in pain and his knees collapsed to the soft, straw bedding.

Before leaving, she gave him an injection of antibiotics and drew some more blood. "Help Dusty heal, Lord." She knelt to kiss the horse, knowing she'd already lost her heart to him.

Minutes later, Mattie climbed the steps to her apartment and flipped on the kitchen light. Silence greeted her, except for the clock ticking on the wall and the whistle of the north wind as it whipped against the side of the house. She grabbed a dinner from the freezer and stuck it in her microwave. Thankful for a chance to relax, Mattie rested her head on the overstuffed arm of the couch and punched the television remote to hear the news. Instead, she caught the end of a reality program filmed in the jungle.

Didn't these people have lives?

She changed the channel and a familiar face filled the screen, his upper lip rimmed by a milk moustache.

"Got milk?" the advertisement prompted, and the football player smiled straight at her. Even thousands of miles away, the man managed to infiltrate her life.

The commercial segued into a news clip of Gil's retirement.

"Gil, you had a great season of 14–2, with a tough ending in the playoffs," the journalist said. "Let's take a moment to highlight your career. You began as a pro-quarterback fifteen years ago with the Denver Broncos and have played with the 49ers the last ten. In that time, you passed for over 39,000 yards, made 4200 pass completions, and threw 310 touchdown passes. How do you feel about ending your career with one MVP on your record, and what are your plans for the future?"

Mattie punched the remote and stared at the blank screen. Gil McCray might be a sports celebrity, but he'd shown her what kind of man he was when he criticized her veterinary skills—and he called himself a Christian. Ha! To her, he was nothing more than a spoiled, selfish man, no matter how great a quarterback or cowboy he used to be. Let him have his ranch in California. Charris County would be better off without him.

She got up to check the food in the microwave and as she set it to cook for a few more minutes, a multitude of sparks emitted from the oven, followed by a deafening bang and a burnt electrical smell. So much for a warm supper. She pulled the half-baked dish out of the microwave and ate the lukewarm meal in silence.

Three hours later, Mattie awoke to the incessant beep of her alarm clock. She reached out from under her warm blankets to turn on the lamp, and it flickered on, then off.

No electricity.

Managing to dress in the dark, she fumbled along the cold floor. As she headed for the kitchen for a flashlight, she caught the distinct odor of something burning. Sniffing the air, she decided it must be lingering fumes from the microwave or maybe the wind carrying smoke from a distant brush pile. She found the flashlight, then pulled on her leather boots and grabbed her coat. Not eager to go out into the wintry night, she made her way down the squeaky stairs to the clinic, then out to the barn where the overhead lights came on.

Surprised that the power worked in the barn, Mattie checked Dusty's vitals, then got him up to clean his stall. Thirty minutes later and eager to return to her warm bed, she led him in a large circle to exercise his swollen legs. When they neared the barn entrance, Dusty's ears perked and he snorted. Mattie glanced outside and her breath caught in her chest.

Bright orange flames raged inside her apartment window above the clinic.

GIL OPENED HIS FRONT DOOR AND WAS GREETED BY A HANDFUL OF his teammates on the stoop.

"Hey buddy, you can't spend the first night of your retirement cooped up by yourself." Johnson, one of his favorite running backs, pressed in through the doorway, followed by his best friend Charlie and a few more players.

Gil glanced at his pocket watch. "It's nine o'clock. Shouldn't you guys be in bed?"

"Not tonight. We have reservations," Johnson said and a couple of the men chuckled.

This aroused Gil's suspicions. "Why don't you fellows come in, and we'll put a movie on? We could study the clips from our playoff game with Green Bay." He awaited their reaction, anticipating it to be loud.

"Our friend thinks he's a comedian." Johnson latched on to Gil's shoulders and steered him to the door. "Grab your jacket. We're taking you out for a fine culinary experience."

Again, the guys snickered. Gil had a hunch it wasn't because they were hungry.

Half an hour later, he sat at a long table crammed with twelve or more hulking football players on plush pillowed benches. Smoke hung in the dark canopied room, as four costumed musicians created intoxicating rhythms on their stringed instruments. One man passed between the tables with his violin, followed by a scantily dressed woman with a tambourine.

Gil figured the guys would take him to one of their favorite spots in the Marina District but never guessed they'd end up at a fancy Moroccan restaurant. "Which one of you dreamed up this wild idea?"

Johnson's lips formed a cocky grin. "Me and my girlfriend tried this place out a few weeks ago. I thought bringing you here would be worth a few laughs. A man only retires once."

Gil nodded, able to read between the lines. The guys intended to get him drunk and embarrass him with a belly dancer.

Not gonna happen, guys.

He laughed with them and studied the luxurious tapestries on the wall until a waiter, his outfit complete with a red felt hat and black tassels, approached their table.

"Welcome, I am your personal servant, Niko. I understand you're here for a *kutlama*—a celebracíon." His thick accent flowed from his mouth like honey. "For your dining pleasure, we are preparing for you, *Kuzu Tandir*, a succulent roast lamb on a spit, served with grilled vegetables and an onion salad, sprinkled with only the finest herbs." The satin-dressed attendant clapped his hands and a veiled woman in a harem outfit brought an ornamented jug of wine to their table. She poured the dark liquid into everyone's glasses, then proceeded to sway her arms and hips to the sultry music of the harpsichord and mandolin.

Uncomfortable with the dancer's undulations, so close he could smell her musky perfume, Gil steered his eyes away from the curvaceous legs and bosom and trained his vision instead on the exotic features of her face, her eyes, the flashing jewels on her ears entangled in long spirals of thick, black hair.

Though half a continent apart, he couldn't help but compare the dancer to Dr. Evans. Mattie was spirited but nothing like the woman before him. The doc's innocence shown in her bright eyes and sweet smile, and he much preferred her soft red curls and petite frame to the lush figure that circled their table. Could he have been wrong about Mattie's relationship with his father?

Nearing his chair once again, the dancer tapped her fingers and a tinny succession of jingles echoed in his ears. The guys beside him whooped and whistled, and Gil became exceedingly uneasy from her attention. In an effort to ignore her and get away from the noise, he withdrew to the men's bathroom. When he returned, their red-capped waiter met him at the table with a tray of appetizers.

"And now for your Saganaki, a mild Kasseri cheese soaked with cognac." He took out his lighter and dipped it above the amber liquid, igniting a slow blaze, which eventually engulfed the entire creation.

"Opa!" he said, and those at the table echoed his exclamation.

Gil stared at the golden-blue flames, entranced by the seductive way the fire danced and flickered over the cheese delicacy, his thoughts drifting back to Kansas.

THIRTEEN

Mattie stood transfixed by the blazing fire shooting out her apartment window. Her body filled with terror. Worried about her patients in the clinic below, she dropped Dusty's lead rope and rushed the thirty yards from the barn to the house. Upon entering the clinic door, she pulled her flashlight from her coat pocket and beamed it around the front office. Smoke slithered from the crevices in the ceiling and filled the room.

She needed help. When she felt for the cell phone normally clipped to her jeans, it wasn't there. She remembered leaving it on the nightstand by her bed.

No good to her now.

The fire had not yet reached the downstairs, but Mattie could almost feel her hair crinkle from the intense heat overhead. She covered her nose and mouth and ran to the back where the animals were caged. Even before she opened the door, she heard the insistent yelps of a puppy, her parrot's squall, the spine-tingling yowls of two frantic cats.

With trembling fingers, Mattie unlatched the first gate she came to of a mother cat and her kittens.

"Scoot, kitties. Out with you." She captured the fluffy fur balls one by one, and they brushed past her legs to follow their mama. Next, she aimed the flashlight on the golden retriever she'd operated on earlier. The dog opened its bleary eyes. Still groggy, the patient couldn't walk on its own.

Mattie flung the cage open and struggled to lift the dog. With shaky legs, she carried the retriever out the rear door to a place of safety under a big cottonwood tree. Doubling over to catch her breath, Mattie watched as the office curtains burst into flames. Then came the chinking *pop* of breaking glass.

Twice more she returned to the clinic to rescue her patients, and on her third trip, smoke billowed into the small back room. As she headed for the animals' cages, a monstrous sound exploded in her ears as the ceiling crashed down in front of her. Crackling flames burst through the hole above with a devilish hiss. She ducked out of the way of the blazing embers, which scorched her face with their intense heat. Her hands trembled with fear.

Think, Mattie, think.

Smoke stung her eyes and nostrils. Her mind felt muddled by the haze.

Hard to breathe.

As she gasped, her lungs instantly rejected the foul, tainted stench of burning plastic and synthetic materials, causing her to choke and sputter for her next gulp of air.

Her movements seemed to occur in slow motion, making it difficult to assess what needed to be done next. "Oh Lord, please help me," she called out.

Drop to the floor.

Mattie recalled this childhood instruction from school, so she allowed herself to collapse to the concrete floor. There, her breathing came easier. Using the collar of her coat, she covered her nose and crawled on hands and knees to the cages, her only goal to rescue the patients trapped inside. She reached the pen of the Labrador stray and let her out, then went on to the prairie dog she'd adopted and fumbled to unlatch the gate. Urging it from its confines, she inched onward where two cats paced and howled inside their barred quarters.

Too close to the fire now, Mattie feared she might crumple and incinerate in the heat like a foam plate at a wiener roast.

Blistering, scorching heat.

Her fingers grasped the lock, and the heated metal seared her skin.

She let go at the sudden pain and shook her hand at the stinging sensation.

Too hot.

Sweat dripped from her face as she searched for a glove or rag to use as insulation. She struggled out of her coat sleeves. The more she exerted herself, the harder it was to breathe.

Mattie's throat constricted, parched now. Her lungs could take no more. A bout of coughs besieged her. Salty tears streamed down her cheeks, and her eyes burned even more.

A bird squawked from above.

Her parrot. She'd never save them all, not even her own precious pets.

Mattie squeezed her eyelids shut in an effort to block out this horrible nightmare. How could this happen to her? What had she done to deserve such bitter loss?

So tired.

If she could rest a few minutes, regain her energy, then she'd rescue the animals. The fire raged on all sides of her now. It snarled and licked at her, making fun of her futile efforts.

Her throat felt as dry as sandpaper. Just thinking about the taste of cool water made her desire it more. She gasped for air and in-haled the putrid smoke around her. Her lungs retaliated, and she lurched forward in another fit of coughing. A nine-week-old puppy pranced and yelped in a cage nearby. It clawed for freedom, shred-ding the newspaper flooring as though it were dirt. If someone had only claimed the pup stranded near her clinic three weeks ago, it wouldn't be fighting for its life right now.

She allowed the pup's desperate appeal to purge her terror as she inched closer, determined not to give up until she held the frightened animal in her arms.

The muffled noise of sirens merged with the jeering fire but offered Mattie no hope. She might rescue the puppy from the cage, but no one would save them from the fiery inferno. It was too late.

FOURTEEN

Niko returned with a fourth jug of wine and proceeded to fill the empty glasses. All but Gil's—his was still full from the first round. He'd vowed long ago not to drink and had no intention of giving in to the temptation now. Someone had to be responsible for getting the boys home tonight.

Charlie shared his belief and covered his goblet when the attendant came around. He then reached for his glass of water. "I hope you don't mind our party tonight. The guys wanted to show you their appreciation."

Gil surveyed a handful of his teammates who had joined the exotically dressed female in the center of the restaurant to learn the art of belly dancing. "No offense, but I think they're enjoying the evening more than me. I'm grateful for the effort, though. The food's good." He raised a chunk of marinated lamb to his lips and bit off another piece of the spicy meat. "Well worth the indigestion I'll have later for eating so much."

Charlie chuckled. "You know this isn't the end of the celebration. Coach and the guys are planning a major retirement party for you."

Gil cringed, hating extravagant good-byes. "You don't have to do that."

"Oh, but we do." His friend sipped his water. "You're an inspiration to us all."

He had never considered himself an inspiration to anyone, especially grown men. "I didn't do anything you wouldn't have done. We play the game, that's all."

"That's why we like you, McCray. You love the game. All that other stuff means nothing. You don't let the money, the hype—the good-looking babes—get to you."

"You don't either."

Charlie stole a piece of meat from Gil's plate and smiled. "I've got Linda and the kids. Do you realize we celebrated our sixteenth anniversary last week? Jason will be in high school next year, and Rhonda the year after that. They grow so fast. I can't imagine what life would be like without them."

An unforeseen cloud of jealousy settled over Gil when his friend talked about his family. He half expected a thunderbolt to shoot right through the roof of this establishment and strike him in the heart. After all his years of playing ball, Gil had a few measly memories to show for it and nothing more. He didn't have a wife to go home to, nor did he have anyone to share in his joy or success. At this point, Gil didn't even have a place to call home, certainly not the townhouse he lived in.

"I have my eyes on a piece of real estate up by Healdsburg, north of Santa Rosa."

"No kidding? Are you finally going to buy that home you've dreamed about?"

Gil thought of the two-hundred-acre ranch with its Spanish-style hacienda and front courtyard, and his mood brightened. "Maybe you'd like to go with me this weekend to check it out?"

Charlie frowned and scratched his head. "I'd like to help, but

Linda's got my whole weekend booked with a ballet recital and a visit to her folks."

Typical response. "If I had a wife and family as great as yours, I'd spend my free time with them too, even if it meant going to recitals." He punched Charlie's shoulder and grinned.

The tempo of the music shifted and in his peripheral vision, Gil saw a long line of football players shuffle toward him, led by the gyrating belly dancer. His humor faded when she pulled him from his bench, cajoling him to join the others.

"No way." He tried to wave them off, but his protests were of no use. The guys followed right behind her, ready to take over if she failed. "Okay, but only if Charlie comes too."

Charlie shook his head, but Gil grabbed him by the sleeve. "Huh-uh, buddy. If I go, you go. You were part of this idea, remember?"

As they formed a circle, a woman distributed cheap, white dishes to hold. The gigantic dopey football players stood among the other diners, all embarrassed but willing to go beyond their comfort zones for the sake of a good time. Gil watched them dance about, some with real zeal. When it came time for him to crash his plate to the floor, he splayed his arms and kicked his feet with exaggerated flair.

"Opa!" The entire crowd cheered as the china shattered into hundreds of pieces.

FIFTEEN

Mattie heard a crash and opened her eyes to see flashing lights against the night sky. She lay flat on her back with an oxygen mask strapped to her face. When her vision cleared, she shifted and saw her clinic in flames. Firemen rushed about, hoses in their hands.

Her own palms and fingers burned like never before. She noted the gauze wrapped around them. Cradled next to her was the stray beagle she'd tried desperately to save from the fire. He licked her arm with his soft tongue. Beside her was her good friend, Clara.

Mattie tried to lift the mask, then coughed, her throat raspy and sore. "What happened? I thought I was going to die in there."

Clara squeezed her in a warm embrace, her face tear-streaked and pale. "I've never been so frightened in all my life. When we saw the animals out here, but not you, the crew went in through the rear. They found you on the floor with this puppy in your arms."

A paramedic pushed the mask back against Mattie's skin. "I'm sorry, ma'am, but you'll have to keep that on." He shined a bright light in her eyes and checked her blood pressure. When the medic finished his examination, Mattie pushed herself up on her elbows.

"Did they save the other animals?" she asked, not sure she wanted to know the answer.

Clara shook her head. "I'm sorry, I'm just thankful they rescued you. We thought we'd lost you."

Mattie tried to remember. Her head throbbed, and her body trembled—from the cold night air or shock, she wasn't sure which. She recalled her futile attempt to save the rest of the animals. How had the fire started?

"Do they know what caused it?" As soon as the words left her mouth, she remembered the microwave and the sparks that had emitted from it only a few hours ago.

"Wouldn't surprise me if that old house had a short in its wires. I thank God you're alive."

The paramedics lifted Mattie onto a stretcher. "We're going to take you to the hospital to run some tests," one of them said. "You inhaled a lot of smoke, plus you have first-degree burns on your hands."

As they wheeled her to the ambulance, Mattie thought of Dusty and panicked. "Clara, I left Gil's horse in the barn. He's not tied up or anything, and he's weak because he hasn't been eating. Will you call Travis and make sure he looks after him?"

"Sure thing." Clara squeezed Mattie's arm and walked beside the gurney. "Don't worry. As soon as I get a sitter for my kids, I'll join you at the hospital. We can work out all the details then." Her friend reached for the young beagle cuddled against Mattie's hip, but Mattie clung to the warm pup, relishing the gift of life.

"Let me keep him a while longer."

Clara hesitated. "I'll take good care of him, don't worry."

At Clara's insistence, Mattie reluctantly let go of the creature. Her arms now cold and empty, like her life. Mattie raised her head and watched as the local fire department worked to put out the blazing inferno. Realizing her home would soon be a pile of smoldering embers, she allowed her emotions to release and a single tear streaked down her cheek.

"What will you do now?" Clara sat next to Mattie's bed in the hospital the following afternoon.

Mattie had been asking herself the same question. She might run her practice from the barn for a little while, but not for long without equipment and supplies. Another option was to rebuild. Or move a mobile home onto the site. But with what? She didn't have enough money for a down payment, and unfortunately, her limited insurance coverage would not go far in getting her back on her feet.

Her optimism dwindled.

"Maybe I could rent a place. Work part-time at the meat-packing plant in Emporia." The pay would help build her savings, but the thought of hiring on as a meat inspector soured her stomach. She'd labored too hard to build her clientele in Charris County to see it fade away.

She thought about Dusty and the few animals she'd saved. Unable to care for them, she would need to contact their owners, but all of her records had been destroyed in the fire. Dread slipped its iron grip around her as she imagined what Gil would say about her situation. *Incompetent.*

That alone filled her with disgust.

"You could stay with me."

Mattie appreciated the offer, but declined. "We both know you don't have room for me and my sick animals. What I need is a place with a garage or a nice shed I could turn into a clinic. I'm afraid if I quit, even for a short while, it'd be like starting over again. When I bought Doc Bryant's place three years ago, he was open two days a week," Mattie said, "and then for only half a day. The rest of the time, he made house calls and supplemented his income by working at the local stockyards. I've done the same."

Clara grimaced. "My husband always told me to give the restaurant time, but you don't know how many days I wanted to pack up and move to the city. When he left me stranded with a business to run and three kids to care for after the divorce, I was this close to quitting." She held her fingers an inch apart. "But I stuck it out. You can too."

Mattie thanked the Lord for giving her such a good friend. God had looked after her needs, granted her a business, and an income she could live on in the most beautiful place she could imagine. He'd given Mattie her heart's desire. But what now? Was God testing her faith?

Her father's failure weighed her with doubt. Perhaps his past would fall on her. She could already hear the gossip, people wondering if she was going to go bankrupt like her dad.

Her head throbbed, thinking about her troubles. "Sometimes I wonder if I should even be a vet — I lost all those patients."

"Are you kidding me? You risked your life saving those animals, and you rescued the majority of them. Saved the beagle, didn't you?" Clara offered a warm smile.

A nurse stepped into the room and laid some papers on the bed stand. "The doctor says you can go home. Here are the release papers for you to sign." She handed Mattie a pen. "Do you have some clean clothes to change into?"

Clara lifted an overnight bag next to her chair. "I thought of that already. The pants will be too big for you, but they'll work for now."

Mattie appreciated the kindness, but her friend's generosity only hammered in the truth that she was homeless. She had no clothes, no personal belongings, nothing to call her own. Her eyes filled with tears.

Clara came to her side and squeezed her shoulder. "You'll stay with me and the kids until we figure out what you're going to do next. We don't have a big house, but there's a couch and a shower. I'll find you some clothes to wear too. I might have some jeans packed away from high school you can borrow until we get to a store."

Mattie allowed her friend to pull her from the bed, careful of her bandaged hands, which stung at the slightest pressure despite the ointment applied to them. *Thank you* seemed too small a phrase to express her gratitude. A tear streamed down her cheek. "You're a dear friend, Clara Lambert. I don't know how I'll ever repay you for your kindness."

Clara hugged her and the warmth of friendship caused Mattie's throat to swell with gratitude.

"Oh please, knowing you is a blessing. Now come on, let's get you out of here."

GIL PUNCHED IN HIS FATHER'S NUMBER, HOPING TO GET THROUGH. He'd tried three times this last hour and received a busy signal each instance.

Who could Dad be talking to?

Earlier that morning, he'd called Mattie's office, but no one answered there either. Doubts clouded his mind about Dr. Evans and her practice. How could she expect to gain new clientele if she wouldn't answer her phone?

The phone beeped in his ear, and he hung up, tired of the effort. He needed to leave for his appointment, anyway. The Realtor agreed to show him the estate he was interested in, and his blood surged with excitement. Maybe he'd soon own a place to call home, a place even his father might think worthy of buying.

Ninety minutes later, Gil stepped from his Escalade and met the real estate broker along the property drive. She had long blonde hair swept back from her face and wore a short skirt and heels that looked out of place in the rural setting.

"Nice to meet you, Mr. McCray." The woman held out her slim hand. She wore too much makeup, and her smile seemed contrived. That would probably change when she realized his interest was more than a passing fancy, when actual dollars entered the picture.

"Thanks for setting this up for me. I've been curious about this place for a while now."

"No problem. I must caution you, the estate isn't officially on the market yet. The owners have agreed, however, to let you tour the home and property."

Warning bells went off in Gil's mind, but he waved it off as nothing more than a business ploy, a stratagem to attract buyers and make more money. After all, a person wants most what he thinks he can't have. "I appreciate your time and effort. Shall we start with the horse barn and work our way to the house?"

He'd played this game often enough with investors to know how best to maneuver the players, much like a game of chess. Don't let them see how interested you are until you're ready to take the queen. In this case, though, it might prove difficult to hide his enthusiasm. The more he saw of this property, the more he wanted it. Green irrigated hills, pipe fence, shade trees galore, and a house and barn that made his heart beat as fast as it did on game days.

They walked inside the horse barn, and it was everything he'd imagined and more. Situated near the entrance was an office and, above it, private quarters for two employees. Gil studied the custom stalls that lined the east wall, then turned his attention to the center arena, complete with bleachers and a glass-enclosed announcer's box. A perfect setup for holding clinics, performance events, and for training horses.

The outside arrangement was nice too. Two different-sized round pens, a training arena, various lots for horses and cattle, and plenty of grass for grazing. Gil hid his excitement, but in his heart, he knew he'd purchase the property for the horse facilities alone, without even looking at the residence.

Gil grinned. The notion of appearing disinterested appealed to his sense of sport. He made a fuss of checking his pocket watch. "You know what? I need to get back to the city. Maybe we could finish the tour another day?"

Shock registered on the agent's face. "You don't want to look at the manor? But you've driven all this way ..."

Gil made a cursory glance of the front courtyard as he walked to his SUV. The Spanish-style home suited his taste — heavily ornamented and carved with turrets and columns. The red-tiled roof and stucco walls would provide cool temperatures in the hottest months, and the entrance was grand enough to impress even the most sophisticated critic.

"Perhaps next time." He held out his hand and kept a solemn expression, despite his exuberance. If he could pull this off, he'd feel like the king of Sonoma County. "Another day, then?"

At her nod, he hopped into his vehicle and left the woman standing there with an expression of disbelief. His goal exactly.

Not checkmate, but definitely check.

SIXTEEN

"THERE'S NO WAY I'M GOING TO MOVE IN WITH YOU AND MOM. IT just wouldn't work," Mattie told her dad Sunday morning on her cell phone.

"Only until you find a place of your own. I'm sure with your skills and experience, you'd find a job at a clinic in no time. And who knows, you might decide you like city life."

Mattie clenched her teeth with determination. Kansas City would drive her crazy with its six-lane traffic and concrete walls. "Sorry, Dad, I'll never live in a city."

"Not a city — a suburb."

She settled into Clara's recliner and dabbed her freshly washed curls with a towel. The fragrance of herbal shampoo and conditioner was a welcome change from the clinging stench of smoke, which had stayed with her in the hospital. Though the smell was now gone, the reality of the fire and how it affected her life was not. "I appreciate your concern, but Charris County is my home. I don't intend to leave."

Her dad fell silent for a moment. "At least let us to bring you some clothes and supplies. Your mom's done nothing but shop since she learned of the fire." His gentle voice soothed her, and Mattie suddenly wanted nothing more than the comfort of her parents.

"That sounds good. Be sure to give Mom my love and tell her thanks. I'll see you soon." She made a few arrangements, then said good-bye, sure her parents would keep trying to convince her to go with them.

The little beagle she'd saved bounded into the living room and hopped up on Mattie's legs, ready to play. "But it won't do any good, will it? We're not going anywhere," she told the pup and nudged him behind the ears.

Clara joined them and sat across from Mattie in another recliner. Her two youngest children followed. Sara climbed onto her lap, while her older brother, Nathan, waited at Clara's side. Their pixie faces made Mattie smile, despite her gloomy mood.

"Here's a copy of last week's *Reader-News*. Maybe it'll list some rentals." Clara handed her the folded newspaper and bounced the two-year-old on her knee.

Mattie awkwardly flipped to the last page and read the classifieds. The rental section listed three mobile homes and nothing else. She laid the paper on the end table. "Not many options. Even if I manage to pull a trailer onto my property, I'll still be short either a clinic or a home. One trailer isn't big enough for both."

"Something will work out. We'll have the pastor pray for you at church this morning," Clara said as a knock sounded on the front door. She set Sara on the carpet with the puppy and got up to answer it, four-year-old Nathan in tow.

"Mornin', Clara. I understand you folks had some commotion the other night. Heard Mattie was staying with you."

Mattie recognized the deep voice and rose to greet the older gentleman in the next room. "You didn't need to come to town, John. I planned to call as soon as I figured out what to do with Dusty."

"That's why I'm here. Had Jake drive me in." Deep lines on his face showed his concern.

"I assure you, Dusty's okay." Mattie attempted to sooth his unease. She'd checked on the gelding earlier that morning and had purchased medicine in Emporia yesterday to get him by for at least a week. "The barn wasn't damaged from the fire. That's where I'm keeping the animals until their owners can pick them up. I have no way to care for them until my clinic's restored."

John shuffled into the front room, leaning heavily on his cane. "It's horrible what happened, but it's times like these when you gotta step back and let friends help. Ain't that right, Clara? Can't do everything yourself."

He chucked Nathan under the chin and smiled, his own chin covered by motley gray whiskers. "Jake's got the trailer hooked to his truck, already bedded with straw for Dusty, and we rounded up a few crates for your critters. Not as sophisticated as what you had before, but they'll do until you can get more."

"I don't understand." Mattie's eyebrows arched. "I can't move my patients. I have no place to go."

"You can stay at the Lightning M and hole up in the guesthouse. Not fancy, but it'll work for now. Put the animals in the barn and use the tack room as your office." He swept his hand in the air. "Plenty big for that. Do whatever you need to get set up."

"I wouldn't dream of imposing." Mattie loved the McCray ranch but could never ask such a thing. To have clients traipsing in and out with their sick pets would be too much. She thought of Gil and the angry words they'd exchanged the last time they'd parted. "I'm sure your son wouldn't appreciate me living on your land. I doubt he'd condone your generosity."

"The Lightning M is my home, not Gil's. Dusty needs a place to stay where he'll get 'round-the-clock care. You can do that at the ranch. I'm not hiring another vet."

Mattie sank into an armchair and sat on one of the children's squeaky toys. John's support served as salve to her wounded spirit, and his words made sense, even to her weary mind. She removed the toy from under her leg and gave in a little. "I'd insist on paying rent." Even if it meant laying off her employees for the time being.

The man switched the wooden cane to his other hand and cleared his throat. "I'm sure we can work out an arrangement. The important thing is for you to tend your animals."

He stepped to the divan and used it for additional support. "No sense wasting your hard-earned money on high rent when you can use my ranch. Your troubles won't last forever. If you're careful with your spending, you'll rebuild soon enough."

Mattie squeezed the rubber toy lightly between her bandaged hands, trying to decide. John's proposition would certainly be an answer to her present dilemma. "May I think on this for a bit?" She didn't trust herself to make an impulsive decision right now, especially one so important.

"What's to think about?" Clara stepped forward, all business. "Mr. McCray's offered a perfect solution, and you're in no position to be choosy. You have animals that need attention. How are you going to give them that if you're running around searching for a home and office?"

Clara was right. Getting her business in order would take time and energy, and there were her patients to consider. Now was not the time for indecision. Sara toddled up to her chair, followed by the pup. The little girl took the toy from Mattie's hand and giggled.

One barrier still stood in Mattie's way.

Gil.

"Mr. McCray has a trailer ready to haul your animals." Clara's eyes bore into hers with stern persuasion. "Don't look a gift horse in the mouth, my dear."

Mattie checked her watch. Why should she worry about Gil? He was in California and might never return.

"Okay, John, you have a deal. Would you mind if we held off a couple of hours, though, until after church? I have a lot to thank God for today."

THAT EVENING, MATTIE STEPPED OUTSIDE HER NEW LIVING QUARTERS and braced herself for the cold. She followed her dad to his car and shook her head at the irony of him wearing a gray western coat and a wool Stetson to cover his receding hairline. He didn't live in the country, yet he still dressed like a cowboy.

"Thanks for bringing all these supplies. You and Mom must have raced through the stores to gather this stuff so quickly."

"You know your mother." Her dad grinned and deposited an empty cardboard box in the backseat of his car. "She rallied her ladies' group, and this morning they filled half-a-dozen boxes with food and supplies."

"I'll be sure to send my thanks." She skirted to the passenger side to tell her mom good-bye. "Thanks for coming to my rescue and helping me get settled."

Her mother nodded, eyes teary. "I wish you'd change your mind. You could stay with us until you find a place of your own." She pulled a tissue from her purse and sniffed. "I can't imagine how you'll survive in such a place. For heaven's sake, there's not even a television."

Mattie forced a smile. "I'll manage." She returned to her dad and gave him a hug. Relishing the comfort he offered, she held on a moment longer and rested her cheek on his shoulder.

"I love you, Dad."

He leaned his head against hers, and his freshly shaved cheek brushed her face. "I love you too, pumpkin. I know when you've made your mind up to do something, there's no changing it." He pulled away and nudged her chin. "Call us if you need anything."

"I will." Her dad slid behind the wheel of his car, and Mattie's throat tightened, suddenly hating to see them go. She'd been on her own for several years, so why was this farewell so difficult? Perhaps her insecurity sprang from losing everything in the fire. Whatever it was, she felt like a little girl who'd gotten lost and now wanted to cling to her parents and never let go. Moisture stung her eyes as they backed out of the driveway.

A cold wind buffeted her as she waved good-bye. Shivering against the cold, she dashed to her new residence. Inside, her beagle friend greeted her at the door as the wind whistled against the elongated windows of the limestone cabin. Mattie took the pup in her arms and headed for the fireplace to stir the logs in the hearth. Soon, a blazing fire warmed her body, allowing her to appreciate the coziness of her temporary home.

In one corner, a quilted comforter covered a small pine bed, and in the middle of the room was a wooden table and chairs. Despite the additions of electricity and a small bathroom, Mattie felt like she'd stepped into another century. Primitive perhaps, but she'd never admit that to her mom. She appreciated John's efforts to keep the original homestead in mint condition and was more than willing to do without a few modern conveniences.

A sense of history swept over her as it always did when she set foot on the Lightning M. With a bit of imagination, she pictured the first homesteader, Jacob McCray, waiting at the table while his wife, Emma, made supper on the cast iron stove.

Caught up in the vision, she conjured an image of herself in a long dress and apron, hair pinned atop her head in a bun. Mattie felt the yards of heavy material against her legs and heard the swish of her petticoat as it brushed against the floor. In her hand was a steaming pot of coffee, and when she turned to the table, there sat Gilbert McCray with a fork in his hand.

What a ridiculous thought!

Mattie rose from the hearth and paced the wooden floor. A large mahogany rocker invited her with open arms. She slid into the contoured seat and rocked her puppy, cuddling him beneath a crocheted afghan made from granny squares. The smell of age and use enfolded them as the fire crackled and popped.

She glanced about the room at the many items delivered to her by her parents and was struck by sadness at everything she had lost in the fire. Her childhood pictures, her college diploma, the china given to her after her grandmother's death. Then she noticed the Bible her parents left lying on the nightstand.

Do not store up for yourselves treasures on earth, where moth and rust destroy . . . For where your treasure is, there your heart will be also.

MONDAY MORNING, GIL CALLED HIS FATHER FROM THE FOUNDATION headquarters. This time he answered on the fourth ring. "Hey, Dad, I tried to reach you all weekend. I couldn't get through to Dr. Evans, either. Have you heard how Dusty's doing?"

"Good morning to you too." His father's voice grated over the long distance connection.

"Is everything okay? With you, I mean?"

"We both know you don't care about my health."

Gil clicked his ink pen on the desk. "You're wrong, Dad. I do care."

"Well, that don't matter now. Mattie's clinic burned down a couple nights ago. She lost everything."

Gil dropped the pen. "You're kidding! How did that happen?"

"Still waiting on the inspector's report. Mattie had to spend the night at the hospital for a few minor burns and smoke inhalation, but she's okay. So is Dusty. We moved 'em out to stay with us until she can afford to rebuild."

Gil leaned in his chair and tried to digest this news, particularly the part about Mattie being in the hospital. His stomach tightened. "She's at the ranch now?"

"What's the matter?" His father's voice barked into the receiver. "You got corncobs in your ears?"

"Are you sure that's a good idea, her staying at the ranch?" Gil's suspicions about the doc and his dad returned full force. He shook his head and frowned, trying to shake them.

"She's setting up office here, scrubbing things good and clean."

Gil pictured the red-haired doctor doing just that. "Is she okay?"

His father wheezed into the phone, and Gil wondered how he was handling all the commotion.

"She's a tough lady. Tougher than most."

Gil reached inside his pants pocket and ran his fingers along the smooth metal watch hidden there. He blew out a long breath and recalled his coach's words about reconciliation. His sense of duty dictated his next words. "Is there anything I can do to help?"

"Jake and I finished putting up shelves in the tack room for Mattie's new supplies. We have everything under control."

The hairs on Gil's neck stirred. "You don't have any business toting around a hammer. Next, you'll tell me you're ready to ride horses or fix fence."

Dr. Evans should know better than to allow his father to push himself so hard. That she hadn't objected disturbed Gil. What else might the pretty doc persuade the old man to do? "Sounds like you need me there. I'd better have my secretary arrange a flight home," he said before he had a chance to think it through.

"Don't get yourself all tied in a knot. No reason for you to hurry home."

It didn't surprise him that his dad didn't want him there. The prospect of returning to Charris County didn't make Gil tingle all over, either. He'd have to put the purchase of his land on hold.

Another delay.

He pulled the silver timepiece from his pocket and watched the second hand click past each successive number. "If it's all right with you, I think I'll stay a couple of months this time — if you can stand to have me around that long?"

His dad grunted. Gil took that as a *yes.*

SEVENTEEN

Two days later, Gil arrived at his father's ranch in a new Dodge Ram Laramie he'd bought in Kansas City. He'd left his Escalade in California until he returned, and he had no intention of borrowing Jake's truck again.

The sun dipped below the horizon, the murky clouds tinged with orange and purple. He parked his truck and went straight for the barn. Once his eyes adjusted to the dim light, he spotted Dusty in a large stall, his head hanging low to the ground. It looked like the horse had lost a ton of weight in the two weeks he'd been gone. A knot of dread formed in his gut.

Dr. Evans stepped out from behind the gelding. "John said you were coming home."

The doc wore a canvas coat and jeans with her hair braided in a ponytail. Gil forced down any lingering resentment or suspicions he had. "I'm sorry about your clinic."

She offered a faint smile. "You probably heard I moved to the ranch. I hope that's all right. I'd hate to be a bother to you or your dad."

A bother to me, but no bother to Dad. Gil's jaw tightened with distrust. Or jealousy?

"It'll only be for a while," she went on, "until I get my feet on the ground."

He noticed the dark shadows beneath her lower lashes and guilt besieged him. The little lady had been under great stress from tending his horse, and now she'd lost her home, her business. He rebuked himself for his silent condemnation.

"How's he doing?" Gil nodded toward Dusty, concentrating on the horse instead of the doc.

"His fever's returned and he's still not eating good. I came out to check his bandages and found his lacerations swollen and warm to the touch. He needs a larger dose of antibiotics." Her mouth pinched into a frown. "The last of my supply is in the cabin refrigerator."

Gil's temperature escalated with the news of Dusty's lack of recuperation. Suddenly, getting away from this woman—even for a few minutes—would do him good. "Tell me what you need, and I'll get it."

Dr. Evans wiped the sawdust from her jeans, then informed him which bottles to bring back. Gil took off hastily for the cabin.

What kind of mistake had he made in giving this woman charge over his horse? Why hadn't he listened when she admitted her incompetence? He should have taken her advice and sent Dusty to K-State. At least there, they would have given him proper medical treatment . . .

When Gil returned to the barn, he found Mattie swabbing Dusty's wounds with antiseptic.

"Come on, boy, you have to fight." She patted the horse on his neck, her concern evident.

Gil handed her the medicine she'd requested, his mind in turmoil. He knew the doc had done all in her power to care for Dusty. She couldn't be blamed for the loss of her home and clinic—her supplies and medicines. But that didn't help Dusty. "This was the last of the penicillin."

Dr. Evans filled a syringe with the antibiotic. "There's enough here to alleviate the swelling and stop his fever. I'll keep an eye out for colic and laminitis and will continue his liquids until he's back on feed. Tomorrow, I want to start hydrotherapy treatment."

She'd spoken this way before, when he'd first seen Dusty's wounds. A skilled professional, void of emotion. "Is he going to make it, Mattie?"

Her tormented expression resembled that of a child who didn't have the answer to an important question. When her bottom lip quivered, Gil fought the temptation to take her in his arms and comfort her. He reminded himself that the doc was no child.

She straightened her shoulders and smiled, her insecurity replaced with sheer determination as she injected the medicine. "Prayer and loving attention are the best we can do for him. As soon as I get a clinic set up, I'd like to take another x-ray to see how his fractures are healing."

Gil kicked at the dirt floor with his shoe. "I don't know if you heard, but I've retired from the game. While I'm here, I thought I'd work on the ranch. See if I can get it in shape. I can help with your clinic too—I need to do something to keep busy." He grinned, but the truth was no joke.

She stared at him with no smart reply. It struck him how attractive she was, even in work clothes with her face smudged by dirt and worry. No wonder his father was so besotted. It was a chore not to become that way himself.

"I don't suppose you have any influence with insurance companies?" She grinned and brushed a stray curl from her face. "My settlement won't come close to covering my loss, but it'll get me started."

Mattie collected the items she'd used to treat Dusty and deposited the soiled cotton into a trash bin. "The tack room needs electrical outlets installed to handle x-rays and my other machines. I'll pay for the work done, of course." She stood at the hydrant and sprayed water into a bucket to wash her hands.

Gil inspected the barn. How would they ever turn this place into a proper facility? They could put the smaller animals in hanging cages, but the examining room would require time and funds the doc obviously didn't have.

"We're getting the upgrade, it's only fair we cover the expenses," he said.

Mattie lowered her eyes. "You and your dad have done too much. I don't know how I'll ever repay you."

"You don't have to." That he felt compelled to offer such generosity surprised him. But he couldn't retract his words even if he wanted to—which he didn't.

"I can't tell you how much that means. Truly, I'm overwhelmed. Jake and your dad already helped build shelves to stock my medicine and equipment. I can't accept more."

Gil cleared his throat, his charitable spirit tainted by the reminder of his dad working out in the barn. "Now that I'm here there's no need to trouble Dad with this project. The physical stress can't be good for him."

Mattie frowned. "I hope you don't think I'd risk John's health."

"Are you saying he didn't exert himself?"

Her eyes flashed. "He sat on a stool and gave orders."

Gil's mouth twitched, proven wrong again. He really didn't want to think poorly of the doc, so why was that always his first inclination? "Somehow that doesn't surprise me."

"You're right about one thing, though." An amused giggle escaped her lips. "We could use your muscle for all the heavy work that needs to be done."

Gil questioned her attempt to exploit his help but smiled at the thought that maybe the doc wasn't completely immune to football players, after all.

EIGHTEEN

THE NEXT MORNING, FROST COVERED THE GROUND, AND THE SKY loomed gray and dreary, typical January weather. Mattie entered the barn, and Dusty greeted her with a nicker.

"Hey, boy." She put her face to his neck in a gentle hug, relishing his warm scent. A quick examination revealed the swelling and fever had subsided. Relief washed over her that the medication had worked. She offered him some feed, and this time the horse took in a few mouthfuls. Mattie continued her morning routine, her hands no longer tender from the burns. God was good indeed. He'd looked after her and had given her a home and a place for business. Even her relationship with Gil seemed more positive.

After her chores, Mattie began cleaning the tack room and carried out the first of the saddles. She met Jake in the center of the barn.

"What'cha doing there, Missy? Here, let me get that for you." The old ranch hand took the heavy saddle from her by the horn.

Her burden lifted, she spun to retrieve another item and nearly collided into Gil. He sauntered past in navy sweats, his brow beaded with perspiration.

"I heard you rolled in last night with a brand new truck." Jake set the saddle on the dirt floor. "Now that you're home, I don't suppose you'd have time to help me out this morning?"

Gil mopped his forehead with the towel slung around his neck. "What's the problem?"

Jake scratched his whiskery chin, hesitant to continue. "Well, I hate to bother you ... but one of the bulls got in with some heifers. I need to move him, but he's being cantankerous. Can't herd him or nothing. If I had my wits, I'd load him in the trailer, but I'm not as quick as I used to be."

Mattie waited for Gil's response. If he didn't offer his assistance, she would. She was about to say so when he finally spoke.

"You need me to saddle up?" A grin spread across Gil's face as though warming to the idea. "Been a long time, but I reckon I can help."

Mattie would give a hundred dollars to see Gil work a bull. "Me too," she volunteered, fearing they wouldn't let her go. "You might need an extra hand out there. I can ride Tulip."

The two men exchanged dubious glances, and she half expected them to tell her a woman on the job would cause bad luck, something she'd heard more than once since her return to the Flint Hills.

"Herding a bull ain't no place for a lady. You could git into a world of hurt. Tulip ain't been ridden much, and with this cool weather, she'll likely be sassy." Jake shook his head, but Mattie caught a hint of indecision.

"I'll keep my distance." Her gaze shifted from one man to the other. "I watched my father pen bulls lots of times. And I promise, I'll only help if you need me."

Jake scratched his chin and looked at Gil. "Have any objections?"

Gil raised his hands in the air. "I learned the hard way not to mess with the doc." He grinned, and sheer pleasure trickled down Mattie's backbone.

At Gil's response, Jake retrieved the saddle he'd set down. "Best get going, then. We've got our work cut out for us."

Sitting astride one of his father's dependable horses, Gil twisted in the saddle, the oiled leather foreign beneath his seat and legs. How long had it been since he'd roped a steer? A quick tally revealed it'd been at least four years, since he'd attended charity event in California. And now he was going to help catch a bull?

I must be crazy.

He pushed his old straw cowboy hat further down on his head, surprised he'd found it in his room and that it still fit. It couldn't be harder than riding a bicycle. Trouble was — his childhood wheels always had four legs and a tail, and the speeds he'd known had been walk, trot, gallop, and run — fast and faster. He twirled the lariat above his head several times, then released the fifty-foot coil onto the ground in an effort to get a feel for the rope.

It reminded him of being stowed up with a knee injury for two weeks, then suddenly turned out to walk without a crutch. He gathered the cord and tried again, this time aiming for something solid.

"How's it going?" Mattie came up beside him on Tulip, all smiles on that pretty face of hers. He threw his loop at a wooden post and missed.

"I do believe I've lost my groove." Gil yanked the lariat across the ground and wound it up to try once more. He hated to admit that his time as a cowboy might have come and gone.

"You'll get the hang of it after a few more tosses. After all, you're a professional passer. Throwing a rope ought to be a piece of cake for you." Mattie trotted toward the barn, and Tulip swished her tail at him, as sassy as her rider.

"Why don't you see if Jake's ready to head out," he called to her backside, wishing a hundred times he hadn't agreed to let her tag along. Having her there would only mean trouble, and he didn't need that kind of pressure. She waved her hand in the air, and Gil swore laughter floated back to him. If he had a football, he'd launch it at her and knock the woman off her high horse. He'd show her exactly what a professional passer could do.

Wanting time on the horses, he and Mattie headed through the east pasture, while Jake followed in the livestock trailer. The gray metal frame jostled with every bump of the tires over rocks and ruts. In a couple months, it would be time to burn the prairie grass, something Gil always enjoyed. He once held in awe the monstrous flames that sometimes reached twice as high as his mount, the intense heat and danger of being caught in the backfires.

His mama used to scold that he ought to do like the rest of the ranchers and light the fire by four-wheeler or truck, but that wouldn't have been nearly as fun. His lips curved into a devilish grin as he checked the height of the dead bluestem, which in places reached to his stirrup. He guessed this year would be no different. Ought to burn like hell itself.

"Which pasture is he in?" Gil asked as Jake passed by in the truck moments later.

"We've got the heifers in the lower Knoll pasture."

Two sections away. Gil took the initiative and brought his mount into a gallop, taking the lead. No sense gallivanting when there was work to do. Shortly thereafter, he came to a bumpy halt at the first cattle guard and opened the gate beside it without dismounting from his saddle.

"How old is this dun mare, anyway?" He hollered into the still morning air as Jake caught up to him.

"Eight. We bought her several years ago at a big horse sale in South Dakota." Jake passed over the guard with a big grin. "Rides like a choo choo train, don't she?"

Gil had to admit she was a bit rough—like pegs poking into the ground, but the girl had speed. "Any particular reason you bought her?"

"You know your dad's fondness for mares. He liked her eyes. Said they were honest and packed lots of heart. She's got cow sense too, and is quick on her feet."

Gil laughed. "Dad always was a sucker for a pretty face." Come to think of it, Gil had a soft spot for a pretty face as well, especially if it boasted little reddish freckles against fiery green eyes. He spun the mare in time to see Mattie dig her heels into Tulip's side, careening her up and over the metal cattle guard as though the horse was good and primed.

Fool woman—the horse could have balked, got her foot caught in between the pipes, thrown her rider.

"What were you thinking?" He yelled at her, his whole body heated at the thought of Mattie's small frame lying in a heap on the ground. "You could have been hurt pulling a stunt like that—or worse, hurt the horse."

The woman drew Tulip in a circle and smiled, fueling his anger. "But I wasn't, which leaves you holding the gate."

Gil exchanged looks with Jake, his temperature rising.

"I guess she got you." The old-timer howled and slammed his fist against the door of the truck in a lighthearted gesture.

Gil shut the gate, then took off into the next pasture, the sturdy mare practically jarring him from his seat.

So much for pretty faces.

NINETEEN

Mattie knew Gil would catch up with her in an instant. He didn't disappoint. Within seconds, his horse's hooves pounded against the hard earth.

"Are you always this feisty, or is it only when you're riding a horse?" He strode up beside her, his mount faster paced than Tulip and about a full hand taller.

"I like to enjoy my rare time away from work."

Gil gazed ahead. "Still, you could have run into real trouble back there."

"I can take care of myself." Mattie hated it when men, particularly male ranchers, patronized her because of her size and gender. Had one of Gil's teammates jumped that guard, he would have thrown his hat in the air with delight. "Have you figured out what you're going to do with the bull? We could try to drive him to his pasture."

"I figured I'd try something else first — a little trick someone taught me as a boy."

Mattie recalled a few of her father's narrow escapes trying to force a bull to go a certain direction when it didn't have a mind to do so. "Are you sure?" A bull could be as mean as firecrackers if a person got too close.

"I've penned 'em before. I'm sure it'll all come back to me."

Mattie prepared herself for the trouble that could occur from such assurance.

Twenty minutes later, they arrived in a pasture where close to thirty Black Angus heifers milled about several large bales of hay. Among them stood an eighteen-hundred-pound brute, majestic and black as ebony, looking as though he didn't want to be messed with.

Jake stopped the truck about three hundred yards away and unloaded his horse from the trailer. He swung the gate open wide. "I figure Mattie and I can hold the young ladies while you slip in and drive him from the herd and into the trailer. If that doesn't work, we can always rope him." The ranch hand mounted his gelding and slapped Gil on the back, his confidence evident.

Mattie followed single file behind Jake and Gil. They meandered through the unsuspecting bovine, and Gil ducked in between the bull and heifers, singling him out from the rest. A few young cows followed, but soon peeled off to rejoin the others. Standing watch over the herd, Mattie kept an eye on Gil's progress.

The big beast didn't care to be on his own and began cutting back and forth in an effort to return to the females. Gil's mare was too agile for that to occur, always on his tail, making the bull's progress difficult.

Tiring of this, the unwieldy creature drove a few yards, then tried sashaying to-and-fro, fighting a bit harder to return to the group. His back arched as he flung his hind legs in the air, less than pleased with the disruption. Mattie heard his rumbling bellow from where she waited, and the distressed sound brought goose bumps to her arms.

Excitement fluttered in her stomach as Gil set his plan in motion. It was like seeing a man come to life, the way he handled the mare and his rope. Pure confidence replaced his earlier awkwardness. He definitely had his groove back.

Gil lunged for the bull's rear and pummeled him with the coils of his rope, making a ruckus as he did so. Like clockwork, the animal busted straight ahead a couple of yards. When he stopped and looked at the trailer, Gil eased off. The brute then blasted onward. This time Gil flanked him on the opposite side with his rope.

The rock-iron beast jerked his head and twisted his body to attack the yellow dun's rib cage, snot issuing from his nose. Mattie gasped at the skirmish.

His crown missed by a fraction as the mare spun on her hind hooves out of the way. Mattie guessed the thoughts in Gil's mind must be whirring as fast as the beat of her heart.

Kicking and bucking, the bull charged the dry prairie grass. Within seconds, Gil came up from behind, hooting and hollering, putting the massive bovine in forward motion once more.

He passed the trailer on the left, and Gil sped ahead to turn him around. Using the rope like a whip, he smacked it inches from the triangular head.

Mattie understood the logic. Make any path but the correct one hard to accomplish and eventually, he'll choose the right course. The bull took off on another route, only to be driven to the trailer by the persistent horse and rider. After minutes of this forced exercise, the bull became winded and stood stock-still behind the open door of the trailer. Mattie held her breath, willing the fellow to step inside.

He stared at the enclosure as though considering just that. Bits of dirt flew in the air as he pawed the dirt and blew mucus from his nose. In the next instant, he drew his thick neck low to the ground and sprung up with extraordinary grace, twisting his muscular body in the air, his hooves landing in syncopated time. Then off he shot in another direction.

Straight for the heifers.

"Uh-oh," Jake said, and Tulip's ears shot upward.

Gil loped beside the bull, right on his hip. Mattie saw an opportunity to help—to prove her competence. She sprang forward, ignoring Jake's protests. Flapping her rope against the gray mare, she dug her heels into the horse's belly, urging her to give a little more.

Tulip complied, and they set a course to intercept the raging bull, hoping to sway the creature to turn.

He pressed onward.

Mattie gripped the rope. Felt the hard, twisted cord against the flesh of her palm. She slapped it against her thigh, then raised the coils in the air. Timing was everything. By dashing in front of the brute, she risked having him flip her like a rag doll. But if she could time her approach with that of Gil's, the bull might consider the two-on-one defense more than he cared to mess with, and her efforts would prove successful.

The thud of Tulip's hooves merged with those of the bull. She counted the seconds before she made her move. A massive blur of coal rushed at her. Mattie shoved her heel into Tulip's left side to cross in front of the bull, then felt the impact of the beast's head as it clipped her horse's hip.

Tulip twisted and Mattie's body whipped sideways. The bull narrowly missed getting his head under the horse's belly. Mattie struggled to stay seated as the mare shot off at a dead run, frightened. When she brought the horse to a halt, Mattie jumped off to inspect Tulip's midsection.

Gil hollered in the distance.

Preoccupied with her examination, she glanced up.

Saw the brute running straight for her.

While she'd made her escape, Gil had managed to turn the bull around, and they were headed in her direction, the brute in the lead.

About twenty yards away, the goaded creature stopped and dug his hooves into the ground. He sniffed the earth, then snorted, shaking his head from side-to-side.

Petrified, Mattie watched him charge. Her feet froze to the ground, unable to move.

With the bull less than fifteen feet away and close enough to smell, Mattie tasted fear and grabbed for the saddle horn. As her foot touched the stirrup, Gil's mare plowed headlong from out of nowhere into the beast's ribs at full speed. The forceful blow laid the bull flat on his side. Mattie took this chance to escape and loped Tulip to safety. When the bovine returned to his feet, Gil charged once more, but this time the bull steered clear of the horse and rider.

From then on, the mighty beast went wherever directed—his head low and compliant as he trotted along. Gil circled him around the trailer, and when the bull stopped at the gate, the cowboy backed off, giving him an opportunity to go in a direction that wasn't forced. Mattie watched in awe as the brute stepped right into the trailer.

TWENTY

GIL TOOK A MOMENT TO CALM HIS NERVES BEFORE CLOSING THE GATE on his opponent, then gripped his rope, prepared to throttle Mattie for her foolish behavior.

Didn't the woman practice any common sense? She could have been stomped into the ground.

He rode up to her, blood pulsating. "What are you trying to do? Get yourself killed, or are you plain stupid?"

Mattie's face paled. She slid from her saddle and rubbed her hand over Tulip's hip. "I miscalculated. Haven't you ever made a mistake? Or is that beyond the great and mighty Gil McCray?"

"Miscalculated?" Gil dismissed her words. Then he noticed her unsteady steps. "Are you hurt?"

He swung off his horse and joined her on the ground, conscious that his own knees buckled slightly. Catching her hand, he felt it tremble. Mattie stared up into his eyes, and at that moment, he couldn't scold her. All he wanted was to wrap his arms around her and nestle his nose in the crook of that pretty little neck. He ought to kick himself for being such a wimp.

"I'm all right." She pulled away, her attention once again on the horse.

"Tulip took a pretty hard blow."

"She'll be sore." Mattie leaned her forehead against the gray mare, but not before a tear slipped down her cheek. "I'm sorry for putting her in danger like that. It was a stupid move."

Gil couldn't agree more. "You grew up around cattle — you should have known better."

She continued to hide her face, her voice muffled. "I wanted to prove that I'm not helpless — I'm not incompetent."

Gil placed his hands on his hips, sure he'd never understand the thoughts of a woman. Then again, maybe he understood this woman more than he cared to admit. "You don't have to prove anything to me."

Mattie swiped her cheeks and straightened to her full height, barely reaching his neck. She pulled her shoulders back and cocked her chin, reminding him of the first day they'd met. "I've seen the way you look at me, heard the doubt in your voice."

She lowered her head and kicked her boot in the dirt. "All my life, I've had to prove myself. My sisters and I stacked hay, doctored cattle. You name it, we did it. As good as any boys." She hid her hands in her coat pockets and stared past his shoulder, failing to look him in the eye.

"When I began my practice, none of the ranchers thought a woman could handle the job — except John."

For the first time, Mattie and his dad's unusual relationship began to make sense. Mattie hadn't been after his father. Instead, she was like a daughter. He glanced at the vet with the unruly red hair fighting its way out of the braid. Someone to look after probably made his dad feel younger ... worthy ... after failing with his two sons.

"Out here, a woman has to prove herself," Mattie continued, giving no indication that she understood or even recognized his inner turmoil. "Men expect women to stay home and raise babies. So you see, I never quite measure up."

The hurt in Mattie's expression made Gil forget his own problems.

"I wouldn't say that. You're a good vet. And not all women are cut out to have babies—not that you wouldn't make a good mama," he said, half-embarrassed that he'd expressed this thought.

"What's this about good mamas?" Jake rode up on his horse.

Mattie's face blushed crimson beneath her freckles. "I better go check on Dusty." Without another word, she climbed on Tulip and took off for the ranch.

Jake twisted in his saddle and spit a stream of tobacco. "I need to get this bull to the barn, anyhow. He can stay in the back pen until it's time to put him in with the girls. Wouldn't want this morning's adventure to repeat itself."

"No, we wouldn't." Gil walked to Jake's truck and gathered some fencing supplies. He placed them in his saddlebag. "While you do that, I'll check and see where he got through. Probably needs fixing."

This morning, Gil had retrieved a big part of his past. It felt good to be back in the saddle. Made him wonder what he'd been doing with his life, and even more, it had him questioning where the path might lead now.

Gil climbed onto his saddle and clicked the dun into a trot. He welcomed the motion and the tang of the mare's sweaty lather. It all added up to one thing: *Home.*

"Care to ride with me partway?" he asked once he'd caught up to Mattie.

The doc nodded, and they headed across the pasture toward the fence.

"I never realized how much I missed this life until now," Gil voiced his thoughts. "This morning's brought back some good memories." He restrained his mare to keep her from getting ahead of Tulip's slower pace.

"You were wonderful out there," she said. "How did it return so quickly?"

"Everything started to click, like I hadn't spent the last nineteen years playing football. Makes me think my plan to raise performance horses isn't crazy, after all. Buy some fillies and train them like I did Dusty."

After awhile, they came to the pasture where the bull originated. Gil examined the fencerow, searching for a break in the barbed wire.

"What about your dad? Do you want to work out your problems with him?"

"That's kind of nosy, don't you think?"

"I know how difficult it is when you don't get along with your parents."

Mattie rarely spoke of her family, and Gil's curiosity was aroused. "You mean your mom and dad?"

She dismounted her horse and stared over the fence line. "They don't understand my devotion to this place. Always trying to get me to move to Kansas City." She took a deep breath and let it out slowly.

The fresh morning breeze rustled against the yellowish-brown grass, and he followed her gaze toward the horizon. She didn't appear eager to discuss the matter, but Gil wanted to know more, if for no other reason than to put a lid on his past.

"You mentioned your sisters were married. They probably provided your folks with a few grandkids." Gil fiddled with his reins, ashamed for prying. In truth, he was probably more interested in discovering what made Mattie so different from her older sister Jenna. Like comparing a prairie rose to a pasture thistle.

"Bridgett has a girl and twin boys. Jenna's divorced with no kids. Probably scared she'd have twins, as well."

Mattie's laughter was pure pleasure to Gil's ears, but the news about Jenna stirred unwanted memories. Why did he care whether she was happily married? She lived in Texas and was no threat to him. "Do you talk to them often?"

She shook her head and her smile faded. "We aren't very close. Everything changed when Mom and Dad lost their home."

Gil considered the doc's fierce regard for the Flint Hills. Perhaps this explained why she defended the land, as though it was what held her together. "Is that why you keep trying to convince me to stay on at my father's ranch?"

"Your family roots grow four generations deep. I'd give my right arm to have what you have."

"This place isn't mine, and what's more, it's falling apart." Gil studied the sagging fence and spotted where the bull had pushed his way through to the other pasture. One little repair wasn't going to make any difference in this fence — the bull would simply find another hole to jump through. And if not the bull, a cow or a horse, like Dusty. The ranch needed an entire face-lift. "Most people don't see things the way you do."

"Then make them see."

Gil laughed at Mattie's hopefulness and recognized a bit of himself in her. "I'm not convinced it would be best for Dad to stay here. Considering his poor health, maybe he should sell and move to town."

"You mean, best for you. Easier to walk away knowing you don't have any responsibility to the Lightning M. Sounds cowardly, if you ask me." She led Tulip a few yards and stopped, the tilt of her chin unyielding. "You're the only family your dad has left. Why can't you get along?"

Gil's spine bristled at being called a coward. He'd just tangled with a bull and had done a fine job of it too. He was no coward. "Our troubles began a long time ago."

"But you're here now, so you must care or you'd still be in California."

Gil didn't like the challenge in her eyes. Some people didn't know when to leave well enough alone.

TWENTY-ONE

THE McCRAY MEN'S PERSONAL LIVES WERE NONE OF MATTIE'S business, and she knew it. But how could she stand around and watch Gil and his dad destroy each other with their hardheaded behavior? What kind of friend would she be if she didn't at least try to help them make amends? "Did you and your dad always fight like this?"

Gil hopped off his horse and pulled the fence pliers from the saddlebag. "When I was a boy, Dad and I understood each other. We accepted our differences. I guess when Frank and Mama died, the peacemakers in the family died as well." He bent down to retrieve the broken wires.

"Is that why you didn't come home when your dad was in the hospital?"

Gil's back straightened, and she could tell by his expression that she'd hit a nerve.

"Nobody told me about his heart attack. And even if I'd known, we were at the end of the season, so it would have been impossible to get away. He wouldn't have welcomed a visit from me. That's why he didn't call."

"Maybe he didn't want to worry you." Even as she said this,

Mattie wondered if Gil's words might be true. Would John have been pleased with his son's return? She wanted to think so, but had witnessed a few of his unkind remarks. "He's been happy to have you back at the ranch."

"I wouldn't call it a welcome party. If you'll recall, he didn't open his arms or offer to roast the fattened calf." Gil attached one end of the fence clip to the broken wire and pulled tight to bring the two loose ends together.

Mattie watched as his neck muscles tensed and flexed. Though physically strong, part of him was as insecure as a little boy. "So, you and your dad have issues. Work them out and start over. He's not getting any younger, and whether he lets on or not, he needs his family. You're all that's left."

She climbed up on Tulip, needing to return to Dusty and her work at the clinic. Staring down at the man, she noted how the brown tufts of hair curled above his coat collar, and how his long nose crooked in the middle, probably broken in a football game.

Or during a fight with his older brother?

She admitted to herself that she wanted to know more about Gilbert McCray. "Thanks for coming to my rescue with the bull. You probably saved my life."

"All in a day's work." Gil tipped his hat to her but didn't smile.

BACK AT THE BARN, MATTIE LED DUSTY INTO THE YARD TO GET SOME sun. Her little beagle followed and stretched out on the ground for a nap. The outside air quieted her spirits. Who was she to try and settle the McCrays' dispute when her own family suffered many of the same symptoms? In high school, Jenna fussed with Mom and Dad about not getting to date the boys she wanted, and Bridgett never cared to do chores. Both her sisters had left home right out of high school, eager to be on their own.

Mattie ladled warm Epsom water over Dusty's wounds to ease his discomfort and remembered her own unease when she'd struck out on her own. She'd enrolled in vet school when her family thought she ought to be a teacher or nurse, and her return to Diamond Falls became fodder for even more criticism. By that time, her parents had moved to the city, so the disapproval went both ways.

Her spine bristled thinking about the arguments they'd had at family get-togethers. It hurt to know her parents and sisters didn't understand her. She supposed that's why she'd latched on to Clara and John. They didn't find her way of life strange, and neither seemed concerned about her marital status.

Pouring another cup of water over Dusty's limb, Mattie watched the milky droplets trickle down his leg.

Not that she wasn't interested in men.

An image of Gil on his father's horse came to mind. She considered the way his mouth tilted when he grinned, and her stomach twitched with uncertainty. She and Gil were alike in many ways, but also very different. Mainly in that his dreams carried him far from the isolated hills she loved.

"A penny for your thoughts."

At the masculine voice, Mattie nearly tipped over her bucket of water. "Don't you ever announce yourself?"

"Sorry, Doc. Didn't mean to surprise you." Gil grinned.

Mattie stood and dusted off her jeans, embarrassed by the direction of her thoughts. Her beagle sat up and yawned, his nap disturbed by the commotion. "Did you fix the fence already?"

"I could work for days and not finish. That old wire ought to be ripped out and replaced by a brand new fence, but that would take all summer."

"You weren't serious about moving your dad to town?" She had the distinct impression he might actually consider the possibility. "What would happen to the ranch?"

"I'd rather have it bought by an outside corporation or run by the state than see it auctioned. At least then, I'd know the Lightning M would be cared for."

Mattie shook her head in disbelief. She despised those who claimed to care for the tallgrass more than the people whose blood and sweat paid for the prairie itself. They only wanted to use the property as a tax write-off as they'd done with her family's ranch. "Your father would never sell your inheritance."

"You don't know him as well as you think." Gil went to Dusty's side and slid his palm over the gelding's back.

"Doesn't that bother you?"

Gil's eyes softened in a sad way, filled with regrets. Mattie noticed the cleft in his chin, and her eyes followed the curve of his jaw and the sleek skin of his cheek. Close enough to smell his aftershave, she felt a gentle stirring in her stomach that spread all the way up her throat. Mortified by where her thoughts had strayed, she stared down at Dusty's trimmed hooves.

"That's one of the reasons I returned. Not to convince him to leave me an inheritance—but to make things right between us. Mama would have wanted me to try."

Glad to hear Gil's resolve to do the right thing, Mattie bent down to lift the gelding's right front hoof.

"How is Dusty doing?"

The horse was able to bear the extra weight, and she felt no unexpected warmth on the hoof. "He looks better today." She eased the foot to the ground, then reached into her coat pocket to pull out an apple. With her pocketknife, she cut it in half and held it up to Dusty's mouth.

The gelding nipped at the white flesh, catching it between his teeth. Mattie crunched into the other half while his portion dropped to the ground. "Oh Dusty, you have to be hungry."

Discouraged, she flung the rest of her apple into the barnyard. Dusty flinched at the action but then leaned his head into Mattie's stomach.

"Sorry for scaring you, boy." She stroked the side of his face, ashamed at her lack of consideration. "What are your plans for Dusty once he's recovered?"

Gil removed his hat and brushed his fingers through his matted hair. "Will he be saddled again?"

Mattie studied the gelding and thought of the horse's big heart, the way he nuzzled his nose against her when she tended to his needs. "You mean because of his eye? It might take a while, but he'll develop his senses on his blind side. You shouldn't have any trouble. At his age, he'd make a good kid's horse. Or find him a home on a handicapped ranch." All of these were viable alternatives, but not the one her heart desired.

"Why not keep him here?" she suggested. "Buy some of those colts you mentioned, and let Dusty roam the pastures with them. He'd probably teach them a lesson or two about manners."

"You don't give up, do you?" He caught one of her stray locks and tucked it behind her ear, his fingers warm against her neck. "Mildred ought to be ringing the dinner bell any minute. Will you join us for lunch?"

Mattie stepped away from Gil's touch. "I have lunchmeat at the cabin."

"Consider it a favor to me for saving your life this morning. Be the peacekeeper at the kitchen table." His blue eyes crinkled in a smile.

Mattie's resolve wavered beneath the temptation. As she considered the invitation, Mildred stepped onto the porch and rang the dinner bell. She smiled and waved.

"What did I tell you? Mildred will think you're rude if you don't join us now."

Mattie bit her lip as her stomach growled. "Okay, but I'm doing this for her, not you."

"I'll tell her to set another plate." Gil took off toward the house, while Mattie led Dusty to the barn. When she entered the kitchen minutes later, Gil, John, and Jake sat at the oblong table. She felt their attention as she washed her hands at the kitchen sink.

"Mildred, your ham and potatoes smell wonderful. I hope it's not a burden to feed one more."

"Don't be ridiculous." The older woman patted Mattie on the shoulder. "We could stand a few more females at the table, considering how much hot air these men blow."

TWENTY-TWO

GIL CHUCKLED AT MILDRED'S COMMENT. "IF YOU THINK WE'RE BAD, you should hang around a locker room sometime."

"No thank you," Mildred said and went back to slicing ham on the stove.

While Mattie washed her hands at the sink, Gil thought about the doc's lifestyle. She ate on the run, tended her patients at all hours of the day, and recently had her life turned upside down. Through all that, she was still a joy to be around. His mother had been that way. She always saw the good in people and tried to be thankful no matter what.

Mattie took a seat opposite Jake. Gil removed his hat and laid it on the floor before offering grace.

When he finished, Mildred set a bowl of steaming scalloped potatoes on the table. "I understand you had quite a morning chasing that bull in the pasture."

"You should have seen 'em." Jake smacked the table with his fist. "Ol' Blackie went into that trailer with his tail between his legs." The ranch hand turned to Gil's dad. "You'd be plumb proud of your dun mare. She's as sassy as ever. Slammed right into the side of that bull and knocked him down. Thought I was at a rodeo."

"You don't say?" The old man's eyes piqued with interest. "You penned the bull today? On your own?" He sounded like he didn't believe it—that he couldn't imagine his son riding a horse after all these years.

Gil nodded. "I had a little help from your new tenant."

His dad directed his gaze at Mattie. "You went with them to the pasture?" There was a reproachful edge in his words but also a hint of admiration.

Mattie lowered her eyes.

"If it hadn't been for her," Gil said, "there's no telling how long I would have chased that bull. I was shocked at how well Tulip moved. Never guessed the girl had it in her."

This seemed to please his father. "Always liked riding that mare." He winked at Mattie, then faced Gil. "How'd it feel to throw a rope again?"

"Good." *Real good.* "Makes me long to rope steers like we did when I was a kid." The mention of it made Gil's heart dance.

"What's stopping you? Pen some fall calves and have yourself a little roping practice." His father's voice chimed with enthusiasm.

If Gil wasn't careful, he'd slip into thinking everything was okay—that problems didn't exist between him and his dad. He shook his head, reminding himself why he came home—to make amends. "I thought this afternoon I'd help Mattie with her room, then when the clinic's done, I'd like to start fixing up this place, beginning with the house."

For a long moment, his father stared at the ceiling. "Reckon it's been a while since anything's been done to the exterior. Ain't had a good sandblasting since you were in high school."

Excitement rushed through Gil at the thought of reviving his old home. "When the walls are done, we can shingle the roof. After that, I want to repair some of the old fence."

"Whoa, there." His father cleared his throat. "Before you go making all these renovations, it might be wise to talk with me first, seeing as how I'm still the owner."

Gil wiped his mouth on his napkin. "These things need done, Dad. Now that I'm retired, I have the time and the money, so we may as well get started."

His father glanced at Mattie, then at Gil with a grumble. That the old man gave in without a fight surprised Gil, but it was probably because the doc tended to bring out a gentler side in his dad. Taking another bite of ham, he glanced out the window and noticed a red truck pull up to the barn. "Are you expecting a client?"

Mattie stood from the table and went to the window, showing immediate recognition. "That's Mavis. She's decided to adopt the yellow stray."

WITH THE EXCEPTION OF DUSTY, MAVIS'S LABRADOR WAS THE LAST of Mattie's patients. As the red truck pulled away, Mattie wondered how long it would be before she'd take on more clients. A week? Two weeks? *Or longer, if she didn't get to work.*

Mattie sighed and returned to the concrete-floored room sanctioned off for her in the barn. Half an hour later, she looked up as Gil strolled in with a tool belt strapped around his waist, her beagle right behind.

"I have tools, and there's wood in the barn. How can I help?" Gil had traded his canvas coat for a flannel shirt tucked into denim jeans. The sight of him made Mattie's pulse quicken.

They worked side-by-side all afternoon, clearing the room and building more shelves for medicine. In addition, they constructed two examining tables out of two-by-fours and sheets of plywood. Gil drove the last nail into the wood and let out a long, slow whistle.

"I don't know about you, but I could stand a break. You don't happen to have any snickerdoodles sitting around, do ya?"

A sliver of anxiety rushed through Mattie at the mention of

those cookies, and how Gil once questioned her abilities as a vet.
Yet here he was, helping her reestablish her business.

"I might have something." She laid her hammer down and moved
past him, calling her pup to follow. As they headed for the cabin,
Mattie noticed a flurry of activity in the corral.

"What on earth is going on over there?"

TWENTY-THREE

GIL LOOKED PAST MATTIE AND SAW JAKE ON HIS HORSE, HERDING A dozen steers that had been unloaded from a trailer. His dad stood at the corral gate, cane in hand, with his blue heeler at his side.

"Let's go see what those old-timers are up to," he said and veered toward the corral.

His dad lifted his cane. "What took you so long? Go saddle your horses."

The smile on the man's face reminded Gil of years gone by, before his dad turned cold against him. "What's going on? Whose steers are these?"

"Jake and I decided to create a little roping practice for you. Like the old days. Convinced a neighbor to bring some longhorns over."

Gil swallowed the knot in his throat. What made his father think he'd be interested in reviving this pastime? Acting like nothing's happened, as though the last nineteen years had been a bad dream? Was the man in denial, or did he hope to make the bitterness between them disappear?

How many nights had Gil gone to bed wishing the same?

The difference lay in not getting his hopes up. He knew change wouldn't take place overnight. But this was a start.

Gil squinted into the sun as it dipped behind the clouded horizon, casting golden-pink hues across the western sky. He grinned at the doc. "What do you think? Want to rope a few steers before supper?"

Mattie's eyes lit up, her enthusiasm contagious. "Beats staring at a cabin wall."

They saddled the mares they'd ridden that morning, and Gil handed Mattie a thirty-foot rope. "Try this on for size."

Mattie swung a loop over her head, each rotation bigger than the one before. She released the cord and missed her target by a few feet. Gil tried not to smile, knowing he might not do better. "It's not as easy as it looks, but you'll get the hang of it."

They rode to the arena where Jake, Gil's dad, and the owner of the steers sat on square hay bales waiting for the fun to begin. On the opposite end of the arena, the longhorns bunched together along the fence. An occasional bawl drifted from the herd, adding to Gil's anticipation. He kissed the dun into a trot, then loped a few circles. Mattie did the same.

"You want to go first?" he asked when the horses were warmed up.

Mattie released another practice throw and it fell on empty space to the ground. The woman was full of concentration, her tongue poking out the side of her mouth. "Why don't you? I'm in no hurry to make a fool out of myself, especially in front of our audience."

"Those old geezers? Pretend they're not there. That's what I do." Maybe he should have given her a few pointers before they began. The thought of holding the doc next to him with the sweet smell of her curls in his face sent a jolt through his body. He shook the image from his mind.

"Frank and I used to keep score, but we won't worry about that. Let's just see how many we can catch." Gil led the way and walked his horse through the spotted steers to break them apart. Not wanting to run them, he swung his lariat and relaxed into the smooth rhythm of the wrist to elbow movement, surprised at how comfortable it felt. The dun stepped into position behind a calf, and he released the rope, extending his arm for the follow-through. The loop pitched forward, then curled around the calf's head, twisting into a figure eight over its back.

"Whoo-hoo," Jake called from the side as Gil ripped the slack, elated at his first success.

Mattie appeared beside him and grinned. "Nice job, considering the calf was barely moving. Mind if I give it a try?"

Before Gil could respond, she targeted her steer, which broke from the herd and dashed into the middle of the arena. Mattie followed and roped its head on her first try. "You sure you don't want to keep score?" she hollered to him and giggled.

Gil straightened in his saddle, his chest expanded. The doc wanted competition, did she? He knew all about sport, thrived on it, even. If the little lady wanted to play hard, who was he to let her down?

MATTIE TIPPED HER HEAD IN LAUGHTER AS SHE PULLED THE SADDLE off Tulip an hour later in the barn. "Bet you thought I'd never roped before."

Gil led his golden mare into the barn, and his lips pulled to one side at having been shown up by a woman, seven to five. "You could have said something."

"What, and spoil the fun? I used to help my dad doctor cattle, plus I was on the equestrian team in college." She deposited the saddle onto a rack outside the feed room.

"Next time, we'll go ten for ten and see who comes out on top." He shot her a mock scowl, and they burst into laughter.

Mattie slung her arms around the gray mare's neck and watched Gil put the tack away. His body was strong, his manner confident and sure, even though she'd whipped him at his own sport. And, he was able to laugh about it … at least this time. All of that, combined with his handsome face and curls, made her clutch Tulip's neck tighter. He was the kind of man she could admire, the kind of man she might be tempted to set her sights on if she had a mind to do so.

Finished with the tack, Gil returned to his mare. "How about letting me take you out for dinner? We could stop in at the café and grab some hamburgers, or whatever you feel like eating — winner's choice."

Her face flushed with warmth. Was Gil asking her on a date? Or was he just being thoughtful? Mattie dropped her gaze and concentrated on brushing Tulip. "That's kind of you to offer, but it's been a long day. After I check on Dusty, I think I'll turn in."

Gil led his mare to Tulip. "Come on, you have to eat. It's not even eight o'clock. Only old women go to bed this early."

Mattie's eyebrows elevated, as did her dander. "Listen, you don't have to tend to me like I'm one of the livestock."

The man's gaze drifted down to her boots. "Trust me, I know the difference."

Caught off guard by his sudden interest, Mattie's stomach fluttered with butterflies. She frowned, at odds with her thoughts and this new feeling.

"If you don't want to go, no problem. I didn't mean to make you uncomfortable. I just thought you might enjoy the company." Seemingly impervious to her rejection, Gil took Tulip's lead rope. "I'm going to Emporia on Saturday. If you need anything, let me know, and I can pick it up for you."

Mattie kicked herself for being such a ninny, making too much of his dinner invitation. She considered his second offer and thought of the many items she needed but didn't have the money to purchase until her insurance check came in. "If it's not too much trouble, I could use some medicine. I can call in an order, if you'd like."

"Sounds good, and don't worry about reimbursing me. We can

deal with that later." Gil led the two mares through the barn to a hay ring outside.

Mattie regarded him as he walked away. She enjoyed his sauntering stride, not the cocky, self-assured gate of a professional athlete. Instead, his demeanor seemed to defy expectations, fitting into this environment as though he'd never stopped being a cowboy. Perhaps she'd made a mistake in turning down his dinner invitation. But if he asked again, would she have the nerve to accept? She smiled at the prospect.

TWENTY-FOUR

Saturday afternoon, Mattie met two electricians at the barn door. They wore matching uniforms and looked to be father and son.

"We were told you needed some outlets installed," the elderly man said.

Surprised at Gil's initiative to hire the work done, Mattie moved out of the way and showed the electricians where she wanted the new wiring. "Thanks for coming out on a weekend to do this."

"No problem. We're glad to help Mr. McCray any way we can."

Mattie pursed her lips, certain which McCray they meant. When she'd first met Gil, the adoration he received from the community annoyed her. Now she understood what the townspeople saw in him. The electricians worked for over an hour, then just as they were leaving, another truck roared up the lane. Mattie stepped out to see Gil backing his Dodge to the barn, its shiny new bed full of boxes and supplies.

"What is all this?" She placed her hands on her hips, trying to hide her disbelief.

Gil hopped out of the truck, a smile plastered on his face. "Can't have a doc practicing medicine without her medicine."

"This is a lot more than medicine." She noted a desk and chair piled high among other boxes, a small refrigerator, and a computer. "A coffeepot?"

"A woman's gotta have her caffeine if she's going to work your hours. I hope you don't mind, but I did a little research on what you'd need to get started. We'll have to order the big pieces next week." He lowered the tailgate and began hauling the items to her new office.

"I can't accept this." She felt like blocking his entrance but moved out of the way, afraid he might plow right over her. "It must have cost a fortune."

Gil shook his head. "I told you we'll worry about it later ... or better yet, take it off Dusty's bill." He grinned and lifted another box from the truck.

"Good idea. I should have thought of that." Mattie pitched in to help, her pleasure building with every pound she carried. At this rate, she'd be back in business in no time.

"How can I ever thank you?" she asked when they'd finished unloading the truck.

"Well, I almost hate to ask, considering you turned me down last time." Gil sat on the edge of her new desk. "I've been craving a juicy T-bone ever since I came home. No one grills a better steak than Charlie's Steakhouse."

Mattie's heart thumped in her chest. How could she say no? She stared at the boxes in the room. "Okay."

Gil clapped his hands together. "Okay, as in, you'll go?"

Mattie laughed, the tension inside dissolving. "Don't look so surprised. You're not the only one who likes to eat."

GIL EYED MATTIE FROM ACROSS THE TABLE. IF POSSIBLE, SHE LOOKED even prettier in the dim candlelight than she did in the sunshine. Her hair was pinned in a loose ponytail with one stray curl at her cheek, and she wore a sweater that matched the leaves in fall — colors that suited her red hair and fair skin quite nicely. He found it easy to give her his full attention despite the Saturday night crowd.

"Thanks for coming with me tonight." He handed her a menu. "I hate going to places like this by myself."

"Far be it from me to keep a man from his steak." She chuckled, and the soft lilt in her voice made him smile.

"That's right. When I want something, you better not stand in my way." He placed a cloth napkin on his lap, then sipped his ice water. "Any idea what you want to order?" He glanced over the menu, already knowing the dinner he'd choose.

"I think I'll have the filet mignon with rice and salad."

"No potatoes?" He guessed Mattie to be more of a french fry kind of girl. "You're not trying to impress me with a dainty appetite, are you? Because I've seen you eat, remember?"

She laid the menu on the table and smiled, her eyes sparkling like the ice in her glass. "You're right. Order me some cottage fries. I'm a little rusty at this dating thing."

Gil's eyebrows rose. *The doc considered this a date?* He smiled, feeling even more confident about the evening. "How long has it been, exactly?"

She leaned back and tallied the number on her fingers. "That depends on whether you count going to bingo and sitting by a man twice my age." A grin tipped her mouth. "If not, it's been a couple of years. Not that I haven't been asked."

"I'm guessing every boy in high school has come by your office at least once, as well as ranchers for miles around." He toyed with his next thought. "Maybe even your technician. What was his name?"

Mattie straightened in her chair. "Travis is too young for me. Besides, I would never let an attraction interfere with work."

"You're attracted to him, then?" Gil thought he noticed something between the doc and the college intern the few times he'd seen them together. It made him glad she'd laid off her hired help.

"I never said that." Her voice bristled in defense. "Besides, he has a girlfriend."

Gil smirked. Just as well. The boy was not man enough for a woman like Mattie. He would have told her so too, except a waitress came to take their order.

"Maybe we should change the subject," he said after the server left. "It's my fault, for my poor manners." He lifted his glass to take a drink of water.

"I recall being the target of those ill manners. Something about snickerdoodles and having too much social life?" Her challenge chilled him to the core.

Cold water spilled onto his chin. He dabbed the liquid with his napkin, remembering all too well the night he'd labeled Mattie an incompetent veterinarian. "I never apologized for that, did I? What can I say? I saw you holding Dad's hand and jumped to conclusions."

Gil tucked the napkin onto his lap, then reached across the table for her hand. "I'm glad you proved me wrong."

Mattie slipped her fingers from beneath his and clutched the edge of the table. "There was nothing to prove. As I said from the beginning, your dad and I are good friends. I'm indebted to him for more things than I can count."

"You'll forgive me for thinking the worst?" Gil revealed his most charming smile, hoping she'd loosen up. It seemed to work.

"Is that why you bombarded me with all those gifts today? Guilt?"

"Not gifts—a trade for Dusty's care, remember?"

Mattie shook her head. "You've gone above and beyond the call of duty." She surprised him by reaching out to squeeze his hand. At her touch, he swore he could feel his heart melting.

TWENTY-FIVE

MATTIE TOSSED HER NAPKIN ON THE TABLE, STUFFED FROM TOO many fries. "I can't eat another bite."

Gil stared at her plate. "You're not going to let that steak go to waste, are you?"

"If you want it, be my guest." She pushed her plate toward him, and his eyes lit with pleasure.

"Don't mind if I do." He stabbed the piece of meat, savoring each bite. When finished, he wiped his mouth with a napkin to reveal a satisfied grin. "They don't make steaks like this in California."

"So I've heard."

Two teenage boys edged up to the table, nudging each other as though to build their courage. "Mr. McCray, could we have your autograph?" The one in front offered paper and pen, while the other boy held out his canvas cap for Gil to sign.

Mattie waited while Gil dealt with his junior fan club, amazed at how well he handled the invasion of privacy. He winked at her once the boys left and tucked a hundred dollar bill under his plate. "Shall we leave before someone else decides he needs an autograph?"

She followed him outside, and the cold air sliced through her jeans.

"Care to walk off some of this food before we return to the ranch?" Gil zipped his leather jacket and motioned behind the restaurant toward the Cottonwood River that flowed through the edge of town.

Mattie pulled on the fleece-lined gloves stuffed in her wool coat pocket. "The weatherman said there was a chance for snow tonight."

"I'll believe it when I see it." Gil stared up at the sky.

The north wind bit into Mattie's skin as she lifted her collar around her neck. They hiked the trail to the natural waterfall, their warm breath rising in the frosty night air. As they neared, the sound of the river cascading over stone intensified. Hundreds of stars twinkled above and Mattie sighed.

Gil clasped her gloved hand when they reached the river's edge, and the contact unnerved her, made her self-conscious. The water trickled over the rocks, and the crisp air nipped her nose.

"Do you ever get tired of the attention?" She tried not to let his romantic gesture affect her.

He released her hand. "You mean at the restaurant?" The light above the trail cast a shadow against the side of his face.

"I don't know how you stand it. If I had strangers approach me all the time, I'd be tempted to hibernate."

Gil chuckled. "You get used to it. It's part of being a *celebrity*." He said the word as though making fun of himself.

"Did you always want to play professional ball? I mean, you must have. How else could you tolerate the attention?" She sat on a wooden bench and heard the orchestra of the falls blend with the cry of a nighthawk.

"My dreams were no different than any other boy out here. Horses and rodeo." He hiked his foot to the bench and rested his forearm on his knee. "Never had any desire to play football until high school, and then only because of my friends."

Mattie shook her head, unable to understand how a boy who

cared so little about football had turned into a professional quarterback. "What changed?"

He ducked his chin into his coat collar. "Frank died."

"I didn't mean to pry." She kicked at a broken limb, then stood to follow the dirt trail along the bank.

Gil offered his arm.

"Frank and I team roped together. He planned to go on the rodeo circuit after high school, which was fine with my dad—until he learned I intended to join him." Gil shook his head, and as he talked, Mattie became more at ease. "You wouldn't believe the arguments we had then."

"Worse than those you have now?" She looked up, and Gil's eyes flickered. Her toes freezing, she clung tighter to his arm for warmth. "I take it he didn't approve of your idea."

"I don't think I've ever pleased the man. He wanted me to stay home and ranch with him. Can you imagine the two of us making business decisions together?" He laughed, but it couldn't disguise the heaviness in his tone. "When Frank died, my fascination for rodeo died with him. That's when football started making sense. As a defensive lineman, I could hit the guy in front of me as hard as I wanted and not get into trouble."

Mattie ached for his teenage years. The heartache he endured losing his brother at such a tender age. Something niggled about his words though. "You didn't start out as a quarterback?"

Gil didn't answer for a moment. "Nope ... it's funny how things work out sometimes."

ALL THIS TALK ABOUT FRANK AND HIGH SCHOOL MADE GIL'S STOMACH churn. Now that he'd retired, he wanted to move on with his life, not dwell on the bad times, the bittersweet moments. Nor did he care to reveal what talking about Frank did to him. How his betrayal haunted him.

He much preferred thinking about Mattie and repositioned his arm around her shoulders, glad for the opportunity to pull her close. Hovering over her, he caught a whiff of her hair, clean and sweet like roses. "What about you? Did you always want to be a veterinarian?"

"I got along well with animals, plus I excelled at science."

"Don't tell me — you were one of those girls who never studied and always got straight A's." She nudged him in the ribs, and he welcomed her tolerance for teasing. The little lady could take as much as she could give. He liked that about her.

"The summer I worked for Doc Bryant convinced me to become a vet," she said. "After that, I knew I wanted to return to Charris County where I could help the ranchers."

"A noble cause." Most girls he'd known at that age were interested in makeup and going to the prom, not in serving others.

"Not entirely." She stopped and grinned. "Doc promised to sell his business to me when he retired. I figured if I worked in Diamond Falls, I might eventually own some land, maybe even a ranch."

"Or better yet, marry a rancher?" He couldn't resist.

At that, she pulled away and went to stand by the wooden fence bordering the trail. "If the right man ever comes along . . . and I don't mean your father."

"What about now? Have you considered how long it'll take to rebuild?"

Mattie shook her head. "I figure once my clinic's set up, I'll start visiting ranchers, let them know I'm back in business. From there, I guess we'll see how long it takes."

"You're not worried?" Her practice had been unsteady before the fire. Considering her own father's bankruptcy, it had to weigh heavy on her mind.

She shifted her feet and pulled her coat tighter around her neck. "I'd be lying if I said I wasn't. But the Lord tells us not to worry about tomorrow, so I'm going to take things one day at a time."

"Do not worry about what you will drink or what you will wear."

"That's right. I'm not as pretty as a lily in the field, but God's going to look after me just the same."

"Even better," he added.

A smile crept onto her face, and the sheer beauty of it, innocence coupled with integrity, made Gil's heart topple inside his chest. He stood before her and studied her face in the dim overhead light. Mattie was far prettier than a flower. Curved brows over thick lashes, green eyes that reflected her every emotion. Long, slender nose.

The two of them were so different. Growing up, he hadn't been able to run from these hills fast enough, and she couldn't wait to get back. Why did he feel so attracted to her, as though God meant for them to be together?

Overwhelmed by an urge to kiss her, he tilted her chin and eased down. Close enough that her breath warmed his skin. He paused. What was he thinking? How could he pursue a relationship with this woman, considering his past — his connection to her sister?

Angered that he couldn't outrun his mistakes, he let go abruptly and stepped away, shoving his hands into his jean pockets. Mattie's home was in Kansas, his was in California, and that's how it needed to stay. Better to keep his distance from this woman who could turn his thoughts to mush.

The river gurgled behind them, and a huge snowflake landed on Mattie's cheek.

"Looks like the weatherman was right." Gil held out his hand and two more snowflakes landed on his palm, melting instantly. "I'd best take you home before you turn into an icicle."

Otherwise, he might be tempted to change his mind and indulge in the feel of her lips against his.

TWENTY-SIX

DRESSED IN FLANNEL PAJAMAS, MATTIE STARED OUT THE CABIN window and watched the giant snowflakes swirl in the yard light's illumination. Her evening with Gil replayed in her mind as she considered his words and behavior. She pressed a finger to her lips and regarded her reflection in the icy glass, sure Gil meant to kiss her. He'd held her so close, his face inches from her own.

But then he'd let go, and from that moment until they awkwardly said good-night, he'd been as cool to her as the crisp evening air.

Mattie turned from the window and added another log to the fire. Warming her hands against the hot flames, her temper flared. Was she not good enough for him? Too short, too many freckles?

She clenched her fists. Why should she care?

Gil might be strong and good-looking, but the man had issues, and oh, how he got under her skin with his casual interest toward the Lightning M. That he wouldn't consider returning to his childhood home gave her enough reason not to care. Then there were moments when she was sure he kept something from her. But what?

Mattie hopped beneath the thick bedcovers, eager to talk to another woman about her conflicting emotions. She knew for certain that she couldn't confide in her mother or sisters. They'd blow this way out of proportion. As she settled against the pillow, the firelight glowed on the ceiling. A flickering flame beckoned to another, then embraced as one. Her lips parted as she allowed herself to imagine what Gil's kiss might have been like.

THE NEXT MORNING AFTER CHURCH, MATTIE GRIPPED CLARA'S ARM and pulled her to the side as people filed out of the pews. "We need to talk ... in private."

Confusion spread over Clara's face as she shifted Sara to her other arm. "What's got into you? You're more restless than all three of my kids." She turned to reprove Jeremy and Nathan, who argued over who would carry their mama's Bible.

Mattie pursed her lips at the comparison, but Clara's assessment was right. She'd been as fidgety as a cat in a cage and had caught only portions of the pastor's sermon. "I need a woman's advice."

This captured her friend's attention.

Clara shooed her boys off to play with their friends in the fellowship hall. "Sounds serious. What sort of advice?"

"Not so loud." Mattie eased them into a deserted alcove, away from the many ears passing by. It was hard enough talking to Clara about her personal life without having anyone else listen in.

"You know ... female stuff." Mattie felt so out of her element, she practically had to force the words from her mouth.

Clara's eyes lit with amusement. "I see. What's on your mind?" She made a face at the toddler in her arms and stuck out her bottom lip, showing no sensitivity to the weight of this conversation, or to Mattie's distress.

Mattie took the girl from Clara's arms to gain her friend's full attention. "Do you think I'm ugly? Too hotheaded? Overly interested in my work?"

Clara blinked. "You're talking nonsense."

Mattie exhaled the turmoil building inside. "I'm serious. Look at me—I'm practically thirty years old. Do you suppose there's a reason men aren't attracted to me?"

"All men, or one in particular?"

"Gil McCray." Mattie mouthed the words and her cheeks grew warm.

Clara's eyes widened. "Why would you care what that man thinks? Didn't he accuse you of having a thing for his dad? The nerve of some men." She chuckled, but when Mattie didn't join in, her eyes narrowed.

Mattie practically heard the siren go off in her friend's head.

"Is something going on between you two?"

Mattie shrugged, still not sure herself.

At her sign of indecision, Clara grasped Mattie's arm. "You'd better be careful with that one. He's rich, good-looking, and used to getting his way." She immediately clammed up, her eyes fixed on something beyond. "We'll talk later," she said through the side of her mouth. "You-know-who is walking this way and is almost to your back door."

GIL SPOTTED MATTIE AS HE SHOOK HANDS WITH RANCHERS AND neighbors from the community. The site of her long red hair against the green sweater made his heart quicken—made him long to touch the wispy curls that escaped her braid once again. Best to continue walking to the door with the rest of the men—make his escape without tempting another awkward moment, but that would seem rude, wouldn't it?

He edged through the departing crowd to where Mattie and another lady stood.

"Good morning, Doc. I didn't realize you attended New Redeemer." At his words, Mattie turned and smiled, though her features appeared strained. She held a curly, brown-haired child who pointed a pudgy finger at him.

"Gil." Mattie spoke his name, and his stomach clenched. He felt like an awkward schoolboy in her presence, and he didn't like it.

"I didn't know you did either." She handed the child to the other woman and repositioned her sweater.

"I'm sure there's much we don't know about each other." He cleared his throat. Of course there was much she didn't know—things he wanted kept hidden—for her sake and for his. He offered his hand to the woman behind Mattie. "Clara, isn't it? From the café?"

"That's right." The woman's eyes narrowed as though sizing him up. Beads of sweat formed on his forehead. Could she see right through him?

Mattie fidgeted with the leather purse on her shoulder and glanced about, her restlessness palpable. His presence obviously made the doc uncomfortable, and after last night, who could blame her?

"Do either of you have plans for lunch?" Gil clenched his jaw. Was he a dimwit? Better to have chucked his loss and walked away.

The two women exchanged odd expressions. "As a matter of fact, we do," Clara said. "Mattie and I were just discussing how we never have a chance for girl talk."

Gil hadn't been around many females in his life, but he knew when something was up.

"Between Mattie's practice and my restaurant and the kids ... I'm sure you understand."

Relief flooded his chest. "Another time, then." As he stepped backward, a hint of regret flashed in Mattie's eyes.

Like a dope, his next words were out of his mouth before he could stop them. "Mattie, if you don't have anything scheduled this afternoon, maybe you'd like to drop by and watch the Super Bowl with Dad and me."

What am I doing?

Why did he feel the need to spend time with the woman? "Never mind, I forgot you don't care for football."

Nice save.

Gil closed his eyes and turned to leave, this time for good.

"Should I bring some chips and dip?" she asked.

His feet stalled in the aisle.

He looked back at Mattie, feeling as though he'd just scored a touchdown pass. "Snacks would be good, or don't worry about it and just bring yourself."

"You're playing with fire," Clara said a few minutes later as she bundled the kids to go out in the snow. "I should know, considering my own failed marriage."

Mattie offered Clara a lopsided smile. She respected her friend's opinion, whether it was something she wanted to hear or not. "C'mon, you gotta help me. How do you know when a guy's interested? I mean, one minute Gil seems attracted, and the next he doesn't."

"He's probably playing a game with you." Clara bent to zip Sara's coat and tie her fuzzy hood at the neck. "My advice is to take things slow — real slow. Make sure you know the guy really well before you give him any part of your heart. Because once you do, all rational thought flies out the window."

She took out two pink mittens and shoved them on Sara's hands, then called to her oldest son. "Take your sister outside to play and keep an eye on her."

Mattie watched the little girl toddle down the church steps with her older brother. "Flies out, huh?" Mattie considered herself a practical woman, a bit stubborn and impetuous at times, but for the most part a clear thinker. "I can't imagine myself brainwashed and googly-eyed over a man. That's a trap for a teenager, not a twenty-eight-year-old veterinarian."

Clara rose from her knees and frowned. "Whatever you say. But don't cry that you were never warned."

"That's just it. I hear warning bells every time I look at Gil."

Mattie wrung her hands, tired of analyzing. "This entire situation with Gil seems hopeless. He doesn't get along with his dad and is determined to own a ranch in California, of all places. For the life of me, I can't understand why, when he could operate the Lightning M and probably own it someday. A part of me knows better than to get involved, but I'm so attracted to him, it's like this huge magnet is drawing us together."

Clara stretched her arm around Mattie's shoulders and squeezed. "Trust me on this one. You can't change a person, no matter how much you think it possible. Only God can change the heart, so love a man for who he is, not who he might be."

Mattie considered her friend's words as they eased their way over the snow-packed ground to their vehicles. She didn't want to change Gil, she only wanted him to appreciate the hills and his home the way she did. That wasn't changing a man, was it? She preferred to think of it as helping him see the error of his ways. Doing him a favor, really, which is the only reason she agreed to spend the afternoon with him and his father.

Watching football.

What on earth had she gotten herself into?

TWENTY-SEVEN

GIL EXCHANGED HIS FOOTBALL FOR THE TELEVISION REMOTE AND SET the leather ball beside him on the couch. "I hope you don't mind my asking Mattie over for the game." He flipped to the channel that hosted the pregame show and relaxed against the couch.

John McCray laid his newspaper on his lap. "Why would I mind?" he grumbled. "It'll give me someone to talk to, now that you gave Mildred the day off."

Gil sat up, reminded of his chili on the stove. "Mildred doesn't need to work every day of the week, especially now that I'm here. She's not your slave." He shook his head and got up to check the soup simmering in the kitchen.

Clutching a wooden spoon, he stirred the thick tomato base, his very own recipe, and the peppery blend of spices drifted to his nose. It made his mouth water, and he lifted the spoon to taste the fiery concoction.

More salt.

He sprinkled the seasoning over the pot of bubbling chili and thought of his teammates who used to like when he'd cook for them. *What were the guys doing now, the rowdy bunch?*

Drinking beer and eating submarine sandwiches, Gil figured, as he assembled a platter of cheese and crackers. All of them watching to see which team would win this year's title. But it wouldn't be them. He shook his head and tried to concentrate on something else, anything but failure ... that it could have been his team competing for Super Bowl rings.

When he returned to the living room, déjà vu hit him square in the face as he spotted Mattie beside his dad's recliner, her hand on his. This time Gil knew better than to challenge the doc's compassionate nature. Instead, he grinned, thinking she was the perfect person to ease him out of this sour mood. She stood from her stooped position and returned his smile.

"John says you gave Mildred the day off. Whatever you're cooking in the kitchen smells wonderful."

His dad snorted. "It'll probably give me heartburn. You know I'm not supposed to eat spicy food."

Gil set the crackers and cheese on the coffee table. "If you can't take the heat, I'll fry you an omelet."

Mattie stepped between him and his dad, thwarting the arrows. She handed him a sack of potato chips and plopped on the couch. "What teams are playing today? Green Bay Packers and Baltimore Patriots?"

Gil chuckled at her attempt to show interest in the sport, guessing his dad didn't know the difference between teams either. "New England Patriots," he corrected and set the chips on the table with the other snacks before taking a seat beside her. "You do understand the basic concept of the game, right? Two teams meet in the middle of the field. One side is offense, one defense, both try to gain possession of the ball?"

At her blank expression, he decided to go over a few fundamentals and ended up charting it out for her on a piece of paper.

"Why don't you leave the girl alone?" his dad said. "I'm sure she'll catch on once the game starts."

Mattie opened the bag of barbecue chips and laughed. "Don't bet on it. When it comes to football, I've never paid much attention, not even in high school."

His dad lifted the newspaper on his lap. "Sounds like you had more sense than some people I know," he grumbled from behind the front page, but Gil heard every word.

He stifled the anger that threatened to boil to the surface like his pot of chili on the stove. Why couldn't his father try to get along? Why did he always have to stir up trouble? Tempted to lash out, Gil bit his words and concentrated on the woman beside him.

She'd changed into a pair of jeans and a flannel shirt, her hair still bound in a braid. To his relief, she no longer emitted the anxiety that surrounded her earlier, but instead, seemed her natural self again.

"Did you and Clara have a nice lunch?"

Mattie popped a chip in her mouth, and it made a loud crunch. "Short but sweet. We ate a quick meal and visited until her mother came to babysit so Clara could go to work." She offered him the bag of chips, and he grabbed a handful.

"She seems like a nice woman. Busy, and I take it not married?"

"Divorced, with three children."

Gil thought of the toddler Mattie held in the church, barely two years old and cute as a doll. How could a guy give up a great wife and kids? His own family had its share of problems, but at least his dad never abandoned them.

"Clara's blessed to have her mother help with the kids." Mattie crunched on another chip.

"Good mothers are a blessing from God—dads too, I suppose." Gil smiled, then considered his father stretched out on his recliner. The anger that burned a short while ago dimmed. He wiped the barbecue residue from his fingers and reached into his front jean pocket for the watch his coach had given him, felt the smooth metal beneath his skin, and was reminded how precious time could be.

As the second hand ticked against his fingers, the big screen roared to life, and the commentators announced the starting lineup. The players ran onto the field, and Gil's excitement grew.

"Do you know any of these guys?" Mattie shifted to the edge of the couch and seemed half-interested in the game.

"Yeah, the Packer's star quarterback for one." He named the various players he respected or in some cases, didn't. Within minutes, Green Bay won the coin toss, and the other team started the game with the kickoff. Gil seized the football on the couch and gripped the laces, wishing he could have been the one throwing the ball.

MATTIE NEVER UNDERSTOOD THE ATTRACTION FOOTBALL HELD FOR people, but she wanted to try and appreciate the game for Gil's sake. He clutched the ball with his thick, wide hands, and she flinched when he faked a pass, patterning his motions after the guy on the television.

"Throw the ball, your split end's wide open!" Gil rose from the couch.

Last Mattie knew, a split end meant you needed a haircut. She regarded John, curious whether he had any interest in the game and discovered he'd fallen asleep on the recliner, the newspaper a tent over his belly.

On the big screen the crowd thundered as the broadcaster announced first down. Without the televised commentary, Mattie would be lost.

"That's more like it." Gil dropped to the couch, football in hand.

"Okay, tell me again what first down means." She expected Gil to complain about having to explain things twice. Instead, his eyes crinkled in a grin, and he referred once more to the sheet of paper on the coffee table.

"The quarterback decides to run, pass, or hand the ball off

to another player. No matter what he chooses, the team has four chances to go ten yards. If they fail, the other team gets the ball." He drew a bunch of zeros on the paper and commenced to outline various playing strategies.

Mattie shook her head, trying to compare Gil's words to what she saw on the television. The ball moved too fast on the screen for her to keep up. How Gil had memorized all these plays and employed them in the blink of an eye was beyond her. It seemed like the man had two identities — the one who rode a horse and the one who threw a football. That he could do both so well caused her estimation of him to climb a few more notches.

She noted their close proximity, how his leg rested against hers, and her attention wavered. Her thoughts drifted to the spicy scent of his cologne, to how he'd held her the night before.

Gil must have noticed her inattentiveness. "Come on, I'll show you."

"Show me what?" Mattie had no idea what he'd been talking about before her preoccupation. He took her hand, causing her skin to tingle.

"I'll show you how the professionals do it."

Again, she had no clue, but followed him through the room to an open area between the living and dining rooms. Cradled against her back, Gil demonstrated with his fingers between the laces how to hold the ball.

"When you throw, you want your index finger to steer the ball into a spiral spin." One by one, he pressed her fingers in place, then guided her arm in a forward pass minus the release. All Mattie could think about, however, was how good it felt to have Gil's arms encircle her — feel his breath tickle her ear. She closed her eyes, savoring the moment.

Too soon, Gil let go and positioned her in another stance. "Now, you be the quarterback, and I'll hike the ball." He bent over with the football between his legs and spouted off a bunch of numbers.

Before Mattie knew what happened, the brown missile shot from Gil's hands and hit her smack in the stomach. In the millisecond it took to cycle thought with reaction, the ball bounced out of reach and crashed into a rose-patterned tea service, knocking the china pot to the floor where it splintered into a hundred shiny pieces.

Mattie gasped.

Gil straightened, his mouth gaping in a horrified expression.

"What in tarnation are you doing over there?" John McCray hollered, his afternoon nap disturbed. He got up from his chair and aided by his cane, crossed the room. When he identified the source of the commotion, his face contorted into an agonized scowl.

"You broke your mama's tea set?" His blue eyes flickered from Gil to Mattie, then settled on his son. "Her favorite tea set?" He struggled to the wooden floor and picked up a shard of porcelain trimmed in gold. His shoulders slumped, outlined by defeat. "I gave this to your mama for her sixtieth birthday. Had tea and cookies with her every afternoon till the day she died."

"I'm sorry, Dad." Gil stepped closer. "We should have been more careful. I was just showing Mattie a few moves."

John glowered at his son. Mattie sensed his rage building and bent to help gather the pieces.

"You always did care more about football than your own flesh and blood." His words came out in ragged breaths as he brandished a portion of the teapot toward Gil. "Left your mother and me to run this ranch by ourselves and took away our hope of watching our grandkids grow up on this land. Broke your mama's heart by denying her one last good-bye."

Mattie glanced at Gil as the arrows shot into his heart.

"We were halfway around the world." Gil pressed his hand to his forehead and squeezed his eyes shut. "Don't you think I wanted to see her before she died? I loved her too. Would have given my right arm to hold her hand and tell her one last time."

Tears stung Mattie's eyes as the two grown men battled out their heartache, as though one's pain was greater than the other. But what could she say? All she could do was be here for them, try to help mend their broken relationship.

No amount of glue would fix the shattered pot in her hand.

But surely Gil and John's relationship could be restored.

Couldn't it?

TWENTY-EIGHT

"One would never know you cared a whit about your mama—never shed a tear at her grave." Gil's dad picked up another shard of the broken teapot.

At the hard tone, Gil froze, incapable of rebuff or movement. He checked Mattie's stunned expression and a part of him withered in mortification. Would she think him a cold monster, incapable of feeling?

Gil forced himself to break through the icy crust to convince his father and Mattie that he wasn't that cruel. He gripped his dad's shoulder. "I never meant . . ."

His father shrugged his hand aside. "Go back to your football. I can clean this up myself."

Gil stared at the high ceiling, wanting to make things better but not having the foggiest idea how to do so. He dropped his gaze to Mattie and offered a silent apology for putting her in the middle of this horrible mess. "I'm going to check on Dusty. Clear the air. Might do us all some good right now."

Mattie rose and clutched his elbow. "Want me to go with you?" The warmth in her eyes offered the understanding he yearned for.

But Gil shook his head. "Stay here. You'll do more for him than I can."

He left the house and plodded across the snow-laden barnyard, his heart heavy in the crisp, cold air. When he opened the barn door, he spotted Jake on a bale of straw next to Dusty.

"Me and Dusty is having us a little chat." Jake tapped his knee and grinned. "Us old fogies have a lot in common. His knees hurt, my knees hurt." He spit a stream of tobacco to the dirt floor next to his father's blue heeler.

Gil knelt beside the gelding and smoothed a hand across his neck. He could feel Jake's eyes studying him.

"Been fussing with your dad?"

"How did you know?"

"I watched you grow up, remember? Seen you take your first ride. Not much has changed since then." Jake scratched his whiskers. "You always wanted to tackle the world. I'm guessing you still do."

Gil's brow puckered as he contemplated the cowboy's words. "I wonder if we'll ever get along—find that place of harmony where we can both be content, or at least communicate with each other without turning it into a brawl."

Jake rubbed his worn jeans as though massaging the tired muscles beneath. "Seems to me you always found your peace on the back of a horse. Might be snow on the ground now, but spring will come. There ain't nothing like spring in the hills—blue skies, fresh green grass, new calves popping out left and right." He twitched his mouth from side to side, then spit another wad of chew. "I'm thinking there's harmony right under your nose." The ranch hand eased from the bale and wiped the dark juice from his mouth. "It'll come to you; jest have to give it some time—for the snow to melt, so to speak."

Jake went off to oil saddles while Gil cleaned Dusty's pen. What the old cowboy said about finding peace on a horse was true, and it solidified Gil's notion of raising horses, top-quality horses like Dusty had been. The ranch he hoped to buy in California would be the perfect setup for a brood mare operation, and having already re-searched the horse industry, he knew where to find proven rodeo stock—right here in Kansas.

When Gil returned to the house, he found Mattie in the kitchen dipping chili into a blue bowl. "How is he?" Gil asked.

Mattie looked up and shrugged. "We swept the broken china from the floor, but he's still upset. I finally convinced him to lie down in his bedroom. Hoped some rest might do the trick."

"I doubt it. Where do you think I got my hard head?" Gil knew his dad would hold this grudge for a good long time. Perhaps as Jake said, the two of them just needed to let the snow melt.

Mattie stirred the pot of chili until Gil stole the ladle from her hand. His clothes reeked of manure and hay ... barnyard perfume. She didn't mind the smell and embraced this side of Gil, hoping to see more.

"What would you think about riding out to Central Kansas with me to look at some horses this spring?"

She grabbed the spoon back. "I think you need to wash your hands before handling the food." She smiled as he followed her com-mand. When he finished wiping his hands on a towel, she handed him a bowl. The steam from the chili tickled her nose but smelled delicious. "What sort of horses are you looking for?"

"Brood mares, maybe even a stud. I want to hire you to do a purchase exam."

"You're serious about raising horses?"

"Dead serious."

John McCray shuffled into the kitchen, one hand on his cane. "What are you dead set on now? Don't tell me you're going back to football?"

"Nope, my playing days are over." Gil took his father a bowl of chili and placed it on the table. "If that's too spicy, let me know, and I'll make you something else."

John scratched his bristly chin and sat down. After a respectable amount of grumbling, he blew on a spoonful and took a bite. He seemed to enjoy it, or at least he didn't complain.

Gil hunched over the counter and attacked his meal with fervor. "I'm going to buy a ranch in California," he said between mouthfuls. "Got it picked out and everything. Beautiful estate, giant barn with an indoor arena. It's not as wide-open as this place, but it's a nice spread."

Mattie dipped a cracker into her chili and pulled it out before it turned soggy. Gil seemed so intent on California. What was he running from? She munched on the cracker and enjoyed the zesty flavor.

"How many acres?" John leaned his elbow on the table with interest.

"Two hundred. Considering the population of the area, that's a lot of land."

Mattie's gaze swung from John to Gil. Populated or not, two hundred acres wasn't enough land to spit on and certainly couldn't compare to the Lightning M. City life had dulled Gil's senses, made him forget the exhilaration of riding on untainted ground. A few weeks in the Flint Hills ought to renew his love for the land and convince him of his mistake. At least, she hoped it would. She ate a spoonful of chili. Within seconds, the fiery seasoning permeated her mouth and radiated from her pores.

John mopped his forehead with a red handkerchief.

"Maybe you ought to fix your dad something else," she said. "You need an iron stomach to eat this stuff."

Apprehension skidded across Gil's face.

John waved off their worry and stared at his son. "Sounds like you got your life all figured out. Seeing as how you're set on owning land in California, I don't guess you have any need for the home place. That's a shame—kind of hoped you'd changed your mind about living here." He rubbed his chest and pushed the half-eaten bowl of chili away.

Mattie lost her appetite too.

"I suppose my niece in Council Grove might be interested in having it, though she's married and has her own home." John's eyes settled on Mattie. "Or maybe I'll hand the ranch over to our good veterinarian here. She's been like a daughter to me these last few years—closer to me than my own kin." He wiped his mouth with a napkin and rose from the table on unsteady legs.

The air in the room was so thick with tension the hair on Mattie's neck prickled beneath her flannel collar. She wanted to diffuse the dynamite sure to explode any minute, but John's statement held such a shock, her words jumbled inside her head.

A daughter to him? Land of her own?

"I never figured you'd give the place to me, anyway." Gil spoke without a hint of offense.

Mattie studied him, suspecting the hurt went so deep it didn't show. Wasn't this exactly what Gil predicted? But John couldn't be so cruel as to deny his only son his rightful inheritance. That would be worse than bankruptcy.

She stepped between the two men. "Now hold on a minute. You don't want to say anything you'll regret later." Her lips twitched as she shot a warning glance at John. "You're not dying, so there's plenty of time to work out this misunderstanding. I know deep down you want Gil to have this place, so don't try to tell me otherwise."

Bunching her hands into fists, she shifted to Gil, prepared to tell him her mind. "And you, standing there as though you could care less. It would kill you if someone else owned this property. Even if you buy your land in California, this will always be your home, the place you grew up with Frank, where you have memories of your mom and dad. How could you let that slip from your lap without so much as a shrug ... or a fight? Don't you know how much this land means—to the both of you?"

Gil shook his head. "It means something to you, Mattie ... not to me." His voice came to her, soft and persuasive.

John let out a disgusted sigh. "I've heard all I care to. Don't need to listen to anymore," he said and ambled from the room.

When he was out of earshot, Mattie turned on Gil like a pit bull. "How can you say that?"

Gil closed the distance between them and lifted her chin, made her look into his eyes. What she saw there contradicted everything that came from his mouth—pain, regret, and a longing for peace. He'd never find that peace by running away from the source of his sorrow.

"I have good memories here, but there are also some really bad ones I'd like to forget. Dad's going to do what he wants with this place. What good will it do to argue about who gets it? My life's in California."

Mattie wrenched her chin from his grasp and stared at the red tiled floor. "But you'll stay until the ranch is repaired? You'll do that for your dad?"

"I won't leave until the work is complete and Dusty's recovered. How about you? Will you help me purchase some mares?"

She stared down at her boots. "I guess I could make arrangements."

"The other day after we caught the bull, you called me a coward. Do you still think that of me?"

Mattie considered their conversation from that day when she'd accused Gil of running away from the ranch and his responsibilities. "That depends on how you handle this mess with your father."

In one smooth motion, Gil seized her hands. "I'm no coward, Mattie. One day you'll see that."

TWENTY-NINE

THE NEXT FEW DAYS, MATTIE SORTED THROUGH THE BOXES IN HER office. Still amazed by Gil's generosity, she took inventory of every item, determined to settle with him cent-for-cent. By Friday, the room began to look like a veterinary office, complete with a sectioned-off examining space where she could perform minor operations.

Mattie sat at the new computer, forced to load client records from a local phone book. Her puppy lay at her feet as she typed in the missing information. She paused to sip her coffee and heard Gil hammering. All week he'd been repairing broken windows and shingles on his father's house, hard-pressed to beat the ice storm forecasted to hit their area on Sunday. Although snow lingered on the ground, the temperature had risen above freezing, which at least made his job easier.

John McCray knocked on the clinic door and entered the room. "Mildred wanted me to check on you. See if you needed anything."

Mattie shook her head, appreciating the gesture. She held up her cup of coffee and smiled. "I'm drinking my morning dose of caffeine now. Tell Mildred I'm good, unless she wants to trade places. I'll gladly cook lunch, if she'll perform a miracle on my accounts."

"Mildred hates computers 'bout as much as I do. She did learn to work that email, though, so she could write to her daughter."

"In Texas, right?"

"She and her family moved to Houston a few years ago. Breaks Mildred's heart not being around her grandkids anymore."

Mattie hoped this wouldn't trigger another tirade about him not having grandchildren. From what she could tell, John and Gil were being civil to one another since their argument, and she prayed it would stay that way. She took another sip, and the robust liquid seared her throat. Her sister, Jenna, lived in Houston, but they didn't talk often, by phone or email. "I ought to keep in touch with my family more than I do. A person gets busy, you know?"

"Everybody's busy." He jerked his thumb toward the house. "Boy's up there making so much ruckus, I can't even sleep. *Bam, bam, bam.* Runs that hammer like a machine."

Mattie smiled. "Gil's excited about the renovations — you should be too. Your house is getting a face-lift."

"I guess I don't mind so much what he's doing — just have to wonder about his motivation." John tapped his hand on his knee to play with the pup, and the beagle, eager for attention, licked his fingers. "Can't understand why Gil came back. He's made it clear he has no desire to stay — no interest in the place. Don't make no sense to me."

"Maybe he's trying to compensate for the time he's been away, all the years apart." She hoped to show the man another view. "Gil's told me he wants to put things right between you two. Says he's tired of fighting."

John snorted. "Could have fooled me."

Mattie's gaze didn't waver. "You're a cantankerous old cuss."

His eyes widened at her frankness.

"What is the problem with you and Gil, anyway?" She got up from her desk and knelt beside him. "Aren't you proud of his accomplishments? He's retiring from fifteen years in professional football.

I don't care for the game, but even I recognize that's a big deal. Why don't you cut him a little slack?"

John wiped his nose with the edge of his hand. Mattie lifted the puppy onto his lap, and the man stared at the beagle without looking up. "Gil walked out on this family long ago. Walked out and didn't look back."

"But that's just it. He was a boy . . . looking for answers, and now he's a grown man . . . still looking for answers. Don't you want to help him?"

"He don't want no help from me."

THE NEXT AFTERNOON, GIL LOOKED UP FROM HIS WORK ON THE roof and saw Mattie lead Dusty out of the barn. From this vantage point, the horse appeared to be in worse shape than Gil realized, the indentations between the ribs deeper and even more pronounced. How much weight had the old boy lost anyway? At least a hundred pounds, maybe more.

Braced against a bitter north wind, Gil bent to pick up a nail and as he stood, he watched Dusty suddenly drop to the ground. The horse then thrashed onto his back with his feet in the air.

"Uh-oh, that can't be good," Gil uttered, his cold fingers already unfastening his tool belt. In haste, he clambered down the aluminum ladder and rushed across the barnyard, making it to the doc's side within seconds. His heartbeat raced as he helped Mattie regain control of the horse.

Dusty sat back on his haunches like a dog. "Colic?" Gil asked, but already knew the answer.

Mattie frowned. "It looks like it. The question is why?" Her warm breath fogged in the frigid air as gray clouds gathered in the sky.

For the next hour, Gil watched as the doc gave Dusty a thorough examination. When finished, Mattie returned to Gil's side and deposited the plastic glove in the trash. "There doesn't seem to be any inflammation of the intestine, which is good. We can pass a nasogastric tube to his stomach to relieve any gas or fluid building there. After that, we'll see how he does."

Gil followed the doc to her office where she retrieved a few more supplies. As a boy, he'd witnessed horses with colic, and it was always of great concern to the owners. He knew it wasn't a disease, but rather an indication of stomach pain. "What were you looking for during your exam?"

"Dusty's been under a lot of stress this past month. He's not eating normally, and he's lost a lot of weight. Plus, he's been on several anti-inflammatory medications — a big indicator that this could be ulcer-related. I'm guessing that's what has triggered the colic, but I need to rule out a few more causes."

"You mean like a stomach ulcer in a human?"

"Yeah, horses get them, too."

When they returned to Dusty's side, they found him kicking at his stomach, obviously still bothered. The doc administered a pain reliever to ease Dusty's anxiety. Gil then helped pass a tube through the horse's nostrils, and they flushed out his stomach. When finished, Dusty seemed more content. The doc wasn't satisfied, however, and stuck him in the stomach with another needle.

Gil stayed behind while she went to her office to test the fluid. "Hey boy, sorry to make you go through all this." He smoothed his hand down Dusty's neck and shoulder, careful of the wounds that were still healing from his accident. "You need to get well, so you and I can go out for a ride. We could go down to the creek, just like when we were young. Would you like that boy?"

Dusty shifted his weight to the opposite side and breathed a heavy sigh through his nostrils, as though agreeing the suggestion sounded like a good idea. Gil sat on a nearby bale of hay and stared at the animal, wondering if his old friend understood. Maybe Gil's presence would have an effect on Dusty's healing after all, as the doc said?

A short while later, Mattie came out of her office, all business.

"In the old days, Doc Bryant would have given Dusty laudanum and linseed oil and let time be the judge. Thanks to modern medicine, we can rule out a lot of guesswork—but not all. I've consulted a colleague of mine, and we agree that performing a gastroscopy on Dusty is warranted."

"I take it that's another test?"

Mattie nodded and sat beside Gil on the hay bale. "I'm ninety percent sure we're dealing with ulcers, but this would tell us for certain. The problem is I don't have an endoscope long enough to do the job. They're rather expensive ..."

Gil straightened. "Where can we get one? I'll buy one for you."

She grasped his hand and smiled. "You don't always have to be in control, Gil. My colleague is going to try to borrow one from K-State. Until then, all we need to do is keep Dusty comfortable."

Gil clenched his jaw. As a quarterback and owner of his foundation, he knew what it took to be in control, to find the answers and call the shots. It defined him as a man and gave him purpose. He stared down at the doc's hand, not sure what to do with the helplessness that washed over him and called him weak. "That's all? Just sit and keep him company?"

Mattie squeezed his hand, and a measure of strength and assurance passed between the two. "Yeah, just sit and be his friend."

For the next two hours, Mattie waited with Gil in the barn, taking turns walking Dusty to help ease the horse's discomfort. Her colleague arrived as the north wind howled against the side of the barn.

"I do believe we're under a winter storm advisory." Jim Wilson removed his wool cap and gloves, then greeted Gil with an enthusiastic handshake. "It's nice to meet you, Mr. McCray. Dr. Evans told me all about you and your horse. I'm glad I could help out, even if it is cold enough to freeze a well digger's—" He stopped suddenly as though remembering Mattie's presence.

"Pardon my language, Dr. Evans," he said, then continued. "You wouldn't believe the paperwork I had to fill out in order to borrow this gadget. According to those boys at the university, this baby is worth its weight in gold. It's a good thing I have connections." The older veterinarian lifted a hard plastic case onto a wooden bench.

Mattie removed the flexible endoscope and waited while her colleague from the next county examined Dusty for himself. Gil came to her side to view the contraption, and she wondered what he thought of the vet. Though Dr. Wilson came off a bit rough around the edges, his reputation in equine science made him the best choice for the job.

"That poor fellow has been through the wringer, hasn't he? It looks like you've patched him up well." He lifted Dusty's eye bandage and nodded his approval. The gelding jerked his head in agitation. "I assume the patient hasn't eaten? Twelve hours at least?"

Mattie raised an eyebrow and indicated Dusty's gaunt size.

"Yeah, that's what I thought," the doctor said, then immediately went to work by injecting Dusty with a tranquilizer.

For the next thirty minutes, Dr. Wilson and Mattie performed the gastroscopy, which allowed them to view Dusty's stomach lining with a small camera. What they found confirmed Mattie's suspicions that the horse had multiple ulcers.

"Thank you for all your help, Jim." She shook the vet's hand an hour later and heard the first wave of sleet spit against the metal roof.

"You best be getting home before the roads turn bad," Gil added.

"I'll take the back way. The gravel won't be nearly as slick," the man said. "You be sure and let me know how Dusty gets along. Treat him with those tubes of medicine I gave you, and we'll examine him in another month to see if the ulcers have healed."

Gil helped carry the doctor's equipment to his truck. Mattie waved from the barn entrance and saw Gil slip a bill into the man's hand.

To her surprise her colleague gave it back. "I don't want your money, Mr. McCray. But if it's not too much trouble, I would love your autograph."

THIRTY

Two severe ice storms hindered Gil's progress in February, but by the end of March, the weather had stabilized enough for him to get some serious work done on the ranch. Dusty's health had stabilized as well, and Gil witnessed progress in the horse's recovery every day.

He wiped the sweat from his brow as he stretched the new barbed wire between corner posts. Jake clipped the wire to the steel posts while his dad's blue heeler lounged on the damp earth.

"Can you believe this weather?" Gil stopped his work and met Jake at the four-wheeler where he took a swig from the water jug.

"Spring is in the air." Jake took his turn at a drink and gave some to the dog. Hank lapped it up as it streamed from the jug. "Good weather for calving too. Counted four baby calves this morning and looks like several more will follow right behind. There's rain in the forecast. A change of weather always brings on a few births."

Gil checked the puffy clouds in the blue sky, then stared out at the rolling hills. He recalled the days when he and Frank rode the pastures in search of baby calves. Usually found them in the gullies or brush, all wobbly and shiny new.

Good memories.

His gaze followed the ridge of the hill and stalled when Mattie came riding toward them on Tulip. He tried to hide his delight. Ever since Dusty's colic incident, he and the doc had grown closer as friends, though he couldn't deny the deep attraction he felt for the woman. Some days, much to his embarrassment, he found himself staring at her, admiring her thick pretty hair and her controlled movements as though she had everything in life perfectly measured. He knew a romantic relationship with the doc would never work and had tried to drown his yearning in ranch labor. Despite his efforts, he didn't know how much longer he could continue the ruse.

Mattie drew the gray mare to an abrupt halt a yard from where they worked and slid from the saddle in one effortless motion. She smiled at Gil, and heat blazed through him hotter than the afternoon sun.

"Mildred thought you guys might be hungry." She reached into her saddlebag and pulled out a plastic sack filled with cookies.

Jake whistled. "That Mildred — she's a good woman."

"None better," Gil said, though if there was a contest, the doc might come in a close second.

Mattie handed the cookies to Gil, and her fingers rested on his to send another jolt of fire clear to his toes. "You've been working real hard lately. If you don't already have plans, I thought I might fix you supper tonight ... that is, if you'd care to come over?" Though soft, her voice had an uncertain edge, as though daring him to accept.

He blinked his astonishment as he considered her invitation. But what was there to consider? The doc was pretty, smart, and strong enough to endure the hardships in life. She'd proven that by how well she'd dealt with the clinic fire. And she didn't let people bully her either — not even him. Her humor made him smile, and the love she offered her patients was a sure sign she'd make a good mother. What more could a man want? Already anticipating an evening in Mattie's company, he cupped his other hand over hers before taking the cookies. "What time?"

"Seven?" She smiled up at him with the exuberance of a young filly who'd been cooped up in a stall too long and wanted to be let out to run.

The dry grass crunched behind him, and Gil cocked an eyebrow.

"Tell her yes, already, and quit mooning over the little lady," Jake said, the smell of wintergreen tobacco on his breath. "And if you ain't gonna eat those cookies, hand them to me."

LATER THAT EVENING, GIL KNOCKED ON MATTIE'S CABIN DOOR, THEN checked his pocket watch. Seven o'clock sharp.

Mattie opened the door, and the smell of fried chicken greeted him. "Come in." She stepped aside and tucked a stray curl into place. "Did you and Jake finish the fence?"

"For today, but we have two more pastures before we're done." He revealed the yellow rose from behind his back, and her smile made his chest swell. "A pretty rose for a pretty lady."

Mattie took the flower, then buried her nose in its petals. She closed her eyes as though immersing herself in the scent. "It's lovely. I can't remember the last time someone gave me flowers."

He kicked himself for not offering her a dozen. If he'd known the reaction one little rose was going to bring, he would have filled the entire cabin. The sizzle and pop of fried chicken drew his attention to the other side of the room. "I see you're getting along with the old cast iron stove."

Mattie placed the rose in a quart jar and set it on the table. "It suits me." She pulled out a chair for him and returned to her work.

Rather than sit, Gil followed her and lifted the lid on a pot of mashed potatoes. "Thanks for having me over—though I have to admit, your invitation surprised me."

She turned the golden pieces of chicken with a fork, then her small hands stilled. "I've been trying to build up the nerve for a few weeks now. But why not? We're grown adults. Live on the same property. I don't see why we can't do things together every once in a while—do you?"

"No, I don't. Not at all," Gil said, determined to enjoy this moment without worrying about the future.

A timer went off, and Mattie opened the heavy oven door to reveal a pan of golden biscuits.

"Can't have fried chicken without homemade biscuits." She grinned, and Gil realized he was in heaven.

When they sat down at the table, Gil tasted every creation—buttery potatoes, crisp pan-fried chicken, flaky biscuits topped with strawberry preserves. The doc cooked like an angel. She looked like one, too, dressed in jeans and a sweater with her hair pulled back in a loose ponytail, little wispy curls on each side of her face.

"I wanted to talk to you about Dusty," she said. "He's doing much better now that his stomach ulcers have healed. His appetite has improved as well. Almost as good as yours," she teased and tore off a piece of chicken with her fork.

"Sorry about that. I guess I got carried away." Gil wiped his mouth on a napkin, conscious of how quickly he was devouring the meal. That's one thing about football players—we like to eat, and this meal you made is very good." He smiled, then made an effort to slow his eating.

Mattie set her fork down and rested her chin on her hand, studying him. "What you've done for that horse's recuperation ought to go in medical books."

Gil stopped chewing. "I'm not sure what you mean."

"I've observed you and Dusty together. You're connected. It's like he knows you're rooting for him, and he finds the strength to go one more step. It's been amazing to watch."

"I'm just being his friend like you instructed."

"And I'm telling you, it's made a difference. You've impressed me with how much you care." Her gaze drifted to her lap, her skin glowing with admiration.

Gil cleared his throat, starting to feel embarrassed yet loving her attention. "I called that ranch in Central Kansas and arranged to see the horses on Saturday. Do you think you'd be able to go with me? Maybe Jake could check on your patients and take care of Dusty for the day?"

The thought of spending an entire day with Mattie made Gil's heart beat faster.

"That's not much notice, but I think Travis could handle it."

Gil stopped chewing. "Travis?"

The doc nodded. "I hired him back part-time to help with the patients. He's supposed to start next week, but I could ask him to come in early."

"Well, if it's not too much trouble," Gil said, but the potatoes in his mouth changed to paste at the thought of the handsome college intern.

THIRTY-ONE

S ATURDAY MORNING, G IL TURNED HIS TRUCK ONTO A PITTED GRAVEL road north of Russell and headed for the Chappell Quarter Horse Ranch near the Saline River. He and Mattie soon passed through the entrance of a spacious property consisting of several barns and a brick ranch house, surrounded by a fenced pasture.

When Gil shut off the diesel engine, a sturdy woman exited the barn, followed by a tall, lanky man wearing a ball cap.

Gil caught the fresh, damp scent of rain as he stepped from his truck onto the sodden gravel. He grabbed his hat and jacket from the backseat.

"You the fellow that called about the mares?" The woman held out her hand to greet him, and he noted her graying blonde hair, firm grip.

"That's right. Gil McCray." He turned to the doc, who was getting out of the truck. "This is Mattie Evans, the vet I spoke of on the telephone."

"Nice to meet you. My name's Yvonne, and this here's my husband, Wayne." The woman smiled, her face tan and wrinkled. "I take it you've traveled all morning. Probably like to stretch your legs a spell?"

At Gil's nod, the couple headed for the metal barn, which housed an indoor arena where a girl with long, jet-black hair worked a bay mare. They watched as she sped through a reining pattern. The young lady rode with precision and sat the horse well.

Yvonne moved to a nearby table and spoke into a speaker system. "You need to practice your rollbacks some more. They're sloppy. Slide to a complete stop and don't rush through it."

"That's Natalie Adams," she said when she returned to her husband's side. "She's riding some of our horses to train for the Miss Rodeo Kansas competition."

Mattie rested her foot on the bottom rail of the arena fence and observed the rider. "How did you get involved in such training?"

Yvonne chuckled with a low, throaty voice. "We've been helping pageantry competitors for years now, ever since our daughter ran for a title. I was a queen myself, a long time ago."

Gil studied the older woman, who probably made quite a sight in her day. Of course, Mattie would have made a fine queen too, with her long hair and flashy smile. Especially dressed as she was today in tan jeans and a suede jacket with fringes that swished and swayed with her every move. In his estimation, the only thing missing was the gold crown.

Mattie turned to Gil, who motioned toward two horses tied up to the arena. She recognized the determined line of his brow and knew he had business on his mind.

"Are those the mares?" he asked.

Yvonne nodded, then frowned, her attention drawn to the rider in the ring who pranced backward on the bay, the horse's head beating up and down in agitation. "Wayne, you want to show them around? I need to help this gal in the arena."

Yvonne headed toward Miss Adams, while Mr. Chappell led Mattie and Gil to the other side of the barn. "Over here, we have the two mares you mentioned on the phone. Some of their offspring are out in the pasture." He stopped a few feet from a red roan, and Mattie had to admit the mare looked dynamic. She stood about fifteen hands tall with nice conformation.

"I'm not sure how much you know about foundation bloodlines, but this ten-year-old has some Driftwood in her. She placed first and second at the National Finals Rodeo two years straight." The man seemed quite pleased, but Gil remained poker-faced.

"If you'd like, you can ride them after lunch," Mr. Chappell said. "Yvonne's got ribs in the oven."

"Thanks for your hospitality," Gil said without consulting Mattie.

"The wife and I like to treat our guests when they come. Gives us a chance to visit and get to know them better." He smiled and moved on to where a big bay mare stood tied. "This girl's refined, with good bones and mind. She has some Doc O'Lena in her and placed in the AQHA World Show a couple years ago. Both our son and daughter have earned top money on her in roping and barrels at the pro level. That's her dam out there that Miss Adams is riding. Quite versatile in the show ring."

Mattie stepped up to the mare and ran her hands down the front legs. Nice and straight, and her forearms were long and muscular. She circled the mare for overall conformation.

When she'd finished her inspection, Mr. Chappell turned to leave. "We can load up in my old truck to look at the others in the pasture. Wouldn't want to get your shiny rig all muddy." He gave an impish grin, then led them to his truck outside.

Gil opened the passenger door for Mattie, and she slid in between him and their host. It seemed that Gil sat particularly close, or maybe that was due to all the jostling she endured as Mr. Chappell drove through several bumpy pastures to a herd of yearlings.

The young horses milled about the parked truck, curious, yet skittish. Gil opened the squeaky door, and they sprang from their hind feet as though a gun had fired, their short tails hiked in the air.

Gil pointed to a colt with a broad chest and muscled rear. Mattie acknowledged his interest right away.

Mr. Chappell noticed too. "That one's an experiment we tried, mixing our Eddy stallion with a daughter of Flying X 6. So far, we like what we see."

"I do too." Gil stepped from the truck to study the colt. "He reminds me of a horse I once trained. How much would you sell him for?"

The man hesitated and shook his head. He got out and rested his elbows on the hood. "I don't think Yvonne's ready to sell that one."

Gil's eyes sparked, and Mattie knew he was prepared for the challenge. "Are you by any chance a football fan?"

"THE WIFE AND I DON'T HAVE TIME FOR SPORTS," WAYNE SAID. "OTHER than watching the grandkids play."

Gil frowned, not what he wanted to hear. He decided to approach the man from another angle. "Name your price, and I'll buy him today."

Wayne removed his cap and brushed his fingers through matted, gray hair. "Mister, I don't know what game you're playing, but if you're that interested, you'll have to haggle it out with my other half." He gave a nervous chuckle.

"The colt would make a good stallion, wouldn't he?"

"Yvonne seems to think so. You interested in standing a stud?"

Gil braced his forearms on the opposite side of the hood, ready to cast his proposition like a well-set fishing line. "Let's say I purchase this little guy, train him up, and put him in some competitions. Maybe he earns high points, maybe a championship or two. Seems to me that would serve you well by bringing you business from the western half of the United States."

The man placed his cap back on his head. "Sounds like a good plan, but I wouldn't count on my wife selling."

Mattie came to Gil's side and squeezed his arm. "Which of these fillies are you prepared to sell—seeing as how we came all the way out here to buy mares?" She smiled sweetly at Mr. Chappell, but the pressure on Gil's arm tightened.

Wayne's eyes shifted from her to Gil. "You two in business together?"

Mattie withdrew her hand from Gil's arm, and his skin felt cold where her fingers had been. "We're friends, good friends." He searched her eyes, hoping to see affirmation of this in their depths.

She lowered her gaze, then turned to Chappell. "I'm providing the health exam ... should you both agree on a deal, that is." At her smile, the two men chuckled.

"Better listen to her. Sounds like she carries a lot of sense in those little boots she wears."

Gil glanced down at Mattie's red ropers. "I'm thinking the same thing." Once the words were out, Gil's heart tugged against his chest.

A little while later, Wayne drove them to the house and went to check on lunch. As soon as he left, Gil reached for Mattie's hands, too excited to contain himself. "If I manage to drive out of here with that Six colt, I'll have you to thank." He wanted to thank her now with a nice warm kiss. Instead, he brushed the few stray hairs from her face that the wind whipped loose from her braid.

"I can't believe you tried to influence him with football." Her mouth curved in mock disapproval. "I'm glad it didn't work."

"This is business, and a man's gotta do what a man's gotta do. If she sells that colt to me, I'll need to hire a private vet to assist with the mares and the breeding of a stallion. How would that strike your fancy?"

"What, work for you in California?" She extracted her hand from his, and the fringes on her jacket swayed. "I don't think so."

Gil captured her by the shoulders, not willing to let her go so easy. Despite her protests, he could tell by the way she melted into his touch that she was right where she wanted to be. "Doesn't the thought of success tempt you a little? There's lots of money to be made in the horse industry. The two of us might make a pretty good team, don't you think?"

"I like being my own boss. Somehow I don't think it would be nearly as fun if you were in charge."

She broke from his grasp, but her eyes shone with anticipation.

THIRTY-TWO

MATTIE'S HEART RACED AT THE LURE OF GIL'S OFFER. SHE REMINDED herself that it was just that—a work proposition, not a marriage proposal. And what if it were a proposal? She'd known Gil for a little over two months, hardly enough time to learn about a person—to know his heart and soul. She took a deep breath to calm her nerves, wishing the damp air would cool the warmth in her cheeks.

"I'm guessing my measure of success isn't the same as yours. You know how I feel about the Flint Hills. And what about my practice? Am I to leave my clients without someone to care for their animals?" She leaned against the horse trailer, glad for the touch of the cold metal.

"California is pretty too. Mountains on one side, ocean on the other, and green hills in between." Gil pulled an envelope from his inside coat pocket. "I received this in the mail this morning. The team's hosting a retirement party for me in a couple weeks—a big shindig. I'd like you to be my date."

Mattie swallowed to soothe the dryness in her throat. "In California?"

"Yes, come with me and meet my friends." His grin beseeched her. "I'll show you the property I want to buy—the place where you'd work. Together we could build you a breeding facility with all the latest technology for artificial insemination."

"Aren't you afraid of getting in over your head?" Mattie reminded herself of Clara's warning to take things slow.

This was not slow.

"I've been thinking about this for some time. What do you say? Will you go to the retirement party?"

Mattie swallowed the dryness in her throat. She'd taken off work from the clinic today. Now he wanted her to take off for a weekend. "I don't know, Gil—I need time to think."

Gil reached out and pulled her into his arms. "Okay, but don't take too long. You know how impatient I am when I want something."

A SHORT WHILE LATER, MATTIE SAT ACROSS FROM GIL AT THE Chappell dining table, Yvonne at one end, Wayne at the other, and the Miss Kansas Rodeo contestant next to Gil. Natalie Adams had perfect olive skin, much prettier than Mattie's own ruddy complexion. Yvonne passed a platter of barbecued ribs, and Mattie pierced a juicy strip and placed it on her plate.

"Wayne showed me a Six colt in one of your pastures this morning but said you're not interested in selling him. What would it take to make you interested?" Gil asked Yvonne.

The older woman's eyes narrowed. "Sometimes no means no."

Gil straightened, and the wooden chair creaked beneath him. "Surely every horse on this property has a price? Aren't you interested in selling horses?

"Wayne tells me you plan to run your operation in California." Yvonne handed Mattie a bowl of fried potatoes. "There's a lot to know about standing a stud. If you lived closer, we could help you—steer potential customers your way."

Mattie smiled as she passed the dish to Wayne. She liked the way this woman thought and hoped Gil would listen.

"You don't know who I am, do you?" Gil shifted his head from one Chappell to the other.

"Gil recently retired from the San Francisco 49ers as their quarterback. He's used to people recognizing him." Mattie half-teased, but Gil's expression crumpled into a frown as though insulted.

Yvonne's face didn't crack, but Mr. Chappell smiled. "I wondered why you asked about football earlier."

"I thought I recognized you," Natalie added. "My dad's a real fan of yours."

"Is that so?" Gil clasped her outstretched hand, his wounded pride easily assuaged.

"Sorry we didn't recognize you, but the wife and I aren't up on sports," Mr. Chappell said. "We appreciate that you like our horses, though."

"They're some of the finest I've seen. While I value your offer to help, I don't think finding customers will be a problem. That is, if you're willing to sell." Gil released Miss Adams' hand and smiled, but his taut cheekbones hinted at agitation.

"I'm not prepared to market that particular colt." Yvonne got up to retrieve a pitcher of tea and placed it on the table. "His mama had problems delivering last year, and we won't be having any more colts out of her. I'd like to see how he's going to turn out before I decide whether to sell."

The woman wouldn't budge and judging by the clouds gathering on Gil's face, Mattie wondered if they were in for a storm.

"I can't believe she wouldn't sell that colt to me." Gil clenched the truck's steering wheel as they headed for Diamond Falls later that evening. He shook his head in frustration, having been prepared to pay top dollar for three of the Chappell mares if she'd sell the colt.

"You ought to be thankful she sold you anything, considering your behavior." Mattie stared at her lap and picked at a piece of mud on her jeans.

"What do you mean, my *behavior?*" Gil's annoyance grew.

"Let's just say when you want something, you don't let anything —or anyone—stand in the way."

Gil clamped his jaw. Had he really behaved poorly? He tried to remember his discussions with the Chappells, specifically those that had made him testy. "I disagree. If anyone behaved badly, it was Yvonne. She invited me out there to buy horses, then she didn't want to sell the one I liked."

"It's her business. She can do whatever she wants. Had I been the owner, I'm not sure I would have sold the colt to you either."

"Why not?" Gil couldn't understand Mattie's change of attitude. She'd been cold and standoffish ever since lunch. Not the sweet, sensitive-natured woman he'd grown fond of, but more the uptight female she'd been when he first met her. "What did I do that was so terrible?"

"For one, you were arrogant. You told the woman you didn't need her help. Big mistake."

"But I don't need her help. I know exactly who my target customers are and how I'm going to attract them."

"Okay ... okay." Mattie raised her hands in the air. "I'm just saying, you could've handled the situation more gently, and Yvonne might have sold you the colt."

"That's not the way I do business. With me, it's all or nothing."

Mattie sniffed. "Natalie Adams certainly gave you all of her attention today."

Gil's neck twitched. Was that jealousy in the doc's voice? "She found my objectives interesting if that's what you mean."

Mattie eyed him with the aloofness of a thoroughbred.

"Fine, let's stop talking about the horses. What about my retirement party? What's your answer, will you go? I need to buy our plane tickets."

She shook her head and stared out the passenger window at the darkening sky. "Right now, the only place I want to go is home."

"You mean *my* home?"

Mattie visibly bristled. "I mean, your *dad's* home."

THIRTY-THREE

Ten days later, Mattie tucked inside her office desk drawer the wedding invitation she received. Just what she needed, another wedding in the family — another chance to catch the bouquet and listen to the old hens whisper behind her back.

No thanks.

There had to be more to life than falling in love and letting your mate drag you wherever he wanted to go. Like California — and who would want to go with an oaf like him, anyway? Gil was so full of himself he couldn't see past his nose to what really mattered.

She forced the man from her thoughts and went back to punching the calculator. Her puppy snuggled in his usual spot right next to her feet. How would she ever make enough money to rebuild her clinic? Even if her business flourished, she'd have to save for a year before she'd have enough to afford the down payment.

Lord, is this what you want for me? To keep trying?

The McCrays had offered her so many kindnesses. Allowing her to live in the cabin and operate her clinic on their ranch, and Gil furnishing her clinic supplies.

All gifts from God.

Gil was like two men — the stubborn, hardheaded guy and the

thoughtful, caring man she couldn't erase from her mind. She considered his retirement party.

You ought to go with him. What harm could it do?

What harm could it do? Going to California with him might endanger her heart. She'd already been tempted beyond her restraint—felt her resolve weaken every time he touched her. When it came to Gil, her mind went blank whenever her heart fluttered—just like Clara warned.

I will not let you be tempted beyond what you can bear. But when you are tempted, I will also provide a way out.

Right ... and her way out was not to go to California. She couldn't traipse off from the clinic for an entire weekend, anyway. Dusty needed her. His rehabilitation was moving forward, and she resolved to keep it that way.

Now all she had to do was inform Gil of her decision.

Gil rounded the corner of the barn and caught Mattie resting her head on Dusty's neck. He stopped, not wanting to intrude on what looked like an intimate moment and watched as she smoothed her hand over the chestnut's back. His heart clutched at the soothing words she spoke to his horse. This was the doc he knew, the woman who put her heart into everything she did.

Since their outing to the Chappell Ranch, she hadn't talked to him unless answering a direct question. It made no sense. Could his buying tactics have really been the cause of her change in attitude? He'd walked away from the Chappell's with one fine mare and a three-year-old filly on the condition that they wouldn't sell the Six colt without first contacting him. Not the outcome he desired, but not altogether disagreeable.

Although Mattie had hinted at jealousy, he couldn't believe a woman as pretty as she was would fret over a girl half his age.

Especially one that bore an uncanny resemblance to Mattie's sister Jenna.

The thought of the dark-haired girl reminded Gil of the complications he would face if a romantic relationship with Mattie developed. Was she worth the risk? Would she understand his past?

He cleared his throat, and Mattie lifted her head from the gelding's neck. She turned and for a brief second her anxiety went unmasked. Then she quickly forced a smile, but her eyes lacked their usual luster.

"I thought I'd find you here." At his words, Mattie's beagle came rushing toward him, its pointed tail whipping back and forth. He bent down to rub the pup, and it rolled over onto its side. "Have you decided about this weekend?"

Mattie kicked at the ground with her boot and nodded. "I can't go with you."

His jaw stiffened. Even though he'd anticipated that answer, he wasn't prepared for the ache it caused in his chest. "Can't or won't?"

She turned to Dusty. "Why don't you ask your dad to go? Maybe you could work out some of your problems."

Gil scoffed at this idea. "You know he'd never agree. He hates football, and he hates even more that I played."

Mattie shrugged. "Couldn't hurt to try."

"Your mind's made up, then?" Gil stopped scratching the pup's stomach and stood. He wanted to run from this humiliation, turn, leave, and never come back. He'd been smart to avoid women all these years. Women were nothing but trouble. "Does this mean you don't want anything to do with me?"

Again, she shrugged. Gil studied the slope of her back, the gentle curve of her waist. How could she give up so easily? A part of him wanted to yank her long braid like a schoolboy, but that thought led to a stronger inclination to loosen her woven hair with his fingers and kiss her into submission.

"I thought we had a good thing started. That we were growing closer."

"We hardly know each other," she said without meeting his eyes.

"I know you, Mattie. I can see through you from where I stand."

She straightened, but still refused to look at him.

"You may not want to acknowledge that there's something between us, Mattie, but I know better. I've heard it in your voice when you've called my name, and I've felt it in your touch." He turned on his heel, tired of the trouble, then glanced back one last time.

"I can't force you to join me, so I'll go to my retirement party — alone. When I return, though, you'd better be ready to finish this conversation."

LATE FRIDAY AFTERNOON, MATTIE ENTERED CLARA'S CAFÉ AND leaned on the counter.

"What brings you to town?" Clara carried a pot of coffee and poured Mattie a cup.

"I was out on a call and figured I'd grab a bite to eat before going home." Mattie studied the menu, though she'd memorized it by heart.

"Is everything okay? You look like you lost your best friend. Don't tell me — you didn't lose another patient, did you?"

Mattie shook her head. "Work is fine." She stared at the list of food options until the words started to blur.

"Hey, what's going on?" Clara snatched the menu from the counter and held it in her hand. "If it's not business, it must be a man. How is Gil?"

Mattie peeked up at Clara, amazed at her friend's ability to read her mind. "I wouldn't know. He left this morning for California."

"What about his dad's ranch? Wasn't he in the middle of fence work?"

"His team's throwing him a retirement party. But I don't care whether he returns. It'd probably be better if he didn't."

"I thought you two were getting along? Didn't you go look at horses with him a couple weeks ago?"

Mattie's eyes started to sting as they'd done all day whenever she let her mind drift to her relationship with Gil. She rested her forehead on the counter and brushed at the tears before Clara had a chance to see. "He asked me to go to California with him."

She raised her head. "Shoot, he asked me to work for him there."

Clara grabbed her dishrag and wiped circles on the counter. "What did you tell him?"

"No, on both counts."

The circles stopped. "You don't seem too happy with your decision."

Mattie's discomfort grew. "He wanted to show me the property he intends to buy — tempt me to work for him."

"Why is that so horrible? Go and see what it's like. You might love it."

"That's exactly why I can't go." Mattie took the cloth from Clara's hand and wiped a grease spot she'd missed. "Do you know how long I've dreamed of owning land in Charris County? — Of reclaiming what my father lost? The Flint Hills are my heritage. I thought I could convince Gil that California was a mistake — that he belonged here. Instead, I find myself being drawn deeper and deeper into his world."

"You're falling for the guy."

Mattie's gaze locked on Clara's. "I never said that."

"You didn't have to. I know the symptoms. When you're with him, your dreams seem less important."

"That's exactly why I didn't go with him."

Clara laid her hand on Mattie's. "Did you stop to consider how much that might have hurt him? Think about it. He has no one to share this moment with."

Mattie's resolve weakened.

"The Lord tells us he won't put more on us than we can bear," Clara said—as though Mattie needed to be reminded.

"It's too late. Even if I did change my mind, his retirement party is tomorrow night. I have no plane ticket and nothing to wear."

Clara smiled and Mattie cringed. She'd seen that look before.

Her friend took three steps behind the counter and returned with a thick, metropolitan phonebook. "The number for the airport ought to be in there." She handed it to Mattie. "And hanging in my closet happens to be a fabulous dress that's never been worn. I bought it on sale last year, hoping to lose enough weight to fit into it. That didn't happen, but I bet it'd fit you like a glove."

THIRTY-FOUR

GIL PAID THE VALET, THEN GAZED UP AT THE MARK HOPKINS HOTEL on Nob Hill. The team had rented the Top of the Mark for this party, a swanky lounge on the nineteenth floor with a near 360-degree view of the San Francisco skyline.

Too bad he wasn't in a mood to celebrate.

He checked his tie and ascended the steps. His black suit confined his shoulders, and his shirt collar threatened to strangle him. As he stepped through the revolving doors, Charlie met him in the hotel lobby.

"Hey, guy." His friend affectionately cuffed him on the neck. "I hardly recognized you in those duds."

"Yeah, you either. I bet your wife likes the shiny shoes." Gil pointed to the designer lace-ups and relaxed a bit.

"You here alone?"

"Is there a better way to be?" He didn't need Mattie's company to enjoy the night. This was his party, held in his honor. No way was he going to let a woman spoil the moment. He'd have fun if it killed him.

"Don't let Linda hear that. She'll be all over you with a list of women a mile long." Charlie laughed mischievously. "There are some real lookers upstairs, but I doubt they'd be on Linda's list — if you know what I mean."

Gil tapped the button to the elevator. "I'll keep that in mind."

They reached the top in seconds. Gil stepped out into a swarm of mingling guests clothed in more black suits and sequined gowns. Makeup adorned the women's faces, their lips bold and shiny, hair sleek and long or arranged on top of their heads with curls streaming down. He noticed one lady with long red spirals, and his heart thumped against his chest at the reminder of the doc.

"Ladies and gentlemen, our guest of honor has arrived," Johnson said and handed him a glass of champaign. At this, several of his teammates whistled from the bar and the guests applauded. From that moment on, Gil couldn't take a step without a lady clinging to his arm or someone trying to monopolize his time with conversation. Despite his determination to enjoy the party, his resolve started to crumble under the onslaught.

Right on cue, Charlie latched onto his elbow and pulled him through the crowd.

"I don't know how much of this I'll be able to take." Gil deposited his drink on an empty tray as he passed by. "I might have to duck out early."

Charlie glanced back with his ever-present grin firmly in place. "The night's young. It'll get better." He led Gil to a table where several of the boys and their wives and girlfriends sat. Charlie's wife gave a slight wave and indicated for Gil to sit beside her.

"You look very debonair this evening," Linda teased.

Gil squeezed her hand. "You clean up pretty swell yourself." He noted her shimmering blue dress and diamond solitaire necklace. "Charlie buy that for you?"

She clutched the pendant and smiled. "He did, and I have you to thank that I have a chance to dress up and show it off."

Charlie reached across the table for a bottle of sparkling cider and poured some in their glasses. "Yeah, I don't wear this penguin suit for just anybody," he said. "Not even my darling wife."

"Can't tell me that. I know better." Gil focused on the blinking lights above the bar in the center of the room, trying to ward off the tightness in his throat. Few couples drew his admiration like Charlie and Linda. Now he understood how fortunate they were to share such an intense love within their marriage.

Not everyone had that opportunity.

As these thoughts filtered through his head, a large television screen flashed to life, commemorating Gil's time on the football field. He watched as a Dallas linebacker plowed him to the ground early in his career.

"Ouch." Gil cringed from embarrassment as those in the room tittered with amusement. One of the linebackers razzed him from the bar. "That's the way to take one for the team, hey Gil?"

Gil raised his drink to his teammate and grinned.

His coach then stood in the center of the room and tapped his champaign glass. "If I can have everyone's attention, I'd like to propose a toast."

The room came to hush.

"I've had the privilege of having Gil McCray on my team for a good long while. We all know that in this sport, superstars come and go, but Gil's managed to stretch out his career for fifteen years—no easy accomplishment in this day of instant fame and instant replay." He chuckled, as did many in the crowd.

"Our team didn't make it to the Super Bowl this year," he went on. "but as many of you know, it's not how many games you win, it's how you play the game—and even more important, how you live your life when the game's over. We're all going to miss you, Gil—me probably the most. So, here's to one of the finest quarterbacks I've ever coached." He lifted his glass to Gil in a toast.

"May your retirement be rewarding and your future a blessing to you and to those you love. And may you never forget how quickly time passes." Coach's eyes narrowed in on him, and Gil understood well the implied message.

"Here, here," the people around him chanted and sipped their drinks.

Gil stood from the table and strode over to his old friend. He squeezed Coach's shoulder with affection. "Thanks for the kind words. I only hope the years will be as good to me as they've been to you," Gil said. Then from the corner of his eyes, he saw her.

Easing through the crowd in a black, satin lace dress that clung to her curves and hung slightly off her shoulders was the doc — *his* Doc.

For a second he doubted his vision, but as she neared, there was no mistaking her identity. Mattie's long, red curls draped loosely about her face and drew his attention to the string of pearls that graced her neck.

He'd never seen her look so beautiful.

"Will you excuse me please," he told his coach, unable to take his eyes off Mattie. He reached her in seconds.

"You came." He caught her hands and stared into her eyes, the sweet scent of roses captivating him. "What changed your mind?"

Mattie offered a sheepish grin. "Clara helped me see the error of my ways."

Gil wondered at her meaning. "But … when … how did you get here?"

Charlie came up beside them and introduced himself. "It's nice to finally meet you, Dr. Evans. Was the limo ride satisfactory?"

Gil's gaze darted to his friend, who stood there with a definite smirk. "You knew about this?"

Charlie winked at Mattie. "Dr. Evans phoned me last night after she'd made her plane reservations and told me everything. After that, I was happy to arrange her accommodations."

"How did you know to call Charlie?"

"You left your invitation with your dad. It listed Charlie's number." Mattie's eyes shone with satisfaction.

Gil gripped Charlie's hand, overcome with gratitude. "Thanks for looking after her."

"You'd do the same for me."

Gil returned his attention to Mattie. Despite their argument, and her abhorrence for the city, she'd traveled all this way for him.

So beautiful.

His chest swelled with emotion. Oh yes, this woman was worth the risk involved. He knew that now. He'd risk just about anything if Mattie would return the affection he felt for her.

"I'm thinking the two of you probably need a few minutes alone." Charlie's voice echoed in Gil's ears as though spoken from a distance. The woman had enraptured Gil's senses.

He grasped her arm and led her to a quiet spot by a window overlooking the white lights of the city. "The last time we spoke, you were determined not to join me. In fact, I thought we were finished."

Mattie looked out the window. "I'm sorry for the way I treated you the other day. I behaved like a switch-tailed mare. Spoiled and unwilling to give an inch. But I was wrong. I want you to know I'm here for you."

"I scared you with my talk of California. I'm not used to people telling me no." Gil tipped her chin to see into her sparkling green eyes. "You're gorgeous with your hair down. It reminds me of the first time I saw you on Dad's mare, with your curls blowing behind you in the wind."

He swept his hand about the room and heard the juiced notes of a jazz orchestra. "Your being here makes all of this worthwhile. Do you know how close I was to leaving?"

She smiled, and Gil's joy radiated all the way to his toes.

"I'm glad you stayed. Who else would give me a tour of this big city?"

Gil considered all the places he'd grown to love that he wanted to show her — Fisherman's Wharf, Chinatown, Union Square, and of course the stadium. "We can start that tour right now." He pointed out the window to a perfect view of the Golden Gate Bridge.

A waiter passed by with a plate of hors d'oeuvres. "Are you hungry?" Gil stopped the man and reached for a slice of pumpernickel topped with smoked salmon and chive cream cheese.

Mattie selected a piece of goat cheese on brioche with fruit chutney. Gil also grabbed one from the plate before the waiter left, his appetite returned now that Mattie was by his side. "Shall we mingle and see what else they have?"

At her nod, he took Mattie's elbow and guided her around the room, introducing her to his friends and teammates. To his surprise, he found the mayor in attendance as well as the team's owner and a dozen Super Bowl champions.

The two stopped at an ice sculpture of a quarterback passing a ball. "How does it make you feel, knowing they did all this for you?" Mattie stared at the replica and a mix of emotions crossed her face. "I can't imagine what it must be like to live in your shoes. This entire city worships you."

Gil shook his head. "It's the image they love. You should have seen what they did for Montana. Now *he* was a man they loved."

Mattie bit the corner of her lip. "I have to admit, most of the time when I'm with you, I don't know how to feel. You're a celebrity, even in our hometown, but when we're at the ranch ... when it's just the two of us, you're a normal person." She stared down at her hands.

"That's nice to know. There for a second, I thought maybe I was made of ice." He tried to ease her embarrassment.

She gazed up with a spark of hope. "I've only known you a short while, yet you know my fears — my deepest hopes and dreams. Sometimes you make me so mad, and then at other times I think I've found my soul mate."

Gil drew back at her words. But wasn't this what he'd hoped for—to gain Mattie's affections? Why then, did he suddenly feel like the world's worst heel? He knew exactly why. Soul mates didn't keep secrets, and they didn't lie to each other. He should have told her about Jenna a long time ago, but he didn't. If he told Mattie now, there was a good chance he'd lose her for good, soul mate or not.

THIRTY-FIVE

THE HESITATION ON GIL'S FACE CAUSED MATTIE TO REGRET HER RASH confession. She should have held her tongue. Waited to see how he felt before throwing all of her sentiments out on the floor before him.

"There's a lot you don't know about me," he said. "I'm not sure I'm worthy of your hard-earned trust."

"What do you mean?" She clutched his lapel, wanting so much to reach out to him. "You're caring, honest, dependable. You have problems with your dad, but who doesn't have issues?"

"I'm not perfect, Mattie."

"I never said you were."

He cupped his hand over hers and concern filled his eyes. "Come on," he said. "Let's go down and get some fresh air." He laced his fingers through hers and pulled Mattie through the crowd of guests, shaking hands with well-wishers as they went out.

"What about your party? You can't just leave." Mattie worked to keep up in her high heels and narrow skirt.

Gil waved to Charlie and a few other friends. "In another thirty minutes, they won't care if I'm here or gone."

They took the elevator to the lobby, and Mattie adjusted her ankle straps, conscious of the low neckline on her dress.

"Everything all right?"

Mattie straightened and pulled on the hem of her skirt, which kept riding up from her knees. "I'm not used to such a fancy dress—borrowed it from Clara."

He leaned closer, and the crisp scent of his aftershave wrapped itself around her. "Quit fussing. You're gorgeous."

The elevator doors opened to reveal the luxurious lobby adorned with giant crystal chandeliers. "Would you like to see Fisherman's Wharf?"

Mattie's sandals already pinched her toes, and her feet ached from the high heels. "How much walking will that involve?"

"Wishing you had your boots?" He grinned, then whirled her through the revolving doors and down the hotel steps. As they neared the sidewalk, the cable car's bell clanged right before it stopped.

Gil grabbed a pole and hopped onto the running board. He swung Mattie up to join him, his hands clasping her arm and waist. Her heart raced at his touch, and she hoped he'd never let go.

But he did, and they settled in for the ride. "Your team really loves you," she said. "What made you decide to retire?"

Gil took a moment before answering. "My age, my aching shoulders and knees." He looked thoughtful. "It's time to start the next stage of my life. I'm nearly forty years old. I want what Charlie has—a loving home, a wife, family. I crave these things even more since I met you."

Despite the cool breeze, Mattie's cheeks warmed at his directness. "You don't mince words, do you?" She rubbed her arms as goose bumps prickled her skin.

Without a word, Gil removed his tuxedo jacket and placed it around her shoulders. "Life's too short for games."

She clutched his jacket, intensely aware of his arm resting on her back. His face hovered over hers, and she gazed into his eyes. "I don't want to play games, Gil."

"Neither do I." He leaned closer, then paused as though waiting for permission. "And you know I don't like to take no for an answer."

Mattie closed her eyes and gave her consent. She pressed her lips to his in a kiss that made her thoughts swirl and turn to mush.

Maybe the two of them could work out their differences. Maybe God had plans for her and Gil, and maybe her visit to California would reveal those plans. It made perfect sense, especially when she considered how much she fought the trip and then how easily the arrangements came together, despite lack of time and money.

His finger trailed down her cheek and lingered on her lips, causing her skin to smolder. Then he enclosed her in his arms and kissed her again, this time with more fervency and passion. His kiss ignited a flame in her heart that threatened to consume her.

The bell above them clanged, and she broke from his embrace.

After a few seconds, she touched her mouth where his lips had been and struggled to think clearly. "Okay ... so we agree we share an attraction ... and that we've at least considered the possibility of a future. But you have to admit, our situation isn't perfect." The cable car lurched over a hill and headed down a steep grade. Mattie gripped the iron handlebar to hold her balance.

Gil reached out to steady her. "As I mentioned, there's a lot you don't know about me — things you should know." His voice murmured softly in her ear.

"You're a football star — I'm sure you've seen and done things that would turn my cheeks red." Again, she swayed with the movement of the car and brushed against Gil's shoulder. "I'm more concerned with our regional differences. My home is in Kansas."

"And mine is in California."

Mattie closed her eyelids at the absurdity of the situation. How could God allow such a connection but provide no clear way for them to be together?

"Before you say more, agree to go with me tomorrow to see the estate I want to buy."

So he could tempt her even more? "I've come this far, you might as well show me everything. But I warn you, nothing will change my mind."

THE NEXT MORNING, GIL MET HER IN THE LOBBY OF THE HOTEL TO take her to the property he wanted her to see. They drove out in his SUV, and as they approached the estate, Mattie's breath caught. When she crossed the threshold of the majestic home, she recalled her taunt from the night before and blushed. In her defense, she'd never considered such a dwelling as this, with its towering ornate ceilings and arched doorways that led to rooms more spacious than her entire apartment had been back home.

The blonde-haired realtor took them past a spiraling staircase, then down a short hallway to a gourmet kitchen.

"Look Mattie, two ovens," Gil teased. "You could bake cookies and biscuits to your heart's content."

Mattie swept her hand along the marble counter and imagined the meals she could prepare. The idea seemed hilarious compared to the antique stove she used now. After a few minutes of consideration, they entered a narrow enclosed porch with a fireplace in the middle.

"This is the solarium," the agent said. "An intimate place to retreat on cold nights with a cup of cappuccino when it's just the two of you ... and then in warmer weather you can entertain out on the lanai." She walked them through an open passageway where an outdoor veranda spanned the entire back of the home, bordered by exotic plants and concrete arches braced with tall pillars.

From that point on, Mattie followed along in a trance, unable to believe people actually lived in such luxury. Gil might be able to fit in to this sort of lifestyle, but how could she with her meager country ways?

She wouldn't know where to begin.

As they neared the end of the tour, they entered the master bedroom, which boasted a private sitting area the size of the kitchen with closets alongside a mirrored dressing room. The adjoining master bath was no less elegant, boasting an oversized spa centrally located behind a huge bay window that overlooked an enclosed view of a privacy garden.

"I'll let you look around for a few minutes before we continue," the agent said, then moved out to the hallway.

Gil came to Mattie's side with a cheeky smile that would rival any Cheshire cat. "Did I tell you, or what?"

"Can you really afford this … palace?" She hated to admit that a part of her enjoyed imagining the possibilities, while her more conservative side argued the place was too pompous for any self-respecting person to own.

"You haven't seen anything yet." Gil kissed her on the nose, completely oblivious to the whirling doubts within her. "Wait till you see the barn."

THIRTY-SIX

"You mean to tell me you weren't impressed?" Gil asked as he headed west toward the coast, wanting to show Mattie another of his favorite spots. He didn't believe Mattie's objections for one minute. What woman wouldn't jump at the chance of being the mistress of such an estate?

"I never said that. I simply suggested the place was too pretentious for my tastes. No one would deny the home was beautiful ... breathtaking, even."

Gil smiled at this description, more fitting of his passenger. She was gorgeous last night, but her outfit today suited her more. Dressed in a tiered skirt and a denim jacket, her simple beauty took his breath away. He especially liked that she'd worn her hair down again and not in its usual braid. "Then you liked it—could even picture yourself there, especially in the barn? With the private clinic I plan to build, you'd be the envy of every vet in the country."

She stared down at her lap and played with the layers of her skirt. "What makes you think I'm so ambitious?"

He thought of how hard she'd worked to build her clientele in Diamond Falls. "I know how much your practice means to you." He reached for her hand, but she evaded his grasp.

"I was mistaken when I said you understood me," she said. "If you think I care about money, then you don't know me at all."

Gil trained his eyes on the road as he went through a series of curves and passed a cluster of weathered businesses. "I know you want to succeed. You want to be accepted."

"But you can't buy my affection with a lavish house and a fancy barn. Can you really picture me in that place, entertaining your football buddies or prospective horse buyers?" Mattie's voice became slightly shrill. "Who are we kidding? You're used to a lifestyle I can't imagine, and my home is on the prairie. I need an uncomplicated life, Gil — not one where I have to pretend to be someone I'm not."

Gil squeezed the steering wheel. Life back home was anything but simple for him. It was extremely complicated. "If we care about each other, we should be able to work through these obstacles. You give a little, I'll give a little."

"That sounds good in theory, but not if it means I have to give up the one thing I care about most — and I don't even understand why." She gripped his shoulder. "What are you afraid of? You're so busy pushing this place on me that you stopped giving Kansas a chance. Why won't you work out your problems with your dad and help run his ranch? Make that your future instead of this overpriced hacienda ... which seems too good to be true, by the way."

Her gaze penetrated and unnerved him.

Swerving off the main highway, he parked alongside the road on a rugged cliff. The salty spray of the Pacific coastline whisked into the cab of the Escalade as he took a deep breath and stared out over the ocean. Far beyond the outcrop of jagged rocks, the white-capped breakers rushed onto the pebbly shore, only to draw back into the dark blue depths, just like his long-buried emotions.

He considered the last few months, his inclination to return home to make amends with his father, only to be swept away by an onslaught of waves — Dusty, Mattie, his dreams of raising horses and owning the California ranch—all of these things had served as deterrents to his original objective.

When had Mattie become his end goal? He'd become so taken with her that he'd glossed over the problems that had followed him all of his adult life. Gil suddenly realized that football wasn't the only thing he needed to retire from; he needed to retire from deceit and the distance he'd put between himself and his dad. He wanted peace. "I'm sorry for pushing you. I guess I have been coming on a bit strong."

"Just a little." Mattie opened the door to get out, and Gil followed her to the scenic overlook. A gusty wind whipped against his shirt, and he went to grab his jacket.

"The view here is beautiful," she admitted as she gazed out at the western horizon. "But to me, these pounding waves are as unsettling as the life they represent."

"No more unsettling than a Kansas tornado."

"Or a California earthquake," she quipped.

"With the prairie, what you see is what you get. It doesn't hide anything." She held down her skirt as it flapped in the wind. "It's not a majestic mountain or hypnotic seashore, but it's honest ... unpretentious and tranquil. Winter snows and summer droughts come, but you prepare for them, and as the seasons change, you get a chance to start anew."

Gil zipped his windbreaker. "Why do I get the feeling you're talking about more than dates on a calendar?"

"I recall a man who wanted another chance with his father." Her eyes challenged him. "Why don't we concentrate on that first, then maybe we can deal with this other stuff ... when and if we have the footing to handle it."

Unable to resist, Gil stepped closer and pulled her into his arms, welcoming her sturdy, yet slight body next to his. She rested her head against his chest as he stared out at the Pacific. The timed surge of the swells as they foamed against the beach whispered in his ears like the distant wind on stems of tallgrass. At that moment, he felt in his heart that he'd do nearly anything for this woman, even if it meant coming to terms with his past and admitting his faults. He just prayed his confession wouldn't destroy their prospects for a future.

"Do you mean you might still give us a chance?" he asked.

Mattie looked up at him with a gleam in her eyes. "All I know is I've been in this state for two days, and already I'm itching to get home. Any chance you'd fly with me tomorrow?"

After a moment's consideration, Gil nodded. A four-hour flight would give him time to build the courage to tell her about his past. And if Mattie took the news about Jenna badly, which he guessed she would, they'd be forced to work it out, talk it out, right there in the passenger seats, thousands of miles in the air.

Where Mattie couldn't run — and neither could he.

"I think that could be arranged, on one condition."

"What's that?"

"There's a shack up the road that serves some of the best crab dinners. Go there with me? Their clam chowder will make your mouth water."

"More so than your chili?" Her voice lilted in amusement.

He scrunched his forehead. "You can't compare beef to chowder. Kansans know their steaks, but if you want seafood, this is the place to be."

MATTIE TURNED THE TAP TO FILL HER HOTEL BATHTUB WITH bubbling water, then adjusted the belt on the white terrycloth robe and considered her day with Gil. Never in her life had she seen such a magnificent home. A part of her felt guilty at having curbed Gil's excitement with her persistent doubts.

But she couldn't help it. The place was too ... extravagant. She much preferred his father's house with its sandstone walls and centuries-old décor. A home like the Lightning M was more than plenty—more than she could hope for.

Mattie watched as the glistening water gushed into the tub. To her dismay, she realized that in her entire time with Gil, neither of them had mentioned love—not once.

Did she love him?

There were moments in his arms when she wouldn't hesitate to think that she did. At times, Gil could be the gentlest, most caring and compassionate man she knew. Those tender moments, however, were offset by tense arguments and the ever-present knowledge that they were too much alike in their bullheadedness and too different when it came to deciding their future.

If she truly loved Gil, wouldn't she be willing to follow him anywhere? It shouldn't matter where they lived, as long as they were together, whether it be the West Coast or the Midwest. If she loved him...

Mattie clipped her hair into a coil on top of her head. By the same token, if Gil loved her, he ought to be willing to sacrifice his dreams and put her desires above his own. In so doing, he would surely come to realize their aspirations were not so different.

They both wanted a ranch, and Gil could raise his horses in the Flint Hills as easily as he could in California. As a bonus, in Kansas he'd have more acreage and be able to work on his relationship with his dad ... *if* he loved her.

THIRTY-SEVEN

"Did you enjoy San Francisco?" Gil asked after they'd settled into their first-class seats on a nonstop flight to Kansas City the next day.

Mattie played with the air controls above her head. "It was ... interesting."

"Meaning you liked it, but you don't care to return?" He tried not to sound offended, but it aggravated him that the city made little impression on her. Their trip to the coast hadn't changed her feelings either, and this discouraged him even more.

"Don't put words in my mouth." Mattie pulled a container of ibuprofen from her purse, then asked the flight attendant for a bottle of water.

"But I'm right, am I not?"

She closed her eyes and pressed her hand to her forehead. "I'm not up to a battle of wits this morning, Gil. But yes, if you must know, I'm glad to be going home where there aren't so many people."

"You get used to it after a while. But you're right, the population of Diamond Falls wouldn't fill the vacancies at the hotel." He grinned, but Mattie covered her eyes with her hand, apparently not up for jokes this morning.

After the stewardess brought a bottle of water, Mattie downed the caplets. When the airplane readied for takeoff, the seat belt light blinked on, and the captain's voice came over the loudspeakers. Mattie clutched the armrest, her body as rigid as a goalpost.

"I take it you don't like to fly?"

Mattie peered at him from the corner of her eye, her head unmoving. "This is the second time I've been on a plane." With that, her face turned a ghastly shade of green, and she covered her mouth.

Gil reached for the little white bag stuffed inside the pocket of the seat in front of him, but by the time he snapped it open, it was too late. She had leaned over her knees and vomited on the floor.

A putrid smell seeped up to his nose, and he dug in his coat for a handkerchief.

"I'm so sorry." Mattie rose from her bent-over position, her forehead beaded with sweat.

Wanting to ease her embarrassment and discomfort, Gil dabbed at her mouth with the white cotton. "Do you feel better now?"

She nodded, and as soon as the plane stabilized, he had them moved to a new location. After a trip to the bathroom, Mattie rested against the seat and closed her eyes. Gil prayed this wasn't an omen of how the rest of their trip would play out.

Halfway through their flight, Mattie woke in his arms, her face revived of its color.

"I'm sorry about before," she said. "It must have been something I ate."

"Don't worry about it. You almost missed my shoes." Her look of distress caused him to laugh. "I'm teasing," he said as an attendant came by to offer Mattie an iced drink and a bag of snack mix.

"Are you brave enough to let me eat?"

Gil checked her color. She looked much better. "You be the judge."

Mattie nodded and tore open the sack. "But give me that barf bag, just in case."

"I'm glad your sense of humor has returned, because there's something I want to talk to you about." Her nap had given him time to consider how to explain the situation between him and Jenna. He wanted to come clean so nothing was hidden between them, and knew he needed to get it over with before he lost his nerve.

"It has to do with why I left Diamond Falls all those years ago," he said, his words somber. "And part of why I've struggled to come back."

Mattie's expression now matched his, and she set her snack aside. "Because of Frank's death, right?"

"Partly, but there were many factors. You already know that Dad and I don't get along. There are reasons for that, other than us both being stubborn." He forced a grin and swallowed the fear crawling up his belly to his throat. "I've told you he got along better with Frank. I was jealous of that, and jealousy can make you do some pretty stupid things."

"We all do foolish things when we're young. Mistakes can be forgiven. God gives us the power to forgive." Mattie squeezed his hand, and her smile willed him to go on.

"I've sought God's forgiveness, but I've never admitted my sins to Dad. Different times I've tried, but I've always fallen short."

The truth was he'd never had the guts. Gil knew from his Bible studies that God could forgive his sins, but accepting this as his own and in his heart was another thing entirely. And if there was even the slightest chance that his heavenly Father wouldn't forgive him, how on earth would his dad, who wasn't a believer?

Once again, doubts stirred within — made Gil question the power of God's grace. His torso flushed with heat, and sweat soaked his shirt. Gil closed his eyes to will back a semblance of control.

Please, Father, help me tell Mattie the truth. Help me not to hurt her. Help her understand.

"Believe me, I want things to be right between us," Gil continued, "for Dad and me to stop bickering. But there are so many things

I want to tell you. I need you to understand, Mattie ... It was a long time ago ..." He pulled his hand from hers and wiped his palms on his jeans.

"If you'll trust me, I'll help you get through this." Mattie rested her hand on his neck and combed her fingers through his hair. The soothing action, combined with the earnest look in her eyes, made him believe it might be possible. "We can do this together."

Oh, how he cared for this woman. No one else had ever been able to comfort him this way, not even his mama. "You say that now ... but there are things you don't know. Things that involve your sister, Jenna."

Mattie drew back at his words, and doubt inched its way into his heart.

"With her dating Frank, you probably shared many secrets, things I know nothing about." Mattie smiled tentatively. "After all, when she was seventeen, I was only eight."

Oh, Mattie, but if you only knew the secrets we share. Father, do I have to risk losing her?

"She's coming back, you know." Mattie played with the hairs on his neck.

Gil's muscles tightened as his heart began to race. "Jenna's coming home?"

Mattie nodded, but her expression seemed void of emotion. "A cousin of ours is getting married. Jenna's flying in for the wedding. Our whole family will be there." Her voice edged with tension, and Gil wondered what was coming next.

"I hate to ask, but ..."

At this point, Gil welcomed any diversion. "Ask away."

Mattie took a deep breath and let it out slowly. "At the risk of having my family swarm around you, I wondered if you might accompany me to the wedding."

To the wedding, where Mattie's entire family would be ... including Jenna?

A shiver spliced through Gil as he considered her request. He suddenly doubted the wisdom in telling Mattie the truth about his relationship with Jenna. The entire situation had disaster written all over it. "Sure. I can do that." He swallowed the dread that lodged in his throat. "When is it?"

"This weekend. I thought I might have Jenna over for supper one night to catch up."

He'd hoped never to see her again, and now Jenna was coming to his father's ranch? Gil could think of nothing worse. "It's been a long time," he said instead.

"What secret were you going to tell me about her? I'm sure it was juicy. Jenna always had a knack for getting into trouble."

Gil stared at Mattie, now the one feeling sick to his stomach. "She'd probably kill me if I told you," he hedged.

Mattie tossed him a mischievous smile. "Then I'll have to get her to tell me, won't I?"

Lord, what am I going to do now? Feeling miserable and his stomach roiling from tension, Gil closed his eyes and pretended to sleep for the rest of the flight.

THIRTY-EIGHT

GIL AND MATTIE CLIMBED INTO HIS LARAMIE AT THE AIRPORT AND headed back to Diamond Falls. As the miles ticked closer to his father's ranch, Gil saw a puff of gray in the distance. A yellowish haze hung in the sky, and a thick musty smell blew into the cab's enclosure through the vents. He lowered his truck window to locate the smoke's origin.

The Lightning M.

Gil gunned the gas pedal, spinning the tires on the loose gravel. A mile down the road, he tore onto his father's pasture, and the big, heavy truck jolted in and out of the hidden ruts. Rather than ease off the pedal, he darted around the gullies and rocks to get in front of the blazing head fires.

"Be careful, Gil." Mattie braced herself against the dash.

Despite her warning, he didn't slow down. "Jake ought to have more sense than to work this fire on his own." He jockeyed through the glowing obstacle course and veered left to dodge an outcropping of jagged rocks. Thirty yards ahead, Jake's four-wheeler shot in and out of the fire, his kerosene-filled pipe dragging along behind him.

Gil swore under his breath. "What's he thinking?"

Then another vehicle emerged from the smoke. Gil accelerated to catch up, and as he neared, he recognized the figure driving the dented black Ford.

Dad?

He slammed on the brake and jammed the gearshift into neutral. "You drive," he shouted to Mattie, then jumped out of the truck.

As Gil approached the other vehicle, his temper raged as hot as the burning pasture. "What are you doing here?"

"What's it look like?" His dad stared back with a scowl.

"Scoot over and let me drive." Gil grabbed the door handle and waited for his dad to shuffle to the passenger side. The truck moved at an idle, and he climbed in without difficulty. Now safely behind the steering wheel, he glowered at his father. "Have you lost your mind? Why didn't you wait for my help?"

His dad held a box of matches and pitched the small burning stick out the passenger window. "How was I to know when you were coming back?"

"You knew I planned to return this week." He checked the rear window to assess the fire's path. "Did you contact the fire department?"

"Jake and I took care of everything. Got a water tank in the back for emergencies."

Gil noted the two-hundred-gallon sprayer in the truck bed, and his anger lessened. "Still, you have no business being out here. Two old men trying to do the work of four. How many acres are you burning?"

"One pasture at a time." His dad rubbed his shoulder, then tossed another match out the window. "Was on my way to start another backfire when you came tearing up from behind. Near scared me to death."

"Think how I felt when I saw you here." Gil scratched his chin, knowing better than to argue with the man. He studied his dad from across the seat and noticed the pallor of his skin, probably from jostling around in the truck. "You feelin' all right?"

"Don't worry about me. I've been burning pastures longer than you've been alive." His words came out choppy.

Trusting his instincts, Gil pressed on the horn to draw Mattie's attention and motioned her to follow him deeper into the pasture, away from the burning flames.

"What are you doing?" His father frowned.

"Getting you out of here. Then I'm going to help Jake manage this fire."

Mattie hopped out of the Dodge and stuck her head in the passenger side window. "Everything okay?"

Neither answered.

Gil peered into her eyes, and she seemed to read his unspoken words. "Come on, John, how about I take you to the house? You can help me unload our suitcases." She opened the door and held out her hand.

He swiped it away. "After all I've done for you, I never expected you to turn on me. Must be the company you're keeping."

Mattie flinched as though slapped.

"There's no reason to take your irritation out on her." Gil grabbed his dad's shirtsleeve. "Mattie hasn't done anything to hurt you. If you want to be mad at somebody, be mad at me." He could handle it, unlike Mattie, who seemed shaken by the hard words.

In a huff, his dad slid out of the truck. "Tell Jake to come see me when it's done. Don't want him thinking I skipped out on him."

The worn look on the man's face belied his gruff demeanor. In that moment, Gil realized his dad's desire to feel needed was what spurred him to lash out. Was that what it was like when a man had nothing to live for? He'd experienced a portion of that when he retired, knowing he'd never play football again, but this seemed nine times greater. "Jake will understand. I'll tell him Mattie needed you at the house."

His dad glanced back with scorn. "Don't you dare lie to him. If

214

you're going to tell him something, tell him I ain't man enough to take care of this land anymore."

Gil's throat tightened, and he turned his attention to the burning prairie, to something he understood from boyhood and could handle. As he went to meet Jake, the crackling flames licked up the dry, dead grass, and he compared the charcoaled ground to his father's life.

Spring rains would charge the roots to grow and burst forth in tender new sprouts so green they would brighten the earth with energy, but what did his dad have to look forward to?

A dead wife, a dead son, and another who antagonized him. Poor health and a ranch that had outgrown his capabilities.

For the first time in his life, Gil felt sorry for the man who'd raised him. A man who once held the admiration and respect of all who knew him, now reduced to a mere shadow of his former self.

His dad wasn't invincible.

Gil ducked his head as this knowledge hit him square in the gut. It didn't matter if he and his dad never made up, or if his dad made Gil's life miserable from now until the end. One thing did matter, however, and it had nothing to do with Gil's past or his own selfish motives. It had to do with things eternal. He had to forgive his father for his shortcomings, and he needed to share what gave his life purpose.

He'd spoken of his faith to Mattie, his teammates, even complete strangers in hospital beds, but not once had he shared it with his father, too afraid of his condemnation.

Now he knew that had to change.

MATTIE PARKED IN FRONT OF THE MCCRAY HOME TO LET JOHN OUT. The man barely said two words since leaving the pasture, and she was concerned about his pale lips and rapid breath.

"I don't know about you, but I'm parched," she said. "Let's go inside and get us a drink of ice water."

Mattie went around to his side of the truck to help him down. As she reached for John's hand, he clutched his chest, his face twisted in agony, beads of sweat on his brow.

She measured the pulse on his wrist and noted the erratic rhythm. "John, are you okay? Is it your heart?"

"Need my pills," he panted. "In room."

Nitroglycerine. Mattie feared what might happen if she left his side. He stared at her, his eyes huge against his ashen face. They seemed to look right through her. Then he slumped against the leather seat of Gil's truck.

THIRTY-NINE

MATTIE DASHED TO JOHN'S BEDROOM AND FOUND THE NITROGLYCERINE tablets on his nightstand. Her heart beat wildly as she called out to Mildred for help. Fumbling with the tiny brown bottle, she hastened to John's side and slipped a pill under his tongue as he labored for breath. She laid him flat on the seat and propped his head on her lap.

Mildred followed close behind and gripped Mattie's shoulder.

"He was burning pasture. Shouldn't have been out there." Tears pricked Mattie's eyes as she forced the words from her mouth.

Mildred turned to go into the house. "I'll call an ambulance."

John opened his eyes, his nostrils flaring. "No ambulance." He rubbed his heaving chest and grimaced. "I'm okay ..."

"No, you're not okay," Mattie told him and checked his pulse again. When his symptoms failed to improve, she gave him another pill. "Mildred, call 911." She looked toward the smoking pasture. "Gil?"

"I'll tell him and Jake what's happened." The woman stared directly at Mattie, her expression sure and composed. "Don't worry. The old goat's in God's hands."

Fifteen minutes later, Mattie followed the ambulance to the

county hospital in Diamond Falls and watched the medics wheel John into an examining room. Unable to join him, she slumped in a waiting chair and covered her mouth. Anxiety washed over her in an overwhelming wave, like the ocean she'd viewed from the cliff less than thirty hours ago.

When a nurse came out of John's room, Mattie rose to meet her. "How is Mr. McCray doing?"

"Are you family?"

Mattie swallowed. "No, but I'm the closest thing to it. His son, Gil, was burning pasture. I'm sure he'll be here soon." She squeezed the nurse's arm. "At least tell me if he's going to be all right. Did he have another heart attack?"

The nurse shook her head. "I wouldn't worry too much. He seems to have a great deal of spunk. Be sure and let us know when his son arrives."

Mattie wrung her hands, hating the helpless feeling. She inched closer to John's room and heard him complain about all the wires and gadgets connected to his body. Her animal patients might bite, but they were more amiable than John McCray.

The emergency doors opened and Gil strode in, his face and clothes covered with soot. Mattie rushed to meet him and launched herself into his arms, her heart hopeful the moment she felt his strong embrace.

GIL BRACED HIMSELF AS HE HELD MATTIE TIGHT. SHE'D NEVER LOOKED so glad to see him. "Where's Dad? Is he okay?" He searched her face for reassurance that his father wasn't dead.

Please don't let him be dead.

"He's conscious. He's in there." She gestured toward a nearby examining room. "What about the fire? Did you and Jake put it out?"

"Jake's finishing up. The fire department arrived to help with the last of it." Though he relished having Mattie in his arms, he reluctantly let her go.

"I take it you're John McCray's son?" The attending physician greeted him, a clipboard tucked under his arm. "Your father appears to have suffered a severe angina attack. We have a heart monitor on him, and we've sent his blood to the lab to test his cardiac enzymes, but at this time, we have no conclusive results. I've reviewed your father's medical history and because of his heart attack in December, I want to send him to Wichita to be cared for by his cardiologist."

Gil's muscles grew weak at the sight of his dad, so pale and fragile. It left him speechless.

The doctor shifted his stance and pulled out his clipboard. "According to your father, these angina attacks are recurring more frequently and with more severity. Were you aware of this?"

Gil stared a hole through his dad. "No, I wasn't."

His father groaned in displeasure. "Don't need more testing." He coughed and a nurse held a plastic basin to his chin.

"He's experiencing quite a bit of nausea," the doctor explained. "I've already spoken to his heart specialist in Wichita, and he's arranging for a heart catheterization to determine the location and severity of blockage in the arteries. Depending on the damage, they may or may not schedule him for surgery."

Gil swiped his forehead and studied his father. Though in pain, the old man still had enough gumption to create a stir. Gil squeezed his dad's foot. "Transferring you to Wichita sounds like a good idea. They'll be able to figure out what's causing your attacks."

His dad shook his head as another spasm hit. "No," he said between coughs.

Gil straightened, praying his father would accept his next words. "Listen, I wasn't home when you were sick before, but I'm here now. I want to be here for you." Gil thought of his mother. He hadn't been at her side when she'd passed away, and he'd regretted it ever since. No way was he going to let that happen again.

"Can I ride with him in the ambulance?" Gil turned and asked the physician.

"It'd be better if you drove. That way you'll have a car."

Gil combed his fingers through his hair. "Of course, I wasn't thinking." In an effort to clear the worry from his mind, he exhaled long and slow. He stepped outside the room to let Mattie know what they'd decided and welcomed her once again into his arms.

"I'm going with Dad to the Heart Hospital for further tests. Will you tell Mildred and Jake the situation?"

"Are you okay to drive?" Mattie surveyed him from head to foot, her concern evident. "At least come to the ranch for a change of clothes. Get a bite to eat before you make the trip."

Gil shook his head. "He needs to know he can count on me."

"It'll be okay, Gil." She seemed to sense his agitation and pressed her fingers to his lips. "I'll have Mildred round up some things for you and John, and I'll meet you there as soon as I've checked on the animals in the clinic."

"You're tired." He grasped her wrists, unable to think of anyone's company he'd welcome more. "I don't want to worry about you on the highway. My suitcase is still in the truck, so I can clean up at the hospital. You get some rest. I'll call when I have more news."

For once, she didn't argue. "Promise you'll call?"

He kissed her forehead gently. "I promise."

MATTIE WAITED FOR GIL'S CALL, TORMENTED BY A RESTLESS SLEEP. The next morning, her cell phone chimed on the nightstand. She fumbled to answer it when she saw that it was Gil.

"Good morning, sunshine."

Mattie welcomed the warm affection in Gil's voice, but that didn't excuse the worry he'd put her through all night. "You didn't call. How's your dad?"

"I'm sorry. He underwent tests all night and is wiped out, but the good news is they've found little blockage."

"No surgery, then?"

"Right now, it doesn't look like it. They want to explore a few more possibilities and are playing with his medicines."

"How are you holding up?" The beagle that lay on the bed at Mattie's feet clambered up to lick her face. She hugged him to her chest, and her voice softened. "Did you get any sleep?"

"Barely. I wanted to tell you I'm coming home to pick up a few things. They're going to let Dad rest this morning and then they'll start in again this afternoon."

"Are you sure you want to leave? I can bring whatever you need."

"You stay and tend to your patients. You've been gone enough."

Mattie closed her eyes and pressed her cheek to the pup in her arms. "Give him my love, then." Her words cracked as she wished she could tell John herself.

"Don't worry, he knows."

Tenderness welled in her heart for Gil. She said good-bye, already reevaluating her day. A short while later, as she poured milk into a bowl of cereal, her cell jingled again. Mattie answered automatically, thinking Gil must have forgotten to tell her something, but a female voice greeted her instead.

"Hey, little sister. What's up?"

"Jenna?"

"Who else? Gosh, it's good to hear your voice. Guess what? I'm here. I took some extra days off work and flew in early. Mom told me about the clinic fire—that you've been staying at the McCray ranch. Do you have any appointments this morning?"

Mattie swallowed. So much for catching up at the clinic. "What do you have in mind?"

Jenna laughed into the earpiece. "I should be there in about half an hour."

"Then I'll see you soon," Mattie said, but her sister had already hung up.

Her cereal now mush, Mattie grabbed her coffee and strode to the clinic to check on her patients. Cup in hand, she went to Dusty's pen and examined his wounds. After fourteen weeks of therapy, the gelding finally seemed to be on the mend, eating better and putting weight back on. He snorted and pitched his head in the air.

Mattie stroked his shoulder. "Hey, boy. Did you miss me?"

Jake stepped up to the stall with a bucket of grain. "Dusty's full of energy this morning. Starting to look like his old self again, thanks to you."

Mattie smiled at the ranch hand's compliment. "Don't thank me. He did it himself, with lots of help from God. I thought I might take him out for a ride — lead him behind Tulip. Maybe after that, we could put him in the large pen by the barn — let him get some grass?"

"He'd like that." Jake removed his hat. "Have you heard anything from Gil?"

She noticed the dark circles under Jake's eyes and guessed he hadn't slept too well. "John's doing better. Sounds like he's going to be in the hospital for a few days, though."

"He won't like that."

"It'll be good for him." *Good for Gil too.* Maybe it would give the two of them a chance to talk.

"I shouldn't have let him start that fire yesterday. I knew it was a mistake, but when Mr. McCray gets an idea in his head, it's hard to stop him."

Mattie opened the gate to continue her chores. "John does what he wants. I'm sure that's where Gil gets his stubbornness." She looked at Dusty, thankful they'd both been stubborn enough to keep him fighting for life. Sometimes obstinacy was a good thing. "His attack would have happened sooner or later, so don't beat yourself up about it."

"I guess this is his season. His time to heal."

Mattie considered his statement, which sounded biblical. Maybe this would be Gil's time to heal, as well. "You read the Bible, Jake?"

The ranch hand spit a stream of tobacco to the ground. "I dabble in it at night," he said, then helped her feed and care for the animals.

When the chores were done, Mattie turned Dusty into the round pen behind the barn. She was studying his progress as he pranced around on the soft dirt when Jake hollered to her from the barn.

"Dr. Evans, you're not going to believe this. You'd best come quick."

She tossed her lead rope to the ground and took off at a run.

What now?

FORTY

"Whoo-wee, I can't believe my eyes. Nobody mentioned you were coming to Kansas," Jake exclaimed, and Mattie watched him twirl Jenna around like a ballerina.

"I hardly recognized you." He whistled between his teeth. "How long's it been?"

"Since I was in high school." Jenna giggled, then waved to Mattie.

Mattie had never seen her sister with short hair. Her dark tresses no longer hung sleek down her back, but curled slightly at the shoulder, more suitable for the career woman she'd become. Dressed in a button-up shirt and capris, Jenna looked thin, but not nearly as wiry as Mattie remembered.

"You've been gone too long, that's for sure." Mattie walked up to her sister and gave her a welcoming hug.

"It's so nice of John to let you stay here."

Mattie stepped away from the embrace. "If it hadn't been for him and Gil, I don't know where I'd be now."

Jenna's white teeth glistened behind a coral smile. "Gil's here? Last I heard, he lived in California and played for the 49ers." She seemed thrilled at the aspect of seeing him. Of course, she would be. They were old friends ... classmates, even.

"He'll be back later this morning." Mattie glanced at Jake, wondering whether to drop the heavy news on her sister's homecoming. "We've actually had a bit of excitement around here."

Jenna raised her eyebrows in expectation. "From what I remember about the McCray household, excitement grows on the trees. Isn't that right, Jake?"

"The only difference is, now our excitement comes from waking up to another day." He kicked his boot against the barn's dirt floor.

"You're not that old." Mattie smiled at the ranch hand's awkwardness. "John had an attack last night," she told Jenna. "They took him to Wichita for heart tests, so we're all a bit out of sorts this morning. But don't worry, he's okay."

"Sounds like you and Jake could use a coffee break." Her sister linked her arm through Mattie's. "Is Mildred here? I want to show her some pictures of her grandkids. Phyllis will tan my hide if I forget to give them to her."

"You stay in touch with Mildred's daughter?"

"She keeps me updated about this dull little town. Never told me about Gil being back, though, so I'll have to give her a hard time about that." She chuckled.

Half an hour later, the four of them sat around Mildred's table looking at pictures and sipping coffee.

"I know Phyllis has told me, but what is it you do in Texas?" Mildred passed a plate of cinnamon rolls around the table.

Jenna took one and peeled a piece off. "I'm a legal aid to an oil producer. A grueling job, believe me."

"I'm surprised they gave you time off." Mattie winked at Jake. "The way Mom talks, the company keeps you busy all hours of the day."

Jenna shrugged. "I enjoy the work, plus I've met some interesting people. You wouldn't believe the sort of men who wear suits down there."

Mattie raised an eyebrow. "Anything you care to share?"

"Just odd ducks, you know? That's one reason they gave me time off, so I could investigate a business deal up here."

"What kind of business?" Jake asked.

Jenna glanced at the back porch. "The kind of business that hides its money," she said with an offhanded smirk that curved into a brilliant smile as the kitchen door screeched open.

"Welcome home, Gil." Jenna leaned back slightly and circled a fingertip around the brim of her coffee cup. "Surprised to see me?"

GIL STARED AT THE WOMAN BESIDE MATTIE. "JENNA?" AFTER MORE than twenty years, he strained to see the carefree girl he knew inside the polished businesswoman before him.

"What's the matter? Don't you recognize me?" She pursed her lips into a sultry pout and rose from the table. When Jenna reached for his hand, he allowed her to pull him to the empty chair next to hers. "Didn't Mattie tell you I was coming?" She gave Mattie a simpering look.

Gil brushed the hair from his forehead. It had been hard enough on his nerves to see his father in the hospital. Now he had to deal with Jenna? He rubbed his temple, his eyes raw from lack of sleep. What he wanted most was a few minutes to hold Mattie in his arms. Then about ten hours of sleep. He sat down at the table, directly across from Mattie.

"How is John? Has he been able to rest this morning?" Mattie asked.

Gil scratched the stubble on his chin and realized he needed a shave. "When I left the hospital, he was dozing. 'Course, when the nurses run in and out every twenty minutes, it's hard for anyone to get much rest."

"Speaking of rest, you look beat." Mildred got up to pour him a cup of coffee.

He stopped her before she went further. "If I drink any more caffeine, I'll be too wired to sleep."

Jake scooted from the table, looking perturbed. "Jenna was telling us about some business deal she's to take care of while here. Sounds like a tax deduction, if you ask me."

"Looking to do some investing?" Gil asked.

Jenna stirred sugar into her coffee. "Investments, deductions, whatever you want to call them. When my boss learned I was coming to the Flint Hills, he asked me to dig around and see if there was any land for sale."

"Don't tell me you work for one of those companies?" Mattie's eyes narrowed and her face blazed. "That's how Dad lost our ranch. How can you betray us by doing the work for such thieves, who prey on decent people struggling to keep their land?"

Jenna glanced from Gil to Mattie. "Don't get all worked up, little sis. What happened to Dad wasn't a bad thing. He and Mom are happy in the city. Now they don't have to worry about all the stuff that goes with ranching."

Mattie slammed her cup against the table and sloshed coffee on her napkin. "I can't believe I'm hearing this. Do you work for the company that bought their land?"

"No." Jenna picked at her cinnamon roll.

"But you do the same thing?"

"Face it, sis. There's money to be made in these hills. And ranching provides these companies a huge tax break." Jenna ignored Mattie's fury and turned to Gil. "How long has your dad been ill? Phyllis told me he had a heart attack in December. Is he still as stubborn as he used to be?"

Gil recognized the smooth voice of deception. *What was Jenna up to?*

He cleared his throat and stood. "Jenna, why don't you come

outside with me? I'd like to have a few words with you … alone." He gave Mattie a reassuring nod and hoped she wouldn't be upset with him for speaking to Jenna in private. There were things he wasn't prepared to share with the doc just yet.

Gil opened the front door for Jenna and followed her to the veranda where they settled in the wrought iron chairs. "Let's cut to the chase. Are you here to try to persuade my father to sell his land?"

Jenna didn't flinch but reached for his hand. "It's good to see you again, Gil. When Mattie told me you were in town, I nearly melted to the ground."

"Do you think you'll get to him through me? I'm afraid you're out of luck with that approach."

She pouted. "I remember a time when you weren't so insensitive, when you actually enjoyed—no, *preferred*—my company."

He pulled his hand away and met her gaze head-on. "That was a mistake we both paid for."

"What about my little sister? It's weird to see her here … and living in the cabin where Frank and I used to meet. Talk about coincidences."

Did Jenna have no pride, no sense of remorse? Gil stared at his boots. How could he have fallen for a woman like this—a woman so unlike Mattie? The differences between the two were like amateur wrestling compared to professional football.

"You're not so gruff with my little sister, are you?" She combed her fingers through her hair and raised it off the nape of her neck. "I heard the softness in her voice when she mentioned your name. And when you walked into the kitchen, her face lit up like a night-time arena with you the star cowboy. I hope you don't plan to break her heart like you broke mine."

To hear her talk about Mattie made Gil's temper burn. He struggled back on course. "You'll be hard-pressed to find anyone in this county who will agree to sell to another outside corporation. There's been enough land eaten up that way."

"Not even your dad? With him in the hospital, I'd think you'd jump at the chance to sell this property so you don't have to worry about him anymore."

"Enjoy your stay, Jenna." Gil forced the words from his mouth. "But don't make trouble where trouble's not wanted—not for my dad, and not for me and Mattie."

Jenna tipped her head, and her laughter rose to the ceiling. "You're too much, Gil. What's the matter? Afraid I'll ruin your little courtship? Let Mattie in on our little secret? I'm guessing my sister doesn't have a clue about our relationship, does she?"

"If she learns you're after the McCray land, she'll never forgive you. She's angry enough the way it is."

The screen door banged shut, and Mattie positioned herself at Gil's chair. "Who's angry, and about what?" She placed a hand on his shoulder, but he noted the edge in her voice and wondered how much she'd heard.

Jenna crossed her feet, her polished toes peeking out from her brown leather sandals. "Gil and I were discussing John's poor health, and how it might be wise for him to sell this ranch. My boss is prepared to pay top dollar for a spread like the Lightning M."

Her gaze riveted on Gil's and defied him to challenge her. "If you have any sense at all, you'll talk to your dad about our offer ... or I can do it, when he gets home."

Mattie's nails bit into his shoulder. "I've always known you to take risks, Jenna, but you've got some nerve to upset this household while John's in the hospital." She stared at Gil, her eyes flashing. "And what about you? Are you actually considering her offer?"

Gil shot a warning glance at Jenna, fearing her next words.

"I guess that's my answer," Mattie said when he didn't respond. She stormed down the porch steps.

"Mattie, wait—" Gil warred with going after her or staying to diffuse the bomb sitting next to him. He chose the bomb. "You like to wreck havoc, don't you, Jenna?"

"In a sense, I'm just protecting my dear sister, Gil . . . from you."

"Mattie doesn't need your protection."

"You sure she isn't a pawn in one of your sordid games? You're good at that, you know." She slipped her foot from its sandal and rubbed it languidly against his jeans. "Do you and your dad still fight like you used to?"

Jenna liked playing cat and mouse. He wanted to take her phony smile and toss it like a football.

"Listen, I know my little sis," Jenna went on. "She sees the best in people, even when it's not there. You and I live in the real world. We know the stakes."

"What are you talking about?" It seemed Jenna still thrived on mind games, but this time, he'd have none of it. He stood to get away from her touch. "I'm going to see if I can straighten this out. I'd appreciate it if you'd keep the past to yourself. Telling Mattie will only hurt both our relationships."

"You haven't told her, then? Bad move, Gil."

He pointed his finger in her face. "I'll tell her when the time is right. If you know what's good for you, you'll keep your mouth closed."

FORTY-ONE

Mattie hitched the leather cinch tight against Tulip's belly.

How could Jenna do this?

And Gil—would he really try to convince his father to sell? She considered their conversations in the past when Gil mentioned this very thing. But she thought he'd changed . . .

"We need to talk." Gil strode toward her in the barn.

Mattie grabbed a bridle from the hook on the wall. "I can't believe my sister's doing this. How can you even consider going along with her suggestion? I thought you cared for me." She placed the curb bit in Tulip's mouth and pulled the headpiece over the mare's ears.

Gil rubbed his jaw. "I do care for you, but it's not my decision to make."

"You said yourself, you wondered if your dad could handle ranch work anymore. His attack last night gives you the perfect excuse to take action." She handed the reins to Gil so she could retrieve Dusty from the round pen. "I almost wonder if you and Jenna didn't plan this entire scenario."

"Don't be stupid. That's ridiculous and you know it." He followed her outside.

She noted the tired lines on Gil's face and regretted her words. "Even if you weren't involved, it's obvious Jenna had this planned from the start. She admitted she knew about John's health problems. I'd guess that's why she agreed to attend our cousin's wedding. It sure wasn't because they were close."

Mattie opened the gate and guided the woven halter over Dusty's nose, careful of his healing wounds. "She probably had ulterior motives for coming to visit me too." That Jenna used her in such a way irked Mattie to no end.

Gil dropped Tulip's reins to the ground and came to Mattie's side. He clutched her elbow and urged her to look at him. "Your sister's been gone a long time. I'm sure she misses you."

Mattie broke from Gil's grasp and snapped the lead rope to Dusty's halter. She led the chestnut gelding to where Tulip waited. "If that's true, she has a funny way of showing it."

"Where are you going?" Gil turned to her, his wide shoulders slumped.

With reins in hand, Mattie hiked her foot into the stirrup and swung her leg over the saddle. Jenna would likely think it rude of Mattie to leave, but right now, she didn't care about propriety. And she refused to be burdened with what Gil may or may not be thinking. "Horses I understand. But you and Jenna are too complicated for my simple mind. If you're here when I get back, okay. If not, okay."

Not wanting to give Gil a chance to reply, Mattie clicked Tulip into a walk and brushed past him with Dusty trailing behind.

She didn't glance back. No way would she turn and look at him. It made her heart ache to leave with their relationship in such a mess, but to continue this conversation would only end in one of them saying something they'd regret.

As she headed for the pasture her willpower caved, and she peered over her shoulder. Her breath caught in her throat.

Gil had already left.

GIL WALKED TO THE HOUSE AND NOTICED JENNA'S RENTAL NO LONGER parked outside the barn. "She didn't stick around long," he said under his breath, then rubbed Hank behind the ears and whistled for the beagle to follow. The old dog had taken to the pup about the same way Gil had taken to Mattie.

He prayed the ride in the pasture would cool the doc down so that when she returned they could talk. Jenna's visit had stirred up a nest of bees worse than any he'd seen in a hayfield, and although he knew better, a part of him saw the logic in exploring the woman's offer on the ranch. After all, his dad just had another attack. What future could the Lightning M hold for the man in his current state of health?

Gil rubbed the muscles in his neck, the tension in his shoulders as tight as a cord. He needed sleep. Then he might be able to think clearly and deal with Mattie's temper. As he neared the house, he met Jake coming out.

"I take it Jenna left?" Gil asked.

"Yep, took off in that fancy sports car." The ranch hand stuffed a wad of tobacco in his mouth. "Said she had folks to visit in town. Told me to tell Mattie good-bye. That she'd call her later."

At least Jenna hadn't disregarded her sister's feelings. Gil hoped she wasn't using Mattie and wondered if their relationship was anything like his and Frank's had been. "What do you think about Jenna's business here?"

Jake's eyes narrowed. "You mean about her wanting to buy the McCray land?"

Gil nodded at the keen observation.

"I'm not a property owner. Never have been. But I've worked

your father's ranch since you and Frank were this high." He gestured to his hip. "I can't imagine someone else owning this land, and I don't want to try. Guess if that's coming, your dad may as well scoot over so I can join him on that hospital bed."

"Think it'd kill you both, huh?" Gil half joked.

Jake chewed on the tobacco. "You're a smart man—all grown up with the wisdom of your parents tucked inside you. Take away a man's dream, and you take his life from him."

Gil didn't respond but walked slowly to the house, Jake's words gnawing on his conscience.

AFTER A SHORT NAP, GIL SAT AT THE KITCHEN TABLE WITH A PLATE of Mildred's stew and two steaming biscuits slathered with butter and elderberry jelly. A packed suitcase waited at the door with clothes for him and his dad. He hoped to talk with Mattie before he left for the hospital, but so far, she hadn't returned.

As though sensing his thoughts, Mildred stared out the kitchen window. "I wonder if Mattie's all right. Hope she didn't have trouble with those horses."

Gil's mouth twisted in concern. Mattie could handle Tulip, but Dusty might have injured himself. He sopped his biscuit in the stew for one last bite. "Maybe I better check on them."

"No need." Mildred smiled. "There she is, coming in from the pasture."

He tossed his napkin on the table and stood, only to have Mildred motion him to sit.

"Finish your stew. You'll be eating cafeteria food soon enough." She refilled his glass of milk, then returned to her dishwashing. "You and Mattie seem mighty friendly these days. With her traveling all the way to California, it must be gettin' serious."

Gil scooped a carrot with his spoon. "I wouldn't call it serious. Too many kinks in the water hose."

The gray-haired housekeeper glanced at him. "She reminds me of your mama. Not many young women like her these days." Her eyebrows raised an inch. "Take Mattie's sister, for example."

Mildred had been with Gil's family almost as long as Jake. She'd helped his mother cook and clean this big house up until the day his mama died. They would have talked about things—shared intimate thoughts. "Did Mama like Jenna?"

Mildred dried her hands on a tea towel. "We all liked Jenna fine."

"What if she and Frank had married?"

She shook her head. "Jenna was too flighty. It would never have lasted. She's not like Mattie."

No truer words had come from the woman's lips. Images of Jenna bathed in moonlight flashed in his mind, and he blinked them away. "You think Mama would approve of Mattie?"

"Course, she would. Mattie's sensible and caring."

An angel compared to her sister.

"Are the two of you making plans?"

Gil's neck grew warm at her question. "Not yet, but I'm sure if that changes, you'll be one of the first to know."

Mildred chuckled. "Someone has to look out for you. You might be big and tough on the outside, but your insides are as tender as a baby's bottom."

He stood and kissed her on the cheek.

She flicked him with her sudsy water. "Scoot out of here and go see that girl of yours."

Gil pressed his lips together, wondering if Mattie had cooled down yet. One glance at his pocket watch confirmed they didn't have time to finish their previous conversation. He gathered his suitcase and jacket and lumbered to the truck. As he loaded the backseat, his cell phone beeped from the dashboard. Thinking the battery low, he checked and saw a text message from his real estate broker in California.

Owners ready to sell. Name your price.

FORTY-TWO

Mattie met Gil at his truck and waited while he checked his phone, her arms crossed in front of her chest.

He tucked the phone in his shirt pocket and turned to face her. His hair drooped to his brow as he shot her a winsome smile. "Still mad at me?"

The ride in the pasture helped calm her nerves, but it hadn't erased her memory. "That depends. Are you going to tell your dad about Jenna's offer?"

"I haven't decided yet."

She resisted the urge to swipe the annoying locks from his forehead, not quite ready to give up her fight. "I think it's a mistake if you do."

"If I don't, she will," he said. "Seems to me an announcement like that would be better coming from his son."

"Or not ... considering your history with your dad."

At her comment, Gil ducked his chin as though she'd hit him.

Mattie's irritation wavered. "I know you're trying to work things out, but still—"

"He's likely to get mad and give himself a genuine heart attack. Is that what you're afraid of?"

That was exactly her fear. "I've seen the way you two fight. His temper shoots through the roof, and yours goes haywire. You can't blame me for worrying."

"I'll try to control myself. Maybe I'll call a nurse in to keep the peace." He grinned and her armor cracked enough to let a smile through.

She didn't try to force it down. "A lot of good that would do. You think he's scared of a little ol' nurse?"

"You haven't seen the nurses in this place."

Mattie uncrossed her arms. "I still don't like it. You should at least wait until he's home — not cooped up in that hospital room where he feels all helpless and trapped."

"Afraid of what he'll say?"

"More afraid of what you'll talk him into." Mattie's smile faded at the thought. For John to give up the ranch at this time in his life might kill him, and it would certainly break her heart.

Gil slid his hands around her waist, and his touch thawed her defenses. "I'm not going to try and talk him into anything. I'll simply tell him the truth — that an offer's been made on the ranch. We'll see what happens from there." He crouched to her eye level.

"Speaking of offers, Mattie ... the estate in California is officially on the market."

Her lungs deflated. *Could there be more bad news this day?* She rested her hands on his chest and saw his excitement. "That's great. I'm happy for you, Gil."

"Save your congratulations, because I know you don't mean it. I'm not going to make an offer until we've had a chance to talk. You and me, alone, after I bring Dad home."

"I suppose we could discuss it after my cousin's wedding. If you still want to go with me, that is."

"I like the sound of that." Gil nuzzled his chin against her cheek and kissed her lightly on the neck. "It'd give us a reason to slip out early."

He did it again. No matter how angry or upset she was, this re-tired quarterback had the ability to melt her with one smooth touch of his lips on her skin. Gil lowered his mouth to hers and kissed her deeply, a penetrating kiss that hinted of a future. His lips lingered on hers, reducing her legs to jelly.

Then he pulled away. He checked his pocket watch and frowned. "I hate to do this, but if I don't leave now, I'll miss what the doctor tells Dad."

Mattie stepped back, surprised her knees didn't falter. "By all means go, but be careful."

Gil tipped her chin. "You'll be okay? You won't let your sister push your buttons, right?"

"I doubt she'll show her face here again ... at least not until John gets home."

"See that she doesn't trouble you. I'll call when I know more about Dad."

Mattie nodded and watched Gil drive away. She pressed her fin-gers to her lips where he'd kissed her, never wanting to forget the sweet sensation.

He lifted Jenna in his arms and twirled her in the swirling creek water. He plunged backward, soaking their glistening bodies as laugh-ter filled the moonlit sky. Jenna faced him, her hands massaging his chest with a sensual touch. Her fingers climbed to his shoulders, and her laughter turned to shrieks as she pushed him under the water and held him there. The water turned to blood, thick and horrifying. Gil couldn't breathe.

Gil awoke with a start in the shadowed hospital room, his face beaded with sweat. The nightmare had returned and with it, the guilt. He should have been the one to die. Not Frank. *Why, God, why?* He shook the thought away and tried to slow his rapid breath—listened to his dad snore, the lights from the heart monitor glowing green and red. When he'd arrived at the hospital that afternoon, he barely spoke to his father before they wheeled him off for a stress test and an echocardiogram. According to the attendant, he did well on both.

The door slid open and a lab technician in a pink blouse came in with more syringes. She went to his father's bedside and pushed a button to elevate his head.

His dad's eyes fluttered open.

"Did you have a nice nap?" Her words were loud as she placed her tray of items on the table.

"Can't get any sleep with you nurses poking me all the time."

Gil forced a chuckle, and the woman gave a hearty laugh. "We need to check your enzymes again," she said and prepared his arm for the needle. "Do you feel like eating some supper?" She worked quickly and attached a bandage to the inside of his elbow where she'd drawn the blood.

His dad grimaced. "What's on the menu? Soy burgers?"

Another nurse stepped into the room with a tray and set the covered dishes on the bedside table. "Tonight you get meat loaf." She lifted the plate's plastic cover to reveal a pale slice of meat masked in ketchup, with a few green beans and applesauce on the side.

The two left, and Gil watched his dad nudge the food with his utensils. "If you ever hear me complain about Mildred's cooking again, punch me in the teeth." He cut into the loaf and held it up with his fork. "Never knew they could make so many things out of soy. It's a plumb embarrassment to the beef association. How dare they call it meat loaf."

Gil chuckled, glad he didn't have to eat the meal. "Part of your heart-healthy diet." He held up the pamphlet he'd been reading that gave the American Heart Association's food recommendations and restrictions.

"Yeah, no salt, no color, no taste." His dad put the slice in his mouth and made another face. "There are some things in life I'm not willing to give up, and meat is one of them."

Gil wasn't sure he agreed with his father's attitude but figured the man had lived a full life and could make his own decisions about what he chose to eat. It reminded him of what Jake said about a man needing his dreams to keep him alive.

"How come you never went to church with Mama?"

The old man looked up from his food. "What makes you ask such a question?"

"She used to take us boys to church and Sunday school, but you stayed home. Do you not believe in God? Or were you too busy?" Gil remembered interrogating his mother about this, but she'd never answered his questions.

"Doesn't matter now. Your mother's dead and gone. Can't do nothing to change that." He cleared his throat and tried to situate himself in the hospital bed by punching on his pillow.

"It seems a good question to ask, with your heart problems and all. Maybe now's the time to make amends with your Creator."

His father's eyes darted to Gil's. "Who says I need to make amends for anything? Did Mattie put you up to this?"

Gil rested his elbows on his knees and grinned. "Has she been talking to you?"

"Been trying to get me to go to church with her for the last several months."

"Why don't you go? It'd be good for you."

"What's good for me is to have some peace in my life and not be pushed by you or anyone else to do something I don't want to do," his father snapped.

The words cast a stone on Gil's heart the size of a boulder. "What do you want in life, Dad? What gives you peace? Living on the ranch where your memories of Mama and Frank are?"

"It's good to have the reminders." His dad nodded. "What would bring me peace, though, is for you to marry and give me grandbabies. Any chance of that happening soon, or will I go to my grave without anyone to inherit the Lightning M, seeing as how you don't want it?"

"Speaking of the ranch ... " Gil scratched his chin, figuring now was as good a time as any to mention Jenna's offer. "There's something I need to talk to you about."

FORTY-THREE

Thursday afternoon, Mattie stopped by Clara's Café after treating a cow's injured leg at a nearby ranch. She sat on a stool at the counter and waited for her friend to finish an order.

"Hey, you, what's going on? You haven't been by all week." Clara winked and handed Mattie a plastic menu.

"I've been called out five times this week for inoculations. You heard about John?"

Clara nodded. "How's he doing? Your sister told me they sent him to the Heart Hospital. She sure surprised me the other night. What's Jenna doing here?"

Mattie pointed to her usual menu choice of a hamburger and fries. "Gil's bringing John home tonight. Jenna returned for our cousin's wedding." She clenched her teeth, trying to forget the real reason for her sister's return.

"She looked good. Her divorce must not have bothered her too much."

"Maybe because she didn't want to be married." Mattie clenched her teeth when the sharp words came out, ashamed of the judgment.

Clara's eyebrows raised as the door to the café jingled. "Let me

242

know if I can order your sister anything." She placed an icy cola in front of Mattie and nodded toward the entrance.

Mattie turned and saw Jenna wave, headed straight for her. "What are you doing, sis? Thought you'd be operating on dogs and cats this afternoon." She sat on a stool next to Mattie and grinned.

"Not today. What about you?" Mattie sipped her soda and fought to maintain a level of composure. "Any success buying land?"

Jenna placed cool fingers on Mattie's arm, and her gold bangle bracelets tinkled against each other. "Still sore about that?"

"If we're going to talk, let's go somewhere more private." Mattie grabbed her glass and moved to an empty booth in the corner. She sat on one side, Jenna took the other.

"Like old times, huh?" Jenna pulled out a menu and browsed the selections.

"Not at all. A lot has changed since we were girls."

Jenna studied her from across the table. "You've done well for yourself, despite staying in this dinky town. I still say you ought to look for a job in the city. You'd make three times as much as you do now, and you wouldn't be stuck in the middle of nowhere."

Mattie let her sister's comment slide. "You never answered my question. Have you found any land to devour?"

Jenna tore open a sugar packet and poured the white crystals into her palm. "Not yet." She dipped a finger in the sugar and stuck it in her mouth.

Mattie watched as Jenna repeated her childhood habit. "Why don't you leave the people in Charris County alone? Tell your boss no one wants to sell."

"And miss out on a hefty bonus? Besides, I'd be doing these folks a favor. John McCray, for example." She licked the rest of the sugar from her hand, then wiped her palm with a napkin.

"Stay away from John." Mattie's tone filled with hostility. "Leave the McCray land alone."

"You're too close to those people, sis. You've let them get under your skin." Jenna tapped the menu on the table and glanced around the café. "Where is that waitress friend of yours, anyway?"

Mattie pressed Jenna's menu to the table. "If you won't do it for me, do it for Frank. Don't steal his family's ranch."

"Frank's dead." Jenna pulled the menu out from under Mattie's hand. "Besides, nobody's stealing anything." She pierced Mattie with her dark brown eyes. "You've got the hots for Gil, don't you? That's what this is about."

Mattie shook her head. "Gil and I are friends. I've grown fond of his father the last few years, and I don't want to see him hurt."

Jenna stared down at the table, her expression sullen. "You're not after Gil? I got the impression the other day that the two of you were an item."

Images of Gil swept through Mattie's mind. Days spent with Dusty and working on the ranch, their trip to Central Kansas, and the most recent time spent in California. Of course, they'd grown close ... but she wasn't after him. That wasn't her way. She might like them to be a couple, if only he'd come around to her way of thinking. And, although he'd spoken some big words about a future together, never once had he mentioned that he loved her. "He's going to the wedding with me tomorrow night, but I wouldn't call us an item."

Her sister's lips twisted into a condescending smile. "Gil's too old for you, anyway, honey. Much too bullish for your sensitive nature." She reached across the table to squeeze Mattie's hand, and the icy touch against her skin seemed too cold to be human.

GIL RELAXED HIS WRIST ON THE STEERING WHEEL AS HE DROVE Mattie to the wedding Friday night. His free hand squeezed Mattie's fingers, warm and dainty beneath his own. Eager to spend a few hours in her company, he'd settled his father in at the ranch and arranged for Mildred to look after him until they returned. The night was theirs.

He peered over at the doc, dressed in the ruffled skirt and denim jacket he'd admired before. "You look good in that color."

"You look nice too." She smiled.

Gil lifted his hand from hers and twirled a long curl in his finger, loving the silky texture as it wrapped against his skin. "You said to dress casual."

"My cousin doesn't like fancy parties. The wedding's a small affair with a barbecue at her parents' house afterwards."

Gil nodded, wondering what it would be like to see Mattie's mom and dad. He vaguely remembered meeting them at Frank's funeral. Then of course, there was Jenna to contend with. He hoped she wouldn't cause trouble, but just in case, he planned to whisk Mattie away so they could talk. "You still willing to leave early?"

Mattie's eyes sparkled. "Most definitely. As soon as we can escape."

THE WEDDING WAS SHORT AND SIMPLE LIKE MATTIE PREDICTED. GIL held her hand as they walked to the outdoor reception, imagining the conversation he would have with her later, and how she'd respond. If it went well, the two of them might be considering a future together.

"Shall we get this over with?" Mattie motioned to where her parents stood by a blossoming redbud tree as the evening dusk settled around them.

"Come on, it won't be that bad." He prompted her forward by the elbow. When they reached her parents, Mattie introduced him with a guarded voice.

He stretched out his hand to Mattie's father, a tall gentleman dressed in a gray western suit. "It's nice to meet you again." He turned to Mrs. Evans and nodded. She smiled up at him, the resemblance to Mattie uncanny.

Mr. Evans scratched his chin. "You're Frank's younger brother, right? I remember meeting you years ago."

"He's the owner of the horse Mattie's treating." Mrs. Evans told her husband in a matter-of-fact way and nudged his arm. "We hoped to meet you tonight, since we missed seeing you when we moved Mattie to the ranch. Mattie told us you played for the 49ers— remember, Owen?"

"Weren't you in Jenna's class in school? I seem to remember you getting a scholarship to Oklahoma State." He skimmed the crowd as though in search of someone. "Have you seen Jenna and Bridgett? They were here a minute ago."

While Mr. Evans went off in search of his missing daughters, Gil pulled Mattie to the side. "Are you thirsty?" His throat felt suddenly dry.

"Yes, but don't leave me alone too long." She squeezed his hand, her fingers lingering on his.

Not prepared to deal with Jenna, he escaped to the barn where they were holding the reception. For several minutes, he stood in line at the punch table and nodded to those he recognized. He listened to the twanging chords of the guitars as a western band warmed up on a makeshift stage. When his turn finally came, he filled two plastic cups with pink punch. Then a woman held out a third cup for him to fill.

He peered up and saw Jenna smiling at him.

"I've been looking all over for you," she crooned. "Mattie said she was bringing you. I'm glad you came. This party is severely lacking."

Gil's lip curled as he politely poured punch into her cup. "What, you don't enjoy talking about the weather, or hearing about Farmer Jones's cows and goats?"

Jenna groaned. "What I want is to hear about you," she said

and latched onto his arm. The flimsy, orange material of her dress brushed against his skin. "It's been a long time, Gil. Too long."

He managed to pull away, then picked up his cups, determined to leave the woman behind. "I'm sorry, Jenna. Mattie's waiting for her drink. Maybe we can talk later."

Jenna took Mattie's cup from him and downed the punch in one long swallow. "Let's talk now." She licked the pink froth from her lips and set his other cup on the table.

FORTY-FOUR

"WHAT ARE YOU UP TO, JENNA?" GIL FOLLOWED HER, WARY OF HER intentions.

She led him behind the barn to a grove of cedars, away from the noise of the wedding party. "I only want a few minutes of your time. Don't worry about Mattie. I'm sure Mother's drilling her with a thousand questions by now." She pulled a cigarette from her purse and offered him one, but he refused. "You should have known better than to accompany her to a wedding. My folks will tear her apart trying to find out how serious your relationship is."

Gil searched for Mattie in the dim light, hoping Jenna was wrong. "What about you? Do they give you a hard time now that you're divorced?" He tried not to enjoy the direct hit too much.

"They know better than to mess with me. If I get mad, I leave." She lit the cigarette and inhaled deeply.

Her remark hit too close to home. Hadn't Gil done the same when he and his dad fought in the past—when things became too difficult? Maybe he and Jenna were not so different after all. "You're a bit old for temper tantrums, don't you think?"

"You should talk. What I want to know is why you're with my sister. She says you're only friends. Is that right?"

Gil checked the darkening yard once more for Mattie, then felt an icy hand on his shirtfront.

"We were friends once too. Is that the sort of friends you are?" She massaged his chest in a circular motion. He remembered when she'd touched him that way before, only then he'd been a teen, thrilled by her attention. Now the sight of her sickened him. She opened her mouth and blew a halo of smoke into the air.

He glared down at her. "You wouldn't understand what Mattie and I have." He wrenched her hand from his shirt.

"Enlighten me," she murmured in a husky voice and took one more drag from her cigarette before tossing it to the ground. "Help me understand why you haven't told Mattie about us. Why you've never married, and why you've stayed away so long?" Her fingers now clutched his pants pockets.

"Do you know I've never forgotten that night?" She yanked him closer. So close, he could smell the heavy tang of her perfume mixed with the stench of cigarette smoke on her breath. "I've kept it with me, even through marriage."

Jenna's words shocked Gil into silence. He stared down at her face and felt genuinely sorry for her. One by one he unwrapped her fingers from his pockets. "We don't share the same memories, Jenna. The only thing that night reminds me of is Frank's death and how I betrayed him."

As soon as he freed himself from her grasp, she clamped down on his fingers, ensnaring them with her own. "You don't remember the caress of our bodies? How it felt when we made love ...?"

Jenna's voice stalled in the cool night air. She slowly released her fingers from his.

Gil wondered at her sudden change in behavior. Then a twig snapped behind him. He turned and saw Mattie, her face contorted with pain and disbelief.

MATTIE WILLED HERSELF TO BREATHE, PRAYING SHE'D HEARD HER sister wrong.

They'd made love? Gil and Jenna? When?

One thought tumbled on top of the next as she realized the two of them shared a past — an intimate past. But that didn't make sense ... Jenna had been Frank's girlfriend. The triumphant expression on her sister's face told Mattie their connection ran deep.

A chorus of frogs moaned from a nearby pond as though to console her. Embarrassed to have been so gullible as to think there might have been a future between her and Gil, Mattie tried to veil her pain.

"I'm sorry to intrude ..." She searched Gil's face, wondering how she'd mistaken their friendship for so much more. "I'm not feeling well, so I'm going to get someone to give me a ride home. You stay and visit."

Gil muttered under his breath, and she tore her gaze from his, desperate to get away from the image of Jenna clutching Gil.

Her vision blurred as she made her way to the barn, the loud music drowning out her thoughts. Gil caught up to her as she neared the cake table. He swung her around by the elbow, and all her hurt and anger erupted in a scathing verbal torrent.

"You lied to me," she lashed out, wanting to pummel him with her fists. "How could you deceive me like that?"

Gil pulled at her jacket, and she struggled free of his grasp, undaunted by the scene she was creating.

"Mattie, please, give me a chance to explain." As he wrapped his arm around her shoulders, Mattie suddenly felt all eyes on them and wondered what everyone must think — her neighbors, clients, friends, and family.

Humiliated, she allowed Gil to lead her to his truck where she could speak her mind away from the curious onlookers. Gil lowered the tailgate and removed his jacket for her to sit on.

"What is going on with you and my *sister*?" She practically spat the word as she swiped the moisture building in her eyes, unwilling to give him the satisfaction of her tears.

Gil picked her up and set her on the tailgate as though she were a child. He stood before her like a guard, blocking her escape. "I'm sorry you had to find out that way. I wish I'd had the courage to tell you before now. I tried, but . . ." The desperation in his voice begged her to listen, his features apologetic in the shadowy night.

"I tried to tell you on the airplane, but something prevented me from spilling my guts. Mostly fear."

Mattie's heart wrenched. "It's true then, you and Jenna . . ." She couldn't force the words from her throat.

"Yes, no matter how much I want to erase the memory, it's true. Your sister and I . . . one time . . . many years ago. I've been sorry ever since."

His words cut into her heart, and Mattie fought to keep the damage to a minimum. She had a doctorate in veterinary medicine. She healed animals daily. Why couldn't she stop her own pain?

"It's a secret I've kept hidden too long," he went on. "One that made me run as far from here as possible. If I'd had the option to move across the ocean, I'm sure I'd have done it."

"I don't understand." Her lips quivered. "Why?" Why had he kept the secret from her all this time, and more importantly, why had he been with Jenna in the first place?

"Why do any of us do stupid things when we're young?" He placed his hands on her knees, and his fingers trembled against her skirt. "I've gone over it in my mind a thousand times. Jealousy, contempt, greed, envy. Childish motives we carry with us into adulthood. All part of the problems I've had with my dad."

Mattie worked to process his words. *Jenna, envy, his father?* "I still don't understand."

"You haven't heard the worst, Mattie. That's really why I couldn't bring myself to tell you. Because when you do, you may never forgive me."

FORTY-FIVE

Gil played over the scene of Frank's death and the incidents leading up to Gil's betrayal. How could he admit such detestable sins to the woman he loved? But with what she now knew, how could he not? He prayed God would grant Mattie an understanding heart able to forgive.

"I want you to know you've changed my life." He clasped her shoulders, fully expecting her to shrug his hands off. She didn't, and he found encouragement in this. "When I returned to Diamond Falls, I wanted to put an end to the pain that haunted me so I could go on with my life. I thought that meant trying to restore a relationship with Dad—visiting him, repairing the ranch. I hoped that would be enough. But it's not.

"My past still troubles me—it comes to me in my dreams. I want it to go away. I've prayed for peace. It's like a scab that grows bigger when you pick it, and I've been picking it for twenty years now." Gil twisted one of Mattie's ringlets around his finger, needing the slightest comfort.

Mattie caught his hand in hers and stilled it. "I don't understand. Is this about Jenna?"

"Yes, and no." He allowed the lock to slip from his finger. "It's mostly about Frank." He turned from her and leaned against the tailgate, unable to look her in the eyes. Instead, he stared at the distant treetops outlined in black against the faint moonlight and forced himself to continue.

"I've told you how Frank was good at everything—the apple of my dad's eye. What I didn't mention was how jealous and tormented this made me. We both liked to rope—he roped better. We both rode horses—Frank had better instincts. We both liked girls, but girls liked him more, and his favorite girl was Jenna.

"I worked hard to outrope, outride, and outwin the girls. I failed on all counts, until one night when Frank and his friends wanted to go to the rodeo grounds and drink some beer. I sensed Jenna's frustration at hanging out with the guys and suggested she stay with me and go for a swim in the creek. The humid August temperature had all of us sweating like dogs, and Frank didn't suspect a thing. I told him we'd meet them at the rodeo grounds once we'd cooled off."

Gil cleared his throat, afraid if he stopped, he might not finish. The cool night air sank into his skin, and he closed his eyes, allowing it to calm him. He refused to go into detail about what happened with Jenna, not willing to hurt Mattie any more than he had to. However, she needed to know the rest of the story.

"I set the scene and one thing led to the next. Jenna and I both knew what we were doing, and we did it anyway. Then we heard the sirens."

Mattie gasped, and he went on undeterred. "We followed the flashing lights to the accident, and that's where I found my dead brother and held him in my arms," Gil choked out the words. His eyes stung from the memory. "I betrayed my brother—not by accident but by a willful act—and in so doing, I failed to take care of him. I might have prevented their deaths. It could have been me driving. If I'd been with him instead of with your sister, I'd have kept the truck from rolling—from crushing them."

He stepped away from the tailgate, away from Mattie's scrutiny.

It killed him to admit this to her, to know that she might condemn him, that he would no longer be a hero.

Not even close.

Mattie followed Gil and gently placed her hand on his back. No words were spoken, but he could imagine what she thought. How could she forgive him—trust him with her heart? If their relationship had been difficult before, it now approached disaster.

"I'm sorry," she whispered against his shirt. "Does your father know?"

Gil closed his eyes. Of course not. How could he admit to the man he wanted to impress the most that he'd killed his oldest son? His pride and joy. Killed him and betrayed him all in one night. "He knows Jenna and I found them in the ditch. After Frank's death, I tried to continue high school rodeo as a single contestant. I rode hard and fast and took my anger out on the calves, ruthlessly flanking them to the ground with pleasure. But even that grew old and couldn't relieve my pain.

"I distanced myself from my family and the things I loved. I turned my attention to football, and there I found release for my anger. Dad never understood, and I never tried to explain. We drifted so far apart over the years that he couldn't even call me when he had a heart attack in December."

Mattie stepped around to face him. "Why do you think he called you when Dusty had his accident?"

Gil shook his head. "I don't know. Maybe on some level he wanted to fulfill his fatherly duty."

"Maybe it was an attempt to get back what you once shared," she said earnestly. "Frank might have held a special place in your dad's heart, but he loved you too. Still does, or he wouldn't bite so hard."

"Where does this leave us, Mattie? I know I have no right to ask … but can you forgive me? Can we go on as though none of this happened? Or has it caused too much damage?"

Mattie turned away. "I don't know, Gil."

Desperation swelled inside his chest at the possibility of losing her. He couldn't allow that to happen.

Tell her. Tell her how you feel.

"When I came here, I didn't have much to look forward to. My career in football was over. I had no one to share my retirement with. No wife, no family. No place to call home. I tried to compensate by putting my energy into buying an estate where I could raise horses and regain part of my past that once gave me joy. I didn't realize how empty this dream was until I began imagining my future—without you."

He spun her around. "I had no idea how much I loved you until tonight, when I thought I'd lost you. Tell me I'm wrong, Mattie. That we still have a chance."

Even in the shadowy night, he could see her tears. He tried to pull her to his chest, but rather than be comforted, she pushed away.

"Do you know how long I've waited to hear those words?" Her voice roared. "For you to say you love me—want me as more than a veterinarian to your horses?" She poked him in the chest, reminding him of the day he first met and fell for her spunk.

"You decide to tell me *now*, after what I've seen and heard? You can't manipulate me, Gil, just because you can't bear to take no for an answer. How dare you be so selfish."

FORTY-SIX

MATTIE SWALLOWED THE ANGER THAT BOILED INSIDE AND ESCAPED to the cab of Gil's truck. She pitched herself against the passenger door, wanting to be as far from him as possible. The man had some nerve to proclaim his love for her after admitting he'd slept with her sister, even if it was a long time ago. In her mind, it felt like it happened yesterday. And it was just like Gil to rush down the field with his declaration of love nevermind how this news might affect her.

"You need time to think, is that what you're telling me?" He joined her in the truck and started the diesel engine.

"Put yourself in my shoes, Gil. Imagine how you'd feel if I told you I'd been with Frank and had kept it from you all this time." She hated being so callous, but he'd asked for it. "I'm sorry for what you're going through, really I am ... but you brought it on yourself. You made choices and now you have to live with them, and that includes having a little patience with me while I deal with this."

Right now, all she wanted was to huddle beneath the quilt on her bed and shrink from reality. She didn't want to think about Gil, or Jenna, or the McCray ranch, or anything.

They drove the rest of the way to the Lightning M in silence.

When Gil pulled up to her cabin, Mattie scrambled out of the cab, eager to be alone.

"May I come in, so we can talk about this?" He called after her, his features illuminated by the truck's interior lights.

Mattie's teeth clenched. "I think we've talked enough for one night."

"Can I see you tomorrow?"

His question hung in the air as she gripped the handle to the cabin door. For a few lingering seconds, she considered answering him, then shut the door firmly behind her.

GIL PLODDED TO THE HOUSE, HIS HEART SO HEAVY AND SORE HE felt like he'd been tackled. After he bid Mildred good night, he approached the kitchen for a drink of water and noticed a light from his father's bedroom. He rapped softly on the wooden door.

"You still awake?" Gil peered inside the room where his dad sat in bed reading.

"How was the wedding?" His father snapped the book closed and hid it beneath the covers, but not before Gil recognized the black leather binding and the engraved gilded cross.

"The wedding went well—the reception, not so good."

His father frowned. "Why's that?"

Gil debated confessing everything as he'd done with Mattie, then considered the outcome. Mattie hadn't taken the news so great ... perhaps his dad wouldn't either. It might affect his health, and Gil refused to take on any more guilt. "Let's just say Jenna put a kink in the evening."

"She after you again? Tell her we're not interested in selling, like I told you in the hospital."

"Jenna doesn't take no for an answer. She's as bullheaded as her sister."

The old man chuckled. "Mattie's not stubborn — she just sees what she wants and goes after it."

Gil wished Mattie would set her eyes on him, but after tonight, he questioned whether she would ever look at him again. He'd intended to discuss their future in California and had planned to ask her to marry him. But he'd fumbled the ball miserably, with no time-outs left in the game.

"What do you think Mattie wants?" Gil sat in the armchair beside his father's bed.

"You ... and these hills. She's been in love with these hills ever since I met her."

"Do you suppose she'd ever leave them?"

"And move to California?" His father tugged on his bedcovers. "Do you love her?"

"Like you and Mama?" Gil prayed for a love that strong. Then, for reasons he couldn't explain, he decided to ask the question that had plagued him for years. "How come you and Mama never came to any of my games?"

His dad's brow puckered. "You sure got a lot of questions."

Gil pointed to the Bible hidden under the covers. "You're reading the Book with all the answers."

"It's your mother's." His father pulled the Bible out and placed his wrinkled hands on the leather. "She seemed to like Psalms — had a lot of those pages marked with pen."

"As for man, his days are like grass, he flourishes like a flower of the field; the wind blows over it and it is gone, and its place remembers it no more."

His dad looked up, curious.

"Psalm one hundred three." Gil smiled. "About the games ... don't you know how much I wanted you to attend?" He squeezed the arms of his chair, not sure he wanted to hear his father's answer. "You could have had the best seats in the stadium."

The old man grumbled. "If I'd known how much it meant to you,

I'd have taken your mother. She wanted to go. I never thought you cared." He slid out of bed in his flannel pajamas and shuffled across the room to a wooden dresser drawer where he pulled out an old scrapbook. "I saved all the newspaper articles your mother cut out. Even have the last game you lost to Green Bay. Cut that one out myself." He sniffed and handed the collection to Gil before climbing back in bed.

Gil leafed through the pages and took in the many newspaper articles collected by his parents through the years.

They'd done this for him?

He clutched the book to his chest. "May I keep it?"

His father waved his hand in the air. "Go ahead, it's yours."

THE NEXT MORNING GIL WOKE EARLY, ENCOURAGED BY THE STEPS HE and his father had taken the night before. He'd come to terms with the situation with Mattie, as well, and decided to give her time to digest his confession.

Right now, the only female he wanted to be around was the young filly he'd purchased in Central Kansas. With the recent trip to California and his father's illness, Gil hadn't done anything with the two horses but put them out to pasture.

That changed today.

He headed for the barn and grabbed his lariat.

Thirty minutes later, after a short, hard fight on the rope, Gil had the three-year-old filly lunging a couple of feet inside the rail of the wooden round pen. As a boy, he'd learned to start his groundwork in a circle and had been taught by the best trainers he knew — his dad, his brother, and his childhood friend, Clive Richards. What his brother didn't know, his dad did, and if neither of them knew the answer to a problem, they turned to Clive, who possessed the finest horse training instincts in the county.

Gil revolved in the center of the ring and noted the bay's

attentiveness. The girl took well to his commands, and at the slightest tug stopped and faced him. He stepped forward and she stood calm, no longer stressed. Grabbing the loop in both hands, Gil prompted her to lower her head. When she did, he lifted the rope off her neck.

"Good girl." He laid his hand on her forehead, then walked to the edge of the pen. A good start.

The sound of clapping echoed from the barn. "A man's most content when he has the submission of a female — wouldn't you agree?"

Gil raised his head to see Jenna coming toward him. "Only if it's given freely and her respect is earned."

Jenna's mouth twisted in an ugly smile. "Whatever you say." She glanced about the barnyard and climbed onto the wooden railing. Hank and the beagle came up and sniffed her black pant legs. She shooed them away with a kick. "I thought I'd come by this morning and have that visit with your dad. Did you mention my offer to him?"

Checking the filly's trust, Gil approached the bay a final time and touched her forehead — sensed her peace. The work done, he turned and walked away without looking back. Once outside the pen, he captured the attention of the two dogs, then headed to the barn, not bothering to answer Jenna.

She ran to catch up. "Well, did you?"

"He's not interested." Gil hung his lariat on a hook on the wall. As he turned to her, his gaze traveled the length of her body in an effort to send a clear message. "I'm not either. I suggest you bother someone else, preferably in another county far from here."

Jenna's eyes bulged with resentment. "That's strong talk for a man who was bound speechless by my sister last night. You chased after her with your tail between your legs. Did Mattie grant forgiveness? I'm surprised she'd even talk to you."

Gil headed outside to fill Dusty's water trough. "If I were you, I'd be more concerned about whether she'll talk to you."

FORTY-SEVEN

Mattie saw her sister approach and opened the cabin door. The black outfit Jenna wore emphasized the dark circles under her eyes. "You're getting an early start on trouble, don't you think?"

Jenna stepped inside and laid her leather jacket on the table. "Very funny, sis. I guess you and Gil made up. At least you didn't kill him, I see."

A foggy haze filled the air and reminded Mattie of the egg frying on the stove. She'd put off going to the clinic this morning, not prepared to face Gil. Now, forced to deal with her sister, she wasn't sure which was worse. "What makes you think I'd want to?"

"Don't play dumb. Did he tell you?"

Mattie turned a piece of bacon in the skillet, and grease splattered her skin. She shook her hand in pain. "Yes, he told me everything." She lowered the flame on the stove, her own temper simmering.

"I thought you loved Frank," Mattie said. "Didn't you plan to marry him? Or is that simply what you led us to believe all those years ago?"

Jenna sat at the wooden table and pulled a pack of cigarettes from her coat pocket. "Mind if I smoke?"

"Yes, I do." Mattie fixed her plate and sat to eat breakfast. "Which brother did you love, Jenna? Frank or Gil? Or do you still love one?"

Her sister slipped the pack of smokes in her coat and grunted. "I'm not interested in your hunky quarterback. I have bigger fish to fry."

Mattie doused her egg with ketchup. "What would you call last night, then?"

"That was nothing more than a test … to see if he loved you."

Test, my foot …

"And by your standards, did he pass or fail?" Mattie bit into her creation, but the distaste of her sister's lies dulled its flavor.

"You tell me." Jenna stole a piece of bacon from Mattie's plate. "Has Gil mentioned anything about the ranch?"

Mattie's gaze darted to her sister's mouth, and she wondered whether this was another game. When had her sister turned into such a pit bull?

"You mean his father's ranch?" Mattie got up to pour herself a cup of coffee. Her hands trembled. "He won't sell."

"I wouldn't be so sure. With a little prodding from Gil, you might be surprised what the old man's capable of, especially in his condition." Jenna rested her elbows on the table and fiddled with the sleeve of her jacket. "I know how upset that makes you. You probably dreamed of settling here with Gil and raising babies, but he'd never be satisfied on this ranch. He and I are the same that way — too confined here."

Mattie lowered her eyes and tried not to let the comment disturb her. "I guess that means you'll be flying to Texas soon." She sipped her coffee, guilt-ridden at wanting her sister gone. There was never any peace with Jenna around.

"I thought I'd spend a few days with the folks. Not that they'll be anymore interested in visiting than you've been. All they talked about at the wedding was Mattie this and Mattie that. I had to beg them to listen to *my* life. They're much more concerned about yours—they always were."

"You're wrong." Mattie pushed the curtains back and watched Gil lead his new roan mare into the barn. "The folks and I hardly ever talked." Sadness welled inside her chest as the words sank into her heart. She didn't feel close to any of her family, not her sisters, nor her parents. The last few months, she'd urged Gil to make amends with his dad. Maybe it was time she took her own advice.

"Well, whatever." Jenna stood and shrugged into her jacket. "Bridgett's the princess who can do no wrong, you're the baby who needs protection, and I'm the black sheep of the family."

Mattie watched her leave. "You don't have to be the black sheep," she said as Jenna stepped out the door.

Jenna turned and smiled. "Like I told Gil—you always see the best in people. That's probably why he loves you so much. I'll admit the thought of going after Gil again was tempting, but when I saw the way he chased after you at the wedding, I knew there wasn't any point. So I willingly concede, and I'm outta here." She blew Mattie a quick kiss and was gone.

GIL HITCHED THE RED ROAN TO A STALL AND HEARD THE HUM OF an engine and the crunch of tires on the gravel outside the barn. He prayed Jenna had left and hadn't bothered his dad about selling the property.

Too bad for her if she did. He certainly knew what it was like to be on the receiving end of his father's tirades.

Footsteps sounded behind him. Light footsteps about the size of a particular doctor's boots. "Did you and your sister have a nice chat?" he asked Mattie without turning.

"No one has nice visits with Jenna." Mattie came up beside Gil. "What about you? I supposed she convinced you to persuade John to accept her offer? You know how much your dad loves this ranch.

How can you do this to him?" She went on before he had a chance to defend himself. "I want to talk to John—to discourage him from selling."

Gil smiled down at her, though tempted to bite back. "After everything I admitted at the reception, what makes you think I'm going to betray him?" He retrieved a currycomb to smooth the tangles from the horse's dark mane, unsure if he and Mattie would ever work out the knots in their relationship.

"Last night I bared my soul to you," he said. "I didn't hold anything back—not even the fact that I love you. I'm not sure what Jenna said, but you need to decide who you're going to trust, Mattie—me or her." He laid the comb down and walked away, just as he'd walked away from the three-year-old in the round pen.

No looking back.

When he reached the house, he took the porch steps two at a time and found his dad reclining in his favorite chair in the living room.

"Did Jenna visit you this morning?"

His father glanced up from his newspaper and frowned. "No, why? Was she here?"

Gil swiped the hair from his forehead, relieved he didn't have to deal with the repercussions of her visit. "She seems to be on a warpath." He checked his jeans for dirt before sitting on the edge of the couch.

"What's going on with her? I get the impression you know more than you're telling." His dad folded the newspaper and waited, his full attention on Gil. "If you're worried you'll upset me, don't be. I feel fine."

This was the moment Gil feared most—the moment when he would come clean about his past—get everything out in the open. He'd told Mattie. Now it was time to tell his dad. He needed to take this step in order to clear his conscience. Hopefully, it wouldn't totally destroy their relationship. His palms dampened with sweat.

"Jenna has her reasons for behaving the way she does." Gil wiped his hands on his jeans. "It started a long time ago, back before Frank died . . ."

GIL WAITED FOR HIS DAD TO SAY SOMETHING . . . ANYTHING TO LET him know he understood or even heard the words spoken the last twenty minutes. At this point, Gil didn't care if his dad hollered in rage. He could deal with anger and frustration. Not silence.

The man twirled his thumbs. "You've kept that hidden all these years? I thought you left the hills because you hated us."

"I've never hated you, Dad. All I ever wanted was your approval — to please you." Gil clasped his hands together. "You don't know how many times I longed to see that gleam in your eyes — the gleam you got when you looked at Frank."

"Was I that bad? I know your mama always took a shine to you . . ." His dad's lips quivered, his eyes downcast. "What happened to Frank wasn't your fault. Not that I approve of what you and Jenna did, but you can't know for sure that Frank would have let you drive his truck. If you'd been with him, I might have lost both my sons that night. I don't blame you for his death, Gil. Neither should you."

Gil knelt by his father's recliner, the way he'd done as a boy, his eyes brimming with moisture.

"What about Mattie? Does she know all this?" His dad laid his hand on Gil's shoulder.

"I told her last night, even admitted I loved her." Gil sniffed back his emotion. "She didn't take it so well."

"I don't suspect she did. Women are funny that way."

He squeezed Gil's neck and seemed at peace, despite everything Gil admitted. The two of them had never spoken so openly to one another, and Gil marveled at it all. "What about the ranch, Dad? You'll have a difficult time running this place with your heart problems. I hate the thought of leaving you, right when things are starting to be good between us."

"Then don't leave. Stay here." His dad reached for his glass of water on the end table.

"You know I want to buy that estate in California. It's a beautiful home, with lots of space and shade. There's even an indoor arena in the barn." Gil stood, hoping to increase his courage. "I want to ask Mattie to marry me, and I'd like you to come with us," he continued. "We can start all over. You can help with the horse operation and watch your grandkids grow up."

His dad took a drink and coughed. "Mattie loves these hills. What's she going to think about California?"

Gil shook his head. "It might take her a while to adjust, but she'll have an easier time with you there. What do you say, Dad? Will you come to California?"

FORTY-EIGHT

Mattie hunched over her desk at the clinic. Her head ached from thinking. What did Gil mean — decide who she trusted? At this moment, she wasn't sure she could trust Gil or Jenna. And certainly not her own heart. Her little beagle traipsed into the room and nestled by her boots. She bent over and picked him up as he licked her hand.

"Why can't everyone be like you?" Except for a few minor incidents when he'd chewed on her boots or some leather tack lying on the ground, the pup had been a perfect companion. Mild mannered, easy to talk to, and better than a pillow to cuddle at night. He didn't argue, either, which made her appreciate him even more. She scratched behind his floppy ears until his hind foot thumped against her thigh.

The pup stared up at her with big brown eyes. "The world would be a better place if more people were like you." She kissed his nose, and he licked her chin. Her phone chimed, and she set the beagle on the floor. She noted the caller ID on the digital display and groaned.

"Hi, Mom." Mattie's forced enthusiasm sounded less than

convincing. "I guess you and Dad made it home okay after the wedding."

"That's why I'm calling." Her mother's voice resonated concern. "Your dad and I were worried about you. We saw you arguing with Gil last night. Is everything okay?"

Mattie squeezed her eyes shut. She'd caused a scene at the reception for all to discuss this morning. "I'm fine."

"You don't sound fine," her mother said. "Your dad wondered if you'd like to come over. Have a late lunch with us tomorrow after church. Jenna's going to be here. We can invite Bridgett and the kids, as well."

The pup gnawed on the toe of her boot, and Mattie nudged him away. "I don't know ..." Although a part of her wanted to be closer to her parents, she didn't care to see Jenna again so soon. "Can I get back to you, Mom? I'm pretty swamped at work right now."

Swamped with worries.

"Sure, but we'd love to see you, Mattie. We never get a chance to talk anymore — you're always so busy." Her mother sighed on the other end, and Mattie's irritation grew. "You know you can talk to us about anything."

"I appreciate that, Mom. I'll call you back as soon as I can."

GIL STARED OUT THE LIVING ROOM WINDOW. IN THE DISTANCE, THE hills they'd burned earlier that week now hinted at buds of pea-green. "I know you love this place." He glanced at his dad in the recliner. "I would never ask you to leave if I didn't think it was best for all of us. We could put the ranch in a trust — come and visit whenever you wanted."

His dad hung his head. "What good would a trust do?" His voice rumbled, thick and gravelly.

Gil returned to the couch and clasped his hands. "We could have an attorney draw up papers. Make provisions for a friend to run the place—maybe Jake, if he'd agree to it. It's the safest way to ensure the land stays in the McCray family. Who knows, one of my kids or grandchildren might decide to live here some day." His heart tugged inside his chest at the thought.

"If you ever have kids." His father pushed himself up from the recliner. Cane in hand, he shuffled to the buffet cabinet where he pulled out a drawer in search of something. Minutes later, he returned with a black velvet box.

"You might try giving this to Mattie the next time you propose." He handed it to Gil and made his way back to his recliner, short of breath. "Your mama would have wanted you to have it. She would have liked Mattie."

Gil opened the box to see a simple diamond solitaire set in white gold. "I can't take this." He closed the lid to give it back to his dad.

"Sure you can. Do it right this time and maybe she'll accept."

"Does that mean you'll come to California with us?" Gil tried to keep the excitement from his voice, knowing the decision would not be easy.

His dad seemed to chew on the question. After a few minutes, he replied, "I always thought I'd live out my days in these hills." His words came out soft and wistful like the leaves on a cottonwood when the spring winds blow. "One lesson I've learned is that life never turns out quite like you expect. I never expected Frank and your mama to die so early in their lives. It nearly ripped my heart apart—but time heals even the worst pain. I never expected you to run off to California to be a superstar football player . . . and I never expected you to come home—but you did."

He rubbed his mouth with wide, thick fingers. "My pride wouldn't let me go to any of your football games. Because of pride, we missed a lot of years—you and I." He sat up in the chair and leaned on his cane. "If going to California will somehow make up for that, I'm willing to give it a try."

Humbled by the man's selflessness, Gil knelt down and offered him a hug. "You won't regret this, Dad. I promise. You'll have a better life than you've ever known in Kansas."

"You don't need to make me any promises. Just get that girl of yours to say yes, 'cause I refuse to die before I jostle a grandbaby on my knee." He stretched in his recliner and stared up at the ceiling, twirling his thumbs.

Gil's throat tightened. He could hardly believe his dad agreed to give up the ranch so easily. No argument — barely a hesitation. Now he had only to convince Mattie that a life with him in California was the right decision.

The next morning, Gil led his father to an empty pew at New Redeemer Church. Scanning the aisles for Mattie's red hair, he spotted Clara and her three children toward the front, but he couldn't distinguish the person next to them. Rather than agonize over Mattie's presence, he put his mind on the hymns and words of Scripture, thankful to have his dad seated beside him. When the sermon concluded, a throng of people gathered around them, welcoming his dad to the service.

"John, I'm so glad you decided to join us."

Gil turned at the familiar voice and saw Mattie shake his father's hand. She looked up at Gil, her eyes like dew on grass.

"You never told me you'd convinced your dad to come to church."

Gil noted how pretty she looked, the sway of her dress, her hair draped over her shoulders in a partial ponytail that complimented her face. "I didn't know until this morning."

He caught her hand and pulled her to the side. "Join us for lunch?"

Mattie stared out at the churchyard where the kids played. "I've made plans already."

"Change them," Gil's father said, having apparently overhead their conversation.

Her brow furrowed, and Gil recognized her struggle.

"No, that's alright." He lowered his voice for her. "If you can't do lunch, maybe we could take Dusty out for a ride in the pasture this afternoon. I need to speak to you about something important."

He gazed into her eyes, hopeful.

Please say yes.

If she refused, what would he do? Beg? Walk away? Gil prayed he wouldn't have to find out.

FORTY-NINE

MATTIE LOWERED HER GAZE, DETERMINED NOT TO GIVE IN TOO easily to Gil's eager demand. "I don't know. As I said, I have another commitment."

She glanced up to see him no longer smiling, his chin firmly set. "What about tonight, then? We could ride before dark."

Mattie struggled for an answer. Oh, how she wanted things to be right between them . . . but how could she get over the fact that he'd been with her sister — as intimate as a man could be with a woman? Not to mention that he'd betrayed his brother in the process. *Had he really changed?*

Could she trust him with her heart, her very soul?

"I'll meet you in the barn around three," Mattie finally said, then rushed outside before she could change her mind. As she walked to her truck, she noticed the land, stretched out into gently rolling hills, barren except for a few trees that dotted the prairie. Soon cattle would graze the bluestem pastures, and all of nature would come out of its long, winter slump.

The wind whipped the soft material of Mattie's dress, and her heels poked into the moist earth, made damp from an overnight shower. Springtime offered much to look forward to—the greening of the hills, wildflowers, cool water from the deep stream wells.

If only Gil would give up his notion of California and stay on at his father's ranch. They could experience this new season in the hills together, and she'd have more time to witness his true character. She watched as Gil and John made their way down the church steps.

Seeing them together, she realized that some miracles do happen. Would a miracle happen for her and Gil too? She dug in her purse for her cell phone. Minutes later, Mattie heard her mother's voice on the answering machine. The poor reception crackled in her ears.

"Hey Mom, something has come up. I won't be able to make lunch this afternoon. Sorry. I'll call you later and maybe we can reschedule."

Mattie placed the phone in her purse. What did Gil want to discuss with her that was so important? She wasn't sure she wanted to know, but she was holding out hope for a miracle.

A LITTLE BEFORE THREE, MATTIE ENTERED THE BARN WHERE GIL saddled Tulip. She debated turning around as fear gripped her stomach.

Gil looked up and grinned beneath his straw cowboy hat. "It's a nice afternoon for a ride. A bluebird day, my mama used to say."

Mattie took the leather straps from Gil's hands, deeply aware of how handsome he looked in a chambray shirt and blue jeans. "I see you've saddled your new mare."

"I worked the filly in the round pen yesterday and figured this afternoon would be a good time to see how the mare performs." He moved to the red roan and placed the bridle on her head.

Mattie adjusted the cinch against Tulip's girth, then went out to halter Dusty. The chestnut gelding snorted at the pasture gate and thumped his hoof into the dirt.

"How you doing there, boy?" She smoothed her hand down his chest and forearms and inhaled the horsy scent, noting the excellent progress in his healing. It'd been nearly four months since his accident. She never believed he would come out of his injuries so quickly. That he'd been brought back to health through tender loving care made her heart swell with affection for the old boy. "Have you thought any more about what you'll do with Dusty, once he's fully recovered?" she asked when Gil stepped out of the barn with the two mares.

Gil rubbed his jaw. "I don't know, maybe I'll turn him out to pasture and let him pick on the new horse like you suggested." He chuckled and climbed into his saddle.

Mattie snapped the lead rope onto Dusty's halter, then mounted Tulip, the leather seat squeaking beneath her as they took off at a walk toward the north pasture. "There's no reason you couldn't ride him. I've been reading about one-eyed horses that perform in reining competitions and much more. You should be able to enjoy him for years to come."

Gil settled in beside her and adjusted his hat. "I appreciate all you've done with Dusty. You put your heart into his recuperation —and you succeeded. I admire you for that."

Never one to take compliments well, and especially not from Gil, she swallowed past the lump in her throat. "I only did my job. That's what you paid me for."

"And you were worth every penny." He grinned, but a hint of sadness marked his cheerful expression. "I thought we might take the horses to Lightning Creek. With all the spring showers, it ought to be flowing good and strong."

Not interested in small talk, Mattie nudged the gray mare into a trot. Gil followed on his roan. The three traveled over the rolling prairie, slowing only to cross the deep ravines and rocky gulches. As they rode, puffy clouds formed in the blue sky. A red-tailed hawk screeched from high above, while an eastern meadowlark flew out in front of them with grass in its beak. They reached the top of a hill and a meandering creek stretched in the valley below, marked by lofty bur oaks.

Mattie reined Tulip to a stop, and Gil halted his mare beside her, his face beaming. "Looks like a good place to rest."

She glanced back at Dusty. The gelding's nostrils flared from exertion, but he also seemed to share Gil's excitement.

They got off and walked the horses down the hill, then let them drink from the clear, rock-bedded stream.

"I haven't had that much fun in a long time." Gil laughed and tied the horses to a fallen log. "You should have seen my mare's tail switch when you took the lead."

Mattie knelt on a large flint outcropping and dipped her fingers into the cool shallow water. "I guess females are alike that way. A little competition tends to make us switchy."

Gil came to her side and stretched his long legs on the slab of rock. "After our argument the other night, I wasn't sure you'd give me the time of day, let alone talk to me."

She concentrated on the clear water as it flowed between her fingers and washed over the white pebbles. "I'm not against you, Gil, but that doesn't mean I'm willing to be with you. I need time to sort things out in my head."

"There's nothing I'd rather give you, but right now I have to make a decision—about the estate in California."

Mattie's stomach fluttered, afraid of what he might say next.

"You know I love you, Mattie. I hope I've made that very clear. If anything, my love for you is greater now because you didn't reject me when I told you about Frank and Jenna. Dad didn't either."

Her eyes darted to his. "You told John?"

Gil nodded.

"We talked last night. I told him everything." He paused for a minute and stared at the ripples created by her fingers. "I asked him to come to California with me … with us … if you'll marry me."

Mattie's throat tightened in alarm. "What did he say?"

Gil reached for her hand and pulled it out of the cool water. "He agreed. I hope you will too."

"He's selling the ranch to Jenna?" Mattie closed her eyes, unable to believe Gil had gone through with her sister's plan.

"No, not to Jenna." He entwined his fingers through hers. "We've decided to put the ranch into a trust, so we can come and visit—hold it for future generations."

Mattie shook her head in disbelief. "How can you do this, Gil? This land is his life. He'll shrivel up and die in California."

"Not if we start a new life, Mattie. He wants to watch his grandkids grow up—our children. He wants to make up for the time we've lost."

"You can do that here. On this ranch ... the land you grew up on. Didn't this ride ... doesn't this beauty ... mean anything to you?" She pulled her hand from his and braced her temple—watched a centipede crawl over the grooves and crevices in the flinty limestone.

"Of course it did. But everywhere I look, I think of my brother."

"Is that so bad?"

"Yes, because it reminds me of what could have been," he said. "I want to move on with my life, not be constantly reminded of my mistakes."

"You think you've confronted your past by admitting your actions from long ago, but you're still running, Gil. If you weren't, you wouldn't be so determined to uproot your dad, to deny him the chance to live out his days on his own land."

"He wants to go."

"You didn't give him an option, did you? It was either the ranch or you."

Gil dug in his front jean pocket. Seconds later, he pulled out a small velvet box. "He could have said no. So can you, but I pray you won't." He opened the box to reveal a beautiful diamond solitaire. "Marry me, Mattie. Build a new life with me and Dad in California."

Mattie covered her mouth with trembling fingers. Her mind raced with the possibilities. Gil wanted to marry her, but could she trust him—completely forgive him? She'd finally have the love she always dreamed of, be able to raise a family, work as a vet in a brand new facility on her own property alongside the man she loved. The proposal seemed almost perfect.

She gazed out at the pasture beyond Lightning Creek. Almost, but not quite.

The green hills swelled and nearly boasted of their beauty. To her, there was nothing more perfect than this tranquil land she cherished, the cattle it fed, and the people who tended it.

A tear coursed down her cheek.

She knew what her answer had to be.

FIFTY

GIL WIPED THE TEAR FROM HER FACE, UNSURE WHETHER MATTIE cried from joy or sorrow. He took the ring from the box and slipped it on the tip of her finger. "Say yes, Mattie. We'll be happy together, I promise."

Mattie stared down at the ring on her finger, and new tears filled her eyes. "It's beautiful, Gil, but I can't marry you."

At her rejection, Gil's muscles tensed. Blood rushed to his head in a flash of frustration and pain. "You don't love me?"

"I do love you. I love you with all my heart. That's why I have to say no."

"That doesn't make any sense. Is it because of Jenna?"

She took the ring from her finger and gave it back to him. "I once believed God meant for us to be together. But I was wrong. We're too different. I could never accept your proposal knowing I'd grow to resent you some day for taking me from here, this land of my heart."

"We can visit as much as you and Dad want. I know you love it here, but you'll grow to love California. We can be together there. At least think about it." He pressed the ring in her palm, praying she'd reconsider.

She shook her head. "I don't need to think about it. I've known all along that we wanted different things. I clung to the hope that you'd remember your love for this place—that it would be enough for you. But it's not." Mattie wiped the tears from her cheek, then gestured toward the pasture. "All of this could have been ours, Gil, if it weren't for the burden you carry." She dropped the ring in his lap and stood. Her boots scraped against the flat stone.

Gil watched as she moved to the oaks where Tulip munched on some fresh new grass. "That's all you're going to say? You're going to turn your back on us because of this silly land?"

Her face pinched, wounded by his callousness. "I'm going to take Dusty and your father's mare to the barn," she said, her words barely audible. "I'd appreciate it if you'd give me some time alone."

With a heavy heart, Gil watched Mattie ride away. He wove his mother's ring between his fingers as the horses' metal shoes retreated against the flint rock. Why had God put Mattie in his path if they weren't meant to be together? He lay on the rock and heard his new mare fuss as the other horses abandoned her. His heart ached with grief, much as it had when the pallbearers carried his mother to her grave—only worse. This hurt even worse.

Mattie had turned him down.

Gil pushed himself hard the next two weeks, forcing Mattie from his head and heart. He longed for earlier days when he could plow into a lineman and crush him to the ground. At least then, he'd work off some of his aggression.

On Thursday, he tore his shirtsleeve on the barbed wire fence he and Jake were stringing. He kicked the fence post, angry at the world and everything around him.

"It's about time we finish this job. I'm sick of building fence on this rocky soil." Gil removed his straw hat and wiped his forehead with a red bandana before taking a swig from the water jug on the four-wheeler.

Jake waited for his turn. "Heard anything from that realtor of yours?"

Gil handed the plastic thermos to the ranch hand. "Nope."

"You surely offered enough, didn't you?"

He glared at the old man. If the estate owners didn't accept his offer, they were stupid. "If my bid doesn't buy it, nothing will."

Jake scratched his bristly chin before taking a drink. "You'd think they'd snatch it up for fear you'll back out."

It did seem strange, which made Gil even edgier. To make matters worse, this first week in May yielded temperatures in the low nineties, and sweat dripped from Gil's nose and down his back. At least in California, he wouldn't have to deal with this lousy humidity.

"Won't be the same here without you." Jake dropped the spout on the water thermos and leaned against the four-wheeler. "When are you and your dad plannin' to head out?"

Gil filed through his mental list of things to do on the ranch. The house had been sprayed with silicone and its roof shingled, the pastures burned, the buildings and windmills repaired. All that remained was the fencing. "We ought to be able to start packing as soon as I hear back on my offer," Gil said. "Hopefully in another week or two."

His stomach clenched as he considered leaving without Mattie. He flung his tools on the cart behind the four-wheeler, then headed on foot toward the ranch.

"Don't you want a ride to the barn?" Jake called after him.

Gil lifted his hand in refusal. "I feel like walking," he muttered into the wind.

One week later, Mattie pulled up to the clinic after a call to treat a horse that had gotten its foot snagged in barbed wire. As she climbed out of her truck, her cell phone chimed. She answered, hoping it wasn't another emergency.

"I see you made it back." John McCray's voice boomed on the other end. "You're a hard lady to get a hold of. I decided if I was going to talk to you, I'd have to call you on your fancy phone."

Mattie glanced at the house and saw John standing on the veranda, phone in hand. She smiled and waved. "Work's been keeping me busy. What did you need to talk about?"

"Mildred's fixing some tea. Come up here and visit an old man for a few minutes. Have some tea with me."

Ever since Gil's proposal, Mattie had purposely steered clear of anyone in the house, fearing they'd want to talk about her and Gil. She knew she couldn't avoid them forever. "Let me check in at the clinic; then I'll be up in a few minutes."

MATTIE SAT AT THE WROUGHT IRON TABLE ON THE VERANDA AND poured chamomile tea into two china cups. "I'm glad you're letting Mildred take such good care of you." She placed the teapot on the table and stirred the amber liquid in her cup.

"Tea in the morning reminds me of when Gil's mama was alive." John lifted the cup to his lips, the handle too small for his big fingers. "Gil tells me you turned down his offer to marry him."

Mattie watched as an orange-bellied swallow worked to build a nest in the corner of the porch. "That's right. If it's all the same to you, though, I'd rather not talk about it."

"I figure your mind's made up." He glanced at the roof and coughed. "Those pesky swallows. Always building their nests here instead of in the barn. I suppose they've been leaving messes on the porch ever since my great-granddad built the place." John poked his cane at the birds.

"You don't have to leave, you know." Mattie felt compelled to discourage the man from moving from the only home he'd ever known.

"Gil wants me to." He drank from his cup and when he finished his tea, he stared at her from across the table. "I know you love this place and these hills. You've been like a daughter to me these past few years." He reached for her hand and rested his thick fingers on hers.

"I have a proposition for you. I want you to serve as the trustee for the Lightning M. Run your clinic here — make this your home. We can create a provision that when I die the land will go to you, as long as no heirs claim the ranch."

Mattie blinked as she processed his words. John wanted to give her the ranch — seven thousand acres of prime grassland in the heart of the Flint Hills. "I can't accept such a generous offer, John. It wouldn't be fair to Gil."

He squeezed her fingers. "Who else can I entrust with the job? Jake will manage the land and cattle as long as he's able and will teach you everything you need to know for when he's gone. Mildred, too, if you want her. If not, she's mentioned moving to Houston to be closer to her grandkids." He puckered his lips, and his eyes glazed with moisture. "I'd hoped to see my own grandchildren before I die, but I'll have to be content with a new life with my son."

Mattie's throat constricted as the man wiped his eyes on a napkin. How could she agree to such a request? To live in the same house where Gil grew up? To surround herself with memories of him and to force herself to stay in touch? "Does Gil know about this?"

"It's my land to do with as I please."

She shook her head. It would be too painful. "I can't do it."

John nodded. "Think long and hard before you say no. You abandoned Gil for these hills. It'd be a shame for you to give them up as well ... especially when they're right here at your fingertips."

LATE THAT EVENING, MATTIE PRESSED THE SPEED DIAL ON HER CELL phone, hoping she wouldn't get the answering machine again.

She didn't. This time her dad picked up.

"Hi, Daddy." Her voice came out a soft whimper. "Can I come home? I need to talk to you."

FIFTY-ONE

Gil sat on the top rail of Dusty's pen and stared into the moonlight. The fence work now complete, all that remained was packing his father's belongings. Then he could get back to his life in California—and start getting over a certain lady veterinarian.

The first three truckloads of cattle would soon ship to their pastures for summer grazing, but by then, he and his dad should be gone. Jake and two hired hands would serve as pasturemen for the season. Every detail had been attended to, including assigning Mattie as trustee for the ranch—if she agreed.

He rubbed the muscles of his neck, which ached from long hours of building fence. It boggled his mind that his dad asked Mattie to serve as custodian, but he guessed it made sense. She would stay on at the ranch, and he would leave.

You're still running.

Mattie's accusation haunted him. He remembered the morning he'd wrestled with the bull when she'd called him a coward. Nearly a month had passed since he'd proposed to her, and other than a brief hello at church on Sundays, the two of them hadn't spoken. His heart ached for her, but what could he do? She was too stubborn to see that he couldn't live here.

Or was he really a coward?

The shuffling sound of boots in the grass prompted him to glance behind into the darkness.

"I thought it might be you out here." Jake came up beside him and rested his arms on the top rail. A full moon shown above and cast an ethereal glow on the old man and his cowboy hat.

"Am I wrong to take Dad from this land?" Gil asked.

Jake spit a stream of tobacco to the ground. "You really wanna know what I think?"

"I wouldn't have asked if I didn't."

"Seems to me you're carrying a world of hurt inside you. Been carrying it a lot of years now. For some reason, these hills don't offer you the medicine they do for others. Don't know why, exactly."

"You believe I'm running too?"

"There are those who love these hills, and those who can't wait to get away." Dusty came up to the fence, and Jake reached out to pet the horse's nose. "When I first started work here, I remember a youngster who couldn't wait to go outside and help his dad, whether that meant mucking stalls in the barn or working cattle in the pasture. That boy wanted to throw a rope and ride his pony, eager for the day and mad at night when his mama made him come in for a bath and supper." The ranch hand grinned, his smile lit by the moonlight.

"He once told me he'd never leave this ranch — couldn't pry him from it with a fence post," Jake added. "You're all grown up now, but I reckon that boy's inside you yet."

Gil zoomed back to the days of his youth, before Jenna, before they lost Frank, to a time when he'd been content following his dad through the many chores on the ranch. He remembered his mama wrapping her arms around him after they'd said their bedtime prayers, and then there was Frank, the big brother Gil looked up to and whose footsteps he wanted to follow.

He closed his eyes and let himself remember.

THE NEXT AFTERNOON, MATTIE SAT ON HER PARENTS' TERRACE WITH her father, having left Travis in charge of her patients for the entire weekend.

"It's going to be nice having you here," he said. "We've been worried about you, Mattie girl. You sounded quite upset last night when you called."

Mattie's face heated, embarrassed at her display of emotion.

He stretched his arm along the back of the gliding bench, and Mattie rested her head against it. She gazed at her mother's patio flowers—irises and pansies in a multitude of colors.

"Come on, talk to me. What's troubling you? Does it have anything to do with the fight you had with that fellow of yours?"

"You could say that." Mattie closed her eyes and prayed for the right words to tell her father. She wanted to share with him everything she'd been going through, but at the same time, she didn't want to hurt him.

"Jenna seemed to think you might still be upset with us for moving to the city." He lifted his arm from her neck and straightened in the metal glider. "Is that part of it?"

Mattie turned to him and noted the new wrinkles on his face, the lines at the corner of his gray eyes. "I wish you lived closer—that we were closer."

Her father nodded. "I've blamed myself a hundred times for not trying harder to keep the home place or resettle there. Your mother has too. But we can't undo our mistakes … I'm not sure we would if we had the chance. You have to understand that times were hard for us then."

"I think I'm beginning to understand how complicated things can become," she said. All her life, Mattie considered the Flint Hills her home, her destiny, especially after her parents lost their ranch. Owning property there—getting back the land they'd lost had become her obsession.

Now that she had the chance to make that dream a reality, the thought didn't hold as much satisfaction as it once had. "I'm so confused," she said, then proceeded to tell about Gil's deception and proposal, and John's offer to let her oversee the Lightning M.

"Sounds like you've got quite a predicament." Her dad scratched his thinning hair. "You know I can't tell you what to do. People make mistakes—some worse than others. I'm sure Gil regrets that he wasn't upfront with you from the start. As for the land, your mom and I made a decision to leave Charris County. I won't lie to you—there are days when my heart aches for the smooth feel of leather reins in my hands, or for the pungent smell of freshly mown prairie hay. But we've adjusted. We made ourselves a new home and life." He offered her a reticent smile. "I traded my cowboy boots in for a pair of loafers."

Mattie nudged his thick waist. "You still wear your boots to church. I've seen you."

He shrugged. "True, but I've discovered loafers can fit comfortably too. Know what I mean, Mattie? The point is, your mom and I loved each other through all those hard years, and we made another life work for us. In the end, the land won't keep you warm at night."

His last statement rang inside Mattie's head. She'd heard similar words from John. But still ... to trade the simplicity of Kansas for California and give Gil her heart? She didn't know if she could take such a leap of faith.

ON A MISSION TO PUT TO REST THE BAD MEMORIES AND REPLACE them with a few good ones, Gil drove past Miller's pond where he and his buddies fished for crawdads and frogs. He revisited the rodeo grounds where Frank and he roped steers, and even spent some time at the football stadium. When he'd reminisced enough, he turned onto a winding dirt road through the Flint Hills, passing over several pasture guards until he finally arrived at the edge of Emporia.

Prompted to visit the Marshall boy again, to see if his recovery had been as good as Dusty's, Gil pulled into the parking lot of the hospital and turned off the diesel engine. A receptionist at the front desk gave Gil directions to the rehabilitation unit where he'd heard Dillon was receiving further care. He headed for the elevators and eventually found the teen in the rehab dining hall sitting in a wheelchair. When he approached the boy's table, the attendant stood to offer Gil his seat.

Dillon looked up, and his lips formed into a lopsided grin. "Didn't think I'd see you again, Mr. McCray."

Gil took the chair opposite the boy. "Me neither. And please call me Gil. Mr. McCray sounds so old," he teased, then latched onto an extra straw on the table, trying not to notice the deep scars on the boy's face. "How are you doing?"

Dillon looked down at his motionless legs. "I'm learning to get around. Me and another boy race the halls."

"That's cool." Gil struggled with the awkwardness, not sure what to say next. Why'd he even come?

"How 'bout you?" Dillon asked, his words slightly slurred. "How's your horse?"

Gil tore the paper from the straw and tied it into a knot. "Dusty's good. I'm good."

"Don't you live in California?"

The boy's sharp memory surprised Gil. "I had some things I needed to take care of here on my dad's ranch."

Dillon took a bite of his lasagna, then shoved the plate to the side. "I've thought a lot about what you said when you were here before. Got lots of time to think now."

Gil forced a smile.

"I've been reading the Bible." Dillon placed his hands on the side of his chair and pushed the wheels backward. "Come on, I have something I want to show you."

Gil followed Dillon down the hall to his room. The football he'd given him sat on the windowsill and a game show blared from a television high on the wall. The teen went straight to a Bible that lay on his nightstand.

"I killed my friend," Dillon said. "I have to live with that. You wished you could have saved your brother. I know what guilt can do—I feel it every day." He opened the Bible, then thumbed through the onionskin pages to a passage in the middle, marked by a red ribbon.

"People tell me I need to forgive myself, so I can go on." The boy's voice shook with irritation. "Why do they say that? Who am I to forgive myself?" He punched a button on the remote control and the television screen went blank. The only sound in the room now came from Dillon's wheezing breath, and the thumping pulse in Gil's neck.

"Forgiveness is important." Gil hoped to calm the boy—make him feel better. "Without it, we'd be lost."

"But I didn't just sin against myself, I sinned against God. This book showed me that." He searched the open page until his finger landed on a verse. "Here, look what else I found."

He handed the Bible to Gil, and Gil read the verses he indicated. "The Lord is compassionate and gracious, slow to anger, abounding in love."

The boy pointed further down the page. "According to this, God won't be angry at me forever. He won't blame me for the awful things I've done—as long as I'm truly sorry."

Dillon took the Bible in his hands and laid it on his lap. "I'm not the smartest kid in my class. But I know who my Savior is. And I know that I'm forgiven."

He stared down at his lap and began reading. "As far as the east is from the west, so far has he removed our transgressions from us."

His voice grew hoarser with every word spoken. "As a father has compassion on his children, so the Lord has compassion on those who fear him; for he knows how we are formed, he remembers that we are dust."

"As for man, his days are like grass ..." Gil finished the familiar passage, the same verse he'd recited to his dad.

It was as though Gil understood the words for the very first time.

FIFTY-TWO

"They're letting me go home tomorrow," Dillon said after the two had talked for over an hour. "I'd give anything to go to the high school rodeo this weekend in Diamond Falls. But Dad won't let me. Says it'd be too much of a strain."

During their visit, Gil learned that Dillon had team roped, and that he'd been good with a horse. An idea began to form. "What if I could arrange for you to go? Would you be willing to speak in front of your peers? Admit to them what you told me tonight?"

The boy nodded. "If it might keep one of my friends from making the stupid mistake I made, you bet I would."

Gil calculated the steps needed to accomplish what he had in mind. He fingered the smooth face of the watch in his pocket. There just might be enough time to put his plan into motion.

Forty minutes later, Gil pulled off the side of the road at an abandoned homestead and picked a handful of purple iris. He had one more stop to make before going home. The sweet scent of the spring flowers filled the truck cab as he drove to the cemetery. He followed the path to the stone markers and knelt beside his mother's grave.

"I'm sorry, Mama, for not telling you good-bye." He laid the flowers on the granite rock. "I wish you could've met Mattie. She's so much like you—I think you would have approved."

He fingered the smooth marble, then turned to Frank's grave. "And you, big brother. I'm sorry I wasn't there for you the night you died. I made a lot of mistakes back then, but that's the one I hate the most—that and what I did with Jenna." Gil looked toward the setting sun and raised his voice to God, his mouth praying the verses he'd read.

"Search me and know my heart, Lord. Do not harbor your anger toward me forever. As far as the east is from the west, so far have you removed my transgressions from me. I believe it, Lord. Help me believe it."

Once the words were out, an immense burden lifted from Gil's chest. For the first time in twenty years he felt truly free—free to live the life God wanted him to live. He lifted himself from the moist ground, and as he did so, the metal timepiece in his pocket seemed to weigh him down. Knowing then what needed to be done, Gil reached into his jeans and pulled out the silver watch his coach had given him in California.

"Coach, I know you'd understand my reason for passing this on," he murmured and laid the watch on Frank's gravestone, no longer needing to keep track of the time.

"I'M GOING TO MISS THESE HILLS," HIS DAD SAID THE NEXT MORNING as the two of them stood out on the veranda. The sun peeked over the eastern horizon and cast a warm yellow glow over the land.

"No, you won't," Gil assured him and squeezed the man's shoulders. "Why don't you and Jake go into town and have breakfast at the café. I have plenty here to keep me busy." He searched the barnyard for Mattie's truck. "You haven't seen the doc this morning, have you?"

"Ain't seen her since Thursday." His father's lips twisted into an ornery grin. "You gonna talk to her again?"

Gil let the question slide. "I'll send Jake to pick you up so the two of you can catch up on all the news in town. Wouldn't want you to miss out on this week's highlights."

"The only talk this week will be about our leaving," his dad said. "Guess now's as good a time as any to say good-bye."

Gil patted his father's shoulders. "It won't be so bad, you'll see," he said, then headed down the steps for Mattie's cabin.

When he knocked on her door, she wasn't there.

He searched the clinic.

Upon finding it empty, he walked out to check Dusty's water. The chestnut nickered and met Gil at the trough. Gil smoothed his hand over the gelding's back and hindquarters. His chest and front legs were healing well, and the scars on Dusty's face had turned a shiny black.

"How you doing there, boy?"

Dusty placed his head in the crook of Gil's arm. He rubbed the horse's nose with affection.

Trust.

Dusty had always trusted him, even when he didn't deserve it.

Gil thought of his plan for Dillon and the high school rodeo.

"Hey, buddy." Gil leaned down and pressed his forehead against Dusty's. "I need you to trust me once more. It's going to be hard, but I have one last job for you to do for me."

GIL DROVE INTO DIAMOND FALLS TO TALK TO SOME PEOPLE ABOUT the rodeo, including Dillon's dad. After he'd taken care of his business, he stopped by Clara's Café.

"Heard anything from Mattie?" he asked when the waitress approached him with a menu.

Clara frowned. "What's it to you?"

The woman either knew about the proposal or had heard the news about them leaving the ranch. The hostility in the air was enough to choke on. "It's everything to me," Gil said quietly, beseeching Mattie's friend with his eyes. "Do you know where she is?"

Clara slapped the menu on the counter by his elbow. "Maybe."

"Come on, Clara. You either know or you don't."

"She went to see her folks this weekend. Maybe her mom finally talked her into applying for a job there." The woman placed her hands on her hips, unmoved by his pleas. "I wouldn't blame Mattie if she gave in. Not much of a future for her here."

Gil stared down at the menu. Was Mattie that desperate? He'd never known her to spend any amount of time in the city, let alone an entire weekend. "When will she be back?"

Clara pursed her lips and shook her head. "Even if I knew, I wouldn't tell you."

Gil had tolerated enough of this woman's antagonism. "Listen, Clara, I know you're sore with me, but I need you to do me a favor." He took a pen from his shirt pocket and scribbled a note on a napkin. "It's important. Make sure Mattie gets this message and comes to the rodeo tomorrow afternoon."

"What if she refuses?"

He stood up from the stool and towered over the woman. "Clara, if you truly want Mattie to be happy, see that she's at the arena at one o'clock. I don't care if you have to hogtie her to your car."

The next afternoon, Gil searched the crowded stands for Mattie's red hair. From where he stood, he couldn't see her anywhere, but he spotted his dad, Jake, and Mildred on the bottom level of the middle bleachers.

Dillon and his parents waited by Gil's side at the arena gates. He gave the boy in the wheelchair a reassuring smile. "You ready?"

Dillon nodded but looked like he might puke his guts out.

"The first minute is always the worst. After that, you'll be fine," Gil said, then turned to Dusty and adjusted the saddle once more.

He patted the gelding, feeling a tad nervous himself. With all his charity work and the crowds he'd spoken to, he'd never done anything quite like this before. The preliminary music played over the loudspeakers—Gil's cue to begin.

"Okay, here goes nothing." He mounted Dusty, then adjusted his hat and took the flag handed him. As he entered the arena, the entire crowd stood as the national anthem began to play. He commenced at a walk, then eased Dusty into a trot, taking it slow as he'd done yesterday in the pasture. When he felt the horse ready, Gil clicked him into an easy lope, and together the two moved as one to the rhythm of the music.

The flag whipped above his head as he circled the arena. When the song neared its end, Gil positioned Dusty in the center of the ring, humbled by the massive applause. An older gentleman and a rodeo queen came out to meet him. He passed the wooden pole to the girl, who turned out to be Natalie Adams. She winked up at him and smiled. Then the gentleman handed him a cordless microphone.

Silence filled the stands. Gil swore he could hear his heart beating inside his chest.

"I want to thank you for allowing me to speak here today," he began. "For those who don't know me, my name's Gilbert McCray. I grew up in Charris County and participated in a few rodeos like this one. Then my older brother Frank died in a vehicle accident. He and his friend were drunk, and both were killed. For a long time, I blamed myself for what happened to Frank. I moved away and became a quarterback for the San Francisco 49ers. Recently I came back, but only because of an accident involving the horse I'm on now.

"Five months ago, Dusty nearly died when a drunk driver ran into him. He lost a lot of blood and injured his upper legs, chest, and eye. The veterinarian handling the case suggested putting him down, but my dad wouldn't let her. Because of my father's determination and the special care Dusty received from Dr. Mattie Evans, I'm able to ride Dusty today, the same horse I trained over twenty-two years ago."

Sighs of disbelief escaped from the crowd, along with a few encouraging whistles.

"I'm telling you this, because I want you to know that good things can come from bad. Even the worst sins can be forgiven. My sins are no exception. Yours aren't either. A young man convinced me of this the other day, and you'll be hearing from him in a few minutes."

Gil swallowed to relieve the dryness in his throat. He clutched the saddle horn to keep his hand from trembling and glanced at the two behind him. They nodded their support. "Dusty's better today and will soon be retired to pasture, like me."

He grinned and returned his eyes to the crowd.

"Some of you may have heard the recent stir that my father and I are leaving the Flint Hills to retire out in California. I'd like to put that rumor to rest."

Gil targeted his dad in the audience and smiled. "California was a nice idea, but it was a mistake. This is my home. Dad and I will not be moving, but will stay at the Lightning M to graze cattle for as long as God allows." He took a quick breath and continued before he chickened out. "There's another rumor floating around that I'd like to tackle, if you'll hang with me for a few more minutes."

He paused and searched the assembly. "Is Dr. Evans in the stands this afternoon?"

The crowd stirred with laughter and a few hoots.

"If you're sitting by Mattie Evans, would you please wave your hand? The doc is kinda short, with red hair and green eyes, and she's probably extremely embarrassed right now."

An older woman on the far end of the bleachers stood and

waved. "Here she is, Gil." She tugged on the lady next to her, and Mattie slowly rose.

The audience began chanting Mattie's name, and Gil beckoned her to come to the center of the arena. Mattie shook her head vigorously, but at the urgings of the crowd, she slowly began making her way down the bleachers.

"Four weeks ago, I asked this woman to marry me." Gil spoke into the microphone and ignored the whoops from the audience, concentrating on Mattie as she walked out across the cultivated dirt. "She turned me down, but I'd like to try again and see if her answer is any different—now that we won't be moving to California."

Mattie stopped halfway between him and the bleachers. Afraid she might change her mind, Gil slipped from the saddle and flipped off the microphone. He closed the distance between them and knelt before her, shutting out the sound of the crowd much like he'd done all those years playing football.

Dressed in blue jeans and a green-checkered western shirt with her long curls flowing in the afternoon sunlight, Mattie looked more beautiful than he'd ever seen her before. He might never remember what she wore this day, but Gil was sure the shiny gleam in her eyes would stay with him the rest of his life.

He took his hat off and held it in his hand. "What do you say, Doc? Will you marry me?"

She sent him a scolding look that promised more conversation later. Then she held out the napkin with words written in blue ink. *I'm sorry—I've been a fool.*

"I'm sorry too," she said, and her mouth twitched as though she might cry. "If you really want to move to California, I'm prepared to go with you."

Gil stood and pulled her into his arms. "Do you know how much I love you, woman? I love that you're willing to sacrifice your dreams for us—that you'd do that for me. But it won't be necessary. I finally realized that holding on to my guilt and sin granted them more power than the Lord's forgiveness. Do you know how stupid that was? If I truly believe that Christ forgives sins, then that includes mine. Once I got that through my thick skull, my love for the Lightning M—these hills—came rushing back. Dad and I are staying." He kissed her then, long and hard, welcoming the taste of her mouth on his with promise of more to come. When he came up for air, he clicked the microphone back on.

"I guess that means yes," he said gruffly, and the audience roared.

He grabbed Mattie's hand, and they hiked to where Dusty stood. "I have one more thing to say before I turn this microphone over." Gil put his hat back on and motioned to the high school rodeo queen who carried a big silver buckle.

"I'd like to present this prize buckle to this weekend's overall winning cowboy, in honor of my brother Frank, and Dusty, and to all of you who have the courage to set a course for yourself and follow your dreams despite troubles that come your way. Our next speaker is a young man many of you know well. He would have been in today's competition had he not been involved in a drunk-driving accident last January. Please welcome Mr. Dillon Marshall."

Applause filled the air as a Ford truck entered the arena with the Marshall family sitting in the back. When the truck stopped, Gil handed Dillon the microphone, then tipped his hat to the young boy, knowing how difficult the next few minutes would be for him. He and Mattie stood beside the truck for moral support as Dillon spoke about stupid mistakes, how much they could cost you, and the grace to go on.

"You did well, Dillon," Gil said when the boy finished. "Let me know if you ever want to do this again, and my foundation will set you up on a high school tour across the nation." Gil shook the boy's hand, then pulled Mattie to his side, not wanting to let her go.

"You never gave up on your dream, either," Gil told her and took hold of Dusty's reins to lead him out of the arena. "You loved these hills, and you never abandoned them."

Mattie gazed up into his eyes. "But I was wrong. I love this land, Gil, but I love you more. These hills don't mean a thing if I don't have you to share my life with."

At that, Gil crooked his arm around her neck and kissed her cheek. His soul stirred at the knowledge that Mattie would be his forever—soul mates. "I'm just glad you brought me to my senses. It took a few kicks—from you, Dad, and some other people God placed in my path, but I'm finally convinced." He twisted one of her curls around his finger and smiled.

"I don't need to run anymore. I've found my home ... right here with you."

His dad met them at the arena gate and held his arms out for Gil and Mattie. "Does this mean I'm finally going to get me some grand-kids to teach how to rope and sit a saddle? You'd better get married quick and get crackin'. I don't know how much time I've got left." He chuckled and thumped Gil's head with enthusiasm.

Mattie's cheeks flushed pink.

Gil grinned as he imagined his kids riding the green hills of Charris County, on horses his family raised—strong, dependable horses with lots of heart. A knot formed in his throat as he thought of the good times ahead.

Thank you, Lord, for all you've given me—for all you've forgiven me for. I couldn't ask for more.

Gil McCray was finally home.

ACKNOWLEDGMENTS

To my Lord and Savior, for quietly whispering in my ear to finish the book so You could do the rest. All praise and glory are Yours.

To my loving husband, Christopher, for all the love and support you gave in the development of this series and especially for agreeing to tag along on all my trips to the Flint Hills. I will forever remember and cherish those days in my heart.

To my lovely daughters, Samantha, Maggie, and Abigail, for listening to me go on and on about my characters and for offering your encouragement and hugs. I treasure your hugs.

To Beth Jusino, for encouraging me to follow my passion for this book and make it bigger. To Rachelle Gardner, at WordServe Literary, for taking on where Beth left off. A huge thank-you for believing in my work and for making me your client. You are the best agent a girl could have!

To Sue Brower, who believed in this story enough to try one more time! And to the many editors, sales, and marketing people at Zondervan. Thank you for your hard work in making this series so beautiful.

To my critique partners, for their help in making this book better, always better. To Tamera Alexander, Beth Goddard, Lisa Harris, Cora Jenson, Jeanne Leach — thank you ladies for being there at the beginning and for being such wonderful friends. Thanks also to Carole Brown, Peg Phifer, and Christy Miller. A special thank-you to my local writer's group, CWF, and especially to Lisa Goins for being my personal cheerleader.

To the many professionals who gave their time and help. To Doctors of Veterinarian Medicine, Scott Baldwin, Paul Cotterill, Carol Hines, and Tracy Hucke; to Jim and Joan Donahue for offering their help and allowing us to stay at the Clover Cliff; to Dr. Jim Hoy for his expertise on the Flint Hills and for teaching the Flint Hills Folklife class at ESU where my passion for the Flint Hills began; to Jenny Cary and Georgiana Daniels for their help with the football scenes.

To the many people who prayed with me and for me during this long road to publication. I could never list all your names, but you know who you are. To my Kansas writing friends Judith Miller, Deborah Raney, and Kim Vogel-Sawyer, you ladies are terrific! To the members at Good Shepherd Church, thank you for your love and support and for always being there for me.

Lastly, thank you, Gayle Ballard, for her help in promotion assistance on the tail end of this project.

May God bless you all,
Deborah

MATTIE'S SNICKERDOODLES

1 cup shortening

1 1/2 cups sugar

2 eggs

2 3/4 cups all-purpose flour

2 teaspoons cream of tartar

1 teaspoon baking soda

1/2 teaspoon salt

2 Tablespoons sugar & 2 teaspoons cinnamon mixed together in small bowl

In large bowl cream together shortening, sugar, and eggs. In a separate bowl sift together flour, cream of tartar, baking soda, and salt. Add to creamed mixture. Chill dough for 30 minutes. Preheat oven to 400 degrees. Roll into walnut-size balls. Roll balls into the sugar and cinnamon mixture. Place two inches apart on greased baking sheet and bake for 8–10 minutes until lightly browned but still soft. These cookies puff up first then flatten out with crinkled tops. Enjoy!

For the latest news and to sign up for a free e-newsletter, please visit www.deborahvogts.com

Deborah would love to hear from you!
Feel free to write her at debvogts@gmail.com or:

Deborah Vogts
PO Box 232
Erie, KS 66733